# The Story
## Part Two – Sable Wyvern

*Peter Lancett*

**THE STORY PART TWO – SABLE WYVERN**
Peter Lancett
Published by Fire Gate Media
www.facebook.com/FireGateMedia
ISBN-13: 978-1539800262
ISBN-10: 1539800261

First published in 2016 by Fire Gate Media

# Preface

## THE STORY - WHEN AND WHY

Sometime in June 2012, when I was still living in New Zealand, it occurred to me that I'd been working on film and television projects for several years and in that time hadn't written any prose fiction. I did wonder then whether I was out of practice and ought to write something to keep my hand in so to speak. I happened to be at my desk with the laptop open and Facebook staring at me and without thinking I started typing. In less than two minutes, the first episode of The Story was posted to my Facebook status timeline. I hadn't planned it, I simply let it flow as a stream of consciousness. One or two friends asked what it was all about and I explained that I was just practicing some prose writing for fun and left it at that.

Next day I wrote the second episode, a direct follow-on from the first, and posted it to Facebook. At this point I realised that I wanted to continue with this exercise because I was already enjoying it and already enjoying the character I'd created, Stevie. The obvious thing to do then was to move The Story to a blog site in order to archive it while still making it available to the few friends who'd expressed an interest in following it. So from then on I'd post an episode a day to the blog site and notify my friends via Facebook to say that the new episode was now available. All in all about thirty people were following Stevie's progress and this following kept me disciplined. An episode a day was expected of me and an episode a day is what I delivered. Every day. Without fail.

## THE STORY - HOW

To make it a more testing exercise for me, I set myself some ground rules. I had to write at least one episode per day and I couldn't spend more than twenty minutes writing an episode. Some days I might write more than one episode, but on those days, each episode had to be written within the twenty minute limit, and there had to be a gap of at least a thirty minutes between writing those episodes. Sometimes

Episodes written on the same day were amalgamated to form a single episode before posting as the narrative structure demanded and this was allowed. As a final kicker, I had to post what I'd written unedited to get me back in the habit, as far as is possible, of getting the good stuff down first time. And mostly this worked out because looking back on the raw blog site posts I'm still rather pleased with what I managed to do.

## THE STORY - WHAT

From the start this exercise in narrative prose composition was called The Story because honestly I had no idea where I was going with it and wasn't much interested in trying to come up with a catchy title. So I got used to calling it The Story and clearly that has stuck. I can't think of it as anything else now. What compelled me to write The Story as a first-person narrative I just don't know, but that's how it came out from the very first words. The daily segments are episodes rather than chapters because they were necessarily short bites of text and often ended with a cliff-hanger, rather like old fashioned radio serials. I'd never considered that The Story would ever be made available for publication but it did occur to me that short bites like this make for an easy read, which is never a bad thing. Pick it up, read a small chunk or two, put it down. Repeat until finished.

## THE STORY - SUBJECT

I enjoyed taking on Stevie's persona as I was writing but it's not true to say - as some people have suggested - that The Story is in any way autobiographical. Yes the occult detail, the ceremonial magic and the detailed knowledge of those things, well I admit it, they *are* part of my biography - *mea culpa*. But Stevie's journey isn't a road I've travelled. Of course some of Stevie's occult experiences are my experiences - as you'd expect given that I've made the depiction of them as accurate as possible while keeping the narrative readable. It's fair to say though, particularly with regard to ceremonial magic, that the preparations and the rituals would be far too long-winded to make for interesting reading in a work of this nature. I've truncated them and I've left lots out. Partly, as I say, for the sake of readability and partly for the sake of safety. There are plenty of books available describing the ceremonial process in full-ish detail if anyone is interested in delving deeper, as a quick scour of Amazon with "ceremonial magic" as the search words will show.

Thinking about it, Stevie's withering and contemptuous comments and his occasional rants are probably as much me as they are him and I apologise if Stevie is sometimes a little sharp with you, gentle reader. Stevie does sometimes go off on a tangent to explain something he's mentioned too, and that is me to a tee. He does acknowledge that he's done it though and almost apologises for it, something that I probably wouldn't do.

## THE STORY - FAMILY
Because the content of The Story was prompting questions from its followers - questions that I was happy to answer - I created a Facebook group for people who were following and that became the question and answer forum. I also used the group to explain things that had come up in the narrative where a detailed explanation in the narrative would have disrupted the flow. This was also a place to have a bit of fun, so I started to post pictures of places and things and sometimes characters mentioned in The Story so that readers could see what I was seeing. I found pictures corresponding to Toni, Hesther, Helen, Maggie, Ella, along with houses, restaurants, cars, clothes and accessories and so on. Characters in The Story have, by and large, exquisite taste - and the means to indulge it. These photos and images can all be found on the Facebook page created for The Story at:

www.facebook.com/TheStoryPeterLancett

## THE STORY - CONCLUSION
So that's it, the story of The Story, and Stevie has come a long way since that initial episode in June 2012. I completed the fourth novel in 2015 but there were a couple of lengthy and announced breaks due to my moving back from New Zealand to England at the end of 2012. There are four novels in the series because The Story took on a life of its own and developed a momentum that I made no effort to check. Thank you for choosing to read it.

## OH, AND ANOTHER THING...
I should perhaps mention that my work with Ceremonial *Haute Magie* - High Magic - began and concluded many years ago in the time before the internet and its quick and easy promises and its

opportunities for fleecing and fooling the unquestioning, the unwary - and those desperate to belong. It's a path I haven't followed for a long long time, but of course you can't unlearn what you've learned, you can't put the Genie back in the bottle. Much of what I learned and experienced has been of great value to me on my spiritual journey, but I feel no regret at having left behind all forms of hierarchical structure, involving as that does, the surrender of personal power and potential to the will of others. It's no longer a way that suits me, though I understand that structure is exactly what others crave. This first novel in the four-novel series following Stevie's quest does concern itself with Ceremonial Magic in particularly dangerous ways. But I'm giving nothing away by saying that in subsequent novels, Stevie's journey is drawn along other paths. For my own part, in case you're interested, I only concern myself with personal journeying through meditation, drumming, chanting and lonely vigils spent in desolate places. Each to their own.

**Peter Lancett, England, December 2015**

*The Story part two – Sable Wyvern*

# The Story
## Part Two – Sable Wyvern

*The Story part two – Sable Wyvern*

# Previously in The Story...

Brought back from New Zealand by his dead wife Helen's best friend Toni, Stevie - aided by Adepts Professor Hanford, the exotic and exquisite Hesther, and Toni herself - has undertaken a dangerous ritual using Enochian magic, to bring immortal beloved and dead Helen back from the 27th Aethyr, where she is trapped and terrified. The ritual has not fared well, the results catastrophic...

*...I CLOSED THE* door behind me with care but I never looked back on the house as I walked around the corner to Toni and my Aston Martin. Toni wasn't sitting behind the wheel as I'd expected. Instead I found her standing by the passenger door. I walked over to her to ask her what was the matter but she held the keys out to me before I could say anything.

'You drive' she said.

As I took the keys from her she opened the passenger door and slid into the leather seat. Something had happened to her. Probably not physically. But mentally. Spiritually. Emotionally. And possibly on unimaginably unattainable levels. This was a great worry because I wasn't experienced enough or wise enough to know how to deal with it.

I tried to engage her on the short drive back to Cheyne Walk but she wasn't terribly responsive. Again, this wasn't the Toni I knew.

'Are you okay?' I asked her. I knew that she wasn't but wondered if she'd open up and share the problem with me.

'I'm fine,' she said. That and nothing more. So I knew that she wasn't.

'What happened in there?' I asked.

'You know. You were there.'

Well now I knew there was something amiss. Because Toni was more experienced at the work we'd done than me. But even I knew that our experiences had been subjective. What I'd experienced, seen, heard and so on would be different to the experiences Toni and Hesther would have had. And not necessarily in subtle ways. Totally different if you look at it the way we view our experiences in the terrestrial world of illusion. So I left it at that. She was in no mood to talk and I didn't want to upset her.

When we got to the house I parked the car and took her straight inside. She was hugging herself as though trying to keep warm against the chilly night air. Except the night air was far from chilly. It was still summer-hot. And humid.

'Do you want a cup of tea or coffee or something? Or a proper drink?' I had to ask her even though I knew she'd answer in the negative. Which she did.

'I just want to go to bed' she said. 'I'm tired. See you in the morning.'

I stood in the hallway watching her shuffle over to the stairs. She made the first stair then halted, gripping tight to the banister rail. So I helped her up the stairs and to her room. I even undressed her and put her to bed. And she let me. Which again was unlike Toni. Very unlike her.

I left her lying in bed with her eyes closed but very much and obviously still awake. I went to my own room to collect my mobile phone and as I wandered unhurried down the stairs I realised I couldn't for the life of me imagine why I'd done that. Force of habit, I supposed.

In the living room I poured myself a drink – Stolichnaya vodka, neat – and sat in one of the deep upholstered chairs taking in the silence and realising I couldn't even hear the sounds of the city outside. I didn't put the room lights on but not wanting to sit in the dark in someone else's house I switched on a tall and exquisite art deco standard lamp. The white light glowed yellow from the globe shading the bulb leaving the room dark in shadow and comfortingly cosy. I wondered about Helen. Wondered if we'd really rescued her from the twenty-seventh Aethyr. She'd been at the gateway with me. And I'd been holding her tight to me as I'd stepped back across that shimmering threshold. Surely we'd freed her from it. I'd got the impression she hadn't even realised she was there.

'Where can we go now Stevie?'

Helen's voice. I looked around frantically but this was just a reflex reaction. I knew she couldn't be there. Not physically. But it wasn't her voice that chilled me. It's what she'd said. Because those were the exact words she'd used when we realised that we weren't safe and needed to get far away. The words that had prompted me to take us to New Zealand.

Right then my mobile phone rang and it was Hesther. She asked me about Toni and I told her. She didn't comment on Toni's condition but something in her silences made me think she was holding something back from me. I wanted to discuss the events of earlier in the evening but she was having none of it.

'You should bring Toni with you tomorrow. To the professor's house. He'll be rested. Come around eleven. I think we have a lot to talk about.'

'How is he?' I asked, meaning the professor of course.

'Exhausted,' Hesther said but with no trace of concern. 'He needs to rest. A good long sleep will do it.' She paused for a moment then asked 'Is Tom there? To look after Toni?'

I told her that the house had been empty when we'd got back. No sign of Tom. Which was true.

She was quiet for a few seconds after that then said 'Well it's good that she's gone to bed. The rest will do her good. And don't forget to bring her with you tomorrow. Even if she says she's not up to it.'

I assured Hesther that the two of us would be there at eleven and she said a short goodbye then hung up. I slipped my phone into my shirt pocket. It had been a strange conversation in some ways. Hesther asking about Tom. Her insistence on my bringing Toni with me on the morrow no matter what. She was definitely keeping something from me. But I didn't twist myself in knots about it. In fact, knowing that we'd be going over things the next day allowed me to put the whole business from my mind at least for the night. And that was a relief I can tell you. First time I'd felt relaxed at all since I'd started to fear the moon in New Zealand. That's how it seemed at any rate. I didn't even wonder about Helen's voice coming out of nowhere just before Hesther's call.

The fact that Hesther *had* called explained one thing to me if nothing else. It explained my impulse to fetch my mobile phone from my room before coming downstairs. That had me smiling. The Adept had wanted to talk to me and she'd made sure that I had what was needed for that to happen. You know, to this day I have no idea how she'd even got my number.

I sat back in the comfortable armchair and actually drifted off to sleep. And was awakened a couple of hours later when the living room door clicked open and I turned to see Tom standing framed in it. I hadn't heard the front door open nor footsteps on the tiled hallway floor to announce his arrival home. Perhaps he'd come back while I was talking to Hesther or while I'd slept. That's what I told myself but in truth I knew that I'd still have heard. And surely he'd have announced himself before now.

'Toni's gone to bed' I said.

He looked at me for a moment until I felt uncomfortable at

the examination then he said 'Yes, I know. She needs to rest.'

Well he must have been upstairs then, to know that. I wondered just when he'd come in. Then it occurred to me that he might never have been out. There was that subterranean citadel in the basement of the house, barely explored by me. He could have been down there. He could have been, but a nagging thought gave me cause to doubt that. His car hadn't been here when we got back.

'Did you have a good evening?' I asked, feeling the need to make conversation.

'No,' Tom said, sharp as you please. 'A dear friend of mine. Passed away suddenly.'

He examined me again and I swear he was gauging my reaction.

'Oh that's sad' I said automatically, the way you do. 'I'm very sorry.'

Tom ignored my condolences. 'It was an aneurism. A blood vessel in his chest. Just above the heart.'

I tried to conceal my shock and don't know what kind of job I made of that. Piss-poor in all probability. Just above the heart you see. The exact place Diana's arrow of dragon-fire had found its mark in the black form that threatened us in the twenty-seventh Aethyr. You're not making that connection? Of course you are. And so did I.

'A close friend?' I asked, wanting to move things along.

'Close enough' Tom said, continuing his close examination of me. 'Actually he was familiar to your wife. And her family.'

Well I understood what he meant by that. Another upper-class knob-sac a hundred times removed from me. But not from Helen. Not from Toni. Not from him.

'He worked behind the scenes for the Royal Household you know. Smoothing things. Fixing things. Held an appointment with the College of Arms. It's a great loss. A great tragedy.'

Why Tom imagined I'd give a fuck about any of this I didn't know. But he was at great pains to explain it to me. And I got the feeling that Tom didn't make idle chit-chat at the best of times.

'Yes, he was a Herald in Ordinary of the College' Tom continued. 'But held an extra-ordinary title. Sable Wyvern. You won't see it in the lists.'

I know a lot more about heraldry now than I knew then so it all sounded gibberish to me as Tom was explaining it. I think he realised that and he stopped. Examined me some more then said:

'We need to talk, you and I. About Toni.'

'I thought we already had' I replied. I wasn't going to let him walk all over me.

'We need to talk more. Shall we say three-thirty again? In the basement?'

'I don't know' I said. 'That depends.'

Tom seemed genuinely surprised by that. 'Depends on what?'

I shrugged. 'On whether you're going to be there or whether you're going to send a proxy.'

Tom's mouth twitched at the corner, the beginning of a smile. 'Three-thirty,' he said. And then he was gone…

# *And now The Story continues…*

*The Story part two – Sable Wyvern*

# The Story Episode # 81
# (Moon phase: Day 21)

I DON'T HAVE a sense of drama. Actually I think I'm something of a dull person truth be told. Well in the sense that I'm not flamboyant at all, I suppose you'd say I'm dull. The clothes I wear are expensive and well-made but they're classic and understated. English-cut Saville Row suits. Oxford shoes and brogues. Cotton Chinos and button-down shirts. You know what I'm talking about, nothing Italian or flashy. Even my car, the Aston Martin. It's beautiful but it doesn't scream at you. I mean, not like a Lamborghini or a Ferrari. I've already mentioned before that I like to allow a woman I'm with to shine, and I'm often with women. So you get the picture when it comes to me.

Well the reason I'm telling you this is because of what happened at three-thirty. I went down there, to that basement. Of course I did. Don't imagine that it was some enchantment of Tom's that made me go. I wanted to go. Of course I did. You would have gone too. I'd already seen two rooms down there and although there'd been nothing but black shadow concealing the rest of the basement, I knew that there was more.

I had just my bathrobe wrapped around me, like last time. I was freshly showered and didn't see the point in getting dressed. It was pitch black dark again, like last time with only the luminous dial of my watch visible. And once again I got to the bottom of the stairs, turned right and felt my way along the invisible corridor until I was touching the nearest doors on either side. I looked at my watch and waited. A minute to three-thirty. I almost started to count the seconds.

'Steven.'

A hissing whisper of my name, reverberating behind me. I turned sharply to face the whisperer but I couldn't see anything through the pitch black.

'Steven.'

Behind me again but no hiss and no reverberation. I turned back, sharp as before and not a little afraid now. But there was Tom. And behind Tom an open door. A very dim light emerged from the room beyond the open door so that I got Tom in partial silhouette.

He wore a hooded calf-length cloak, with the hood pulled up over his head. The cloak was made of a glittering blue fabric embroidered with stars and moons and planets and astrological and alchemical symbols in silver thread.

He'd done it again. Appeared from nowhere. I hadn't heard a door click open. I hadn't heard a footstep – though he wore nothing on his feet. But most curious of all, I'd heard him speak my name before I'd seen the dim light from the room behind him. I surely should have been aware of that before anything else. I mean light travels way faster than sound. But that's not how it happened. A totally different order of events. And I didn't imagine that. That's how it happened.

A flamboyant sense of drama? Tom had it. I didn't. And it was an enchantment, for sure.

'Come in, follow me. And close the door behind you.'

Tom turned and I followed as he stepped into the room. This room was a perfect cube. I'm going to tell you that this cube was the Cube of Space.

An internal steel frame defined the cube. Tubular steel, one inch square. Running along the tops of the four walls, along the floors, down the corners. And the steel was plated with silver. Circular silver-plated rods joined the diagonal corners and the centre of the ceiling to the centre of the floor. And the centres of the walls. Where the circular steel rods running from the diagonals crossed in the exact centre of the cube they held a small silver sphere.

You'll understand that we had to duck and watch our step to find empty spaces we could stand up in. Tom stood in the south east corner of the room and I stood facing him in the north west corner.

You know something? I have no idea what the light source was in that room. A dim yellow glow was what I'd seen from outside the room through the partially opened door. But in the room, with the door closed behind, the light seemed bright and silver. Yes, that doesn't seem right but imagine white light reflecting off polished silver and that's what it was. A glistening magical space.

I have to say that; magical. Because the energy flowed in a specific direction around the cube. The way that it should. You could feel it. I'd be lying if I said that you could see it but it felt like you could. The appropriate symbols were painted on the steel tubes and rods and walls and the floor and the ceiling. The tarot correspondences, the numbers, the alchemical symbols, the musical annotations, the Hebrew flame-letters. I felt a transformation of my physical and psychic entity just from being in that room.

'You're in great danger' Tom said.

No small talk then. I couldn't respond because I didn't feel in any danger and I couldn't know what he meant by that. He waited for a response though, a respectful and polite few seconds that spoke volumes for his upbringing and education I suppose.

And in that time I saw that he was naked beneath the robe he wore. Perhaps I shouldn't mention this, but it's a bit like Hesther. You couldn't help but notice the appearance with Tom; and yes, your eyes are drawn to that special endowment of his. Mine were. Does that make me a homosexual or a bisexual? You tell me. Even back then, I'd gone beyond the squeamish stupidity of prejudice.

I'll tell you this, I was able to appreciate that Tom was in great shape and was a very physically attractive man. And if I'd ever been sexually attracted to a man, Tom would have fitted the bill. And if I'd ever felt that attraction and found it reciprocated, I wouldn't have hesitated. I wouldn't need years of therapy about it either. So now if I get to describe Tom again, you understand where it's coming from. I hope.

But let's get back to it. I was in great danger Tom had told me, and I had nothing to say to that.

'Toni's in danger too. And she's my main concern. Don't doubt that. Whatever you did earlier it's corrupted my wife. She's brought something back from wherever you've been.'

'I know something happened to her. But I don't have the experience to understand it or deal with it.'

'Of course you don't. This is why I'm talking to you now. You're going to see old Hanford tomorrow -' I wasn't getting the impression that Tom held a high opinion of the professor '- and that sorceress.' By this he meant Hesther and an opinion totally lacking in respect. 'You're taking Toni with you. She won't want to go but you're taking her.'

'How do you know this?' I asked.

Tom ignored the question. 'They know what's happened. They know what to do to put it right. Make sure that you're there to look after Toni's interests. I'm going to need you to tell me everything once you get Toni back here.'

I couldn't understand this. 'Look Tom' I said, 'Let's not pussyfoot around here. It's clear what you are.' I looked around the cube of space as dramatically as I could. 'Why don't *you* do what needs to be done for Toni?'

'It's clear what I am? And just what am I Steven?'

'Carry on with riddle-me-a-riddle shit like that and I'm out of here now. Despite what you are. We both fucking know what you are. And what you can do.'

'That was intemperate. But it's the first sign I've seen of passion surfacing in you.'

He examined me in that disconcerting way he had. 'That wasn't you though was it?' he said, as though his examination had revealed something otherwise hidden. 'Salamander, unnatural and barely controlled. That was your wife. You really are in great danger.'

'What kind of danger? From who? From what? And why can't you do what's needed for Toni?'

Tom stood relaxed and in complete synthesis with the energy flowing through the cube of space.

'I'm in a difficult position' Tom said. 'Whatever I might do, there are those who would know. And I can't afford that.'

'What people? Who can be more important to you than Toni? Your wife.'

'There are people. Some involved with the College of Arms... no, I'll say no more. Go to old Hanford tomorrow. Take Toni. And bring her back to me. We can reassess things then.'

'Is that it then?' I said, the salamander burning to the surface again. 'That's all you're going to say?'

Tom raised a hand and held the palm to me. It was like iced water washed over me and calmed me in an instant.

'Go' Tom said. 'And tomorrow we'll reassess.'

I turned to go, opened the door. But I stopped. There was one more thing I wanted to ask him so I turned around. And the room was empty. Despite the fact that I stood in the only visible way in or out of that basement room, Tom was gone.

# The Story Episode # 82 (Moon phase: Day 21)

I HAD TO swelter in the car on the way to Hampstead next morning. Another steamy hot summer day outside and Toni insisted on having the heater on full blast. She said she was cold and she sat in silence in the passenger seat beside me huddled in a thick winter coat. I wore some navy chinos and a blue cotton shirt and I could hardly breathe with the heat.

She hadn't wanted to come with me - as Tom had predicted and Hesther had hinted at. But I managed to cajole her in the end. I had to virtually pull her out of bed and lead her to the shower where she stood under the jets of scalding water unmoving. I even had to towel her dry and dress her. But her choice of clothes not mine. I'd have put her in something summery and light but she chose jeans and boots and a thick woollen jumper. And the winter coat. And honestly, she didn't even break sweat. Unlike me, stuck to the leather seat. This told me that she was chilled to the core. Unnatural and dangerous I'd have said. But whatever ailed her was a result of our adventure in the twenty-seventh Aethyr.

I reflected on the nature of that Aethyr as I turned onto the Finchley Road. The lessons to be learned there were most of all those concerning solitude. A dark cold place. I didn't know how these things worked back then and it seemed to me that Toni hadn't left it behind the way Hesther and I had. She had assimilated that region. Made it a part of her consciousness.

Bear in mind that the Aethyr already existed inside her, as it exists inside all of us. A journey there is an internal one, not to some faraway region somewhere in the heavens. As it is above, so it is below. Never forget that. Solitude and cold. Like a long Polar winter. She seemed to be sinking ever deeper into it. All I could think to do was try to talk to her, despite her reluctance.

'Tom spoke to me last night' I said. 'After you'd gone to sleep.'

'I didn't sleep' she said, turning her face to look out of the side window.

'What's Tom's involvement with the College of Arms?' I asked. 'Well?' I insisted when it seemed she was going to ignore my question altogether.

She continued to look out of the side window but said 'He knows some of the officers. It's a family thing, Old families all-knowing each other.'

I got that but I had something specific I wanted to get to. Since she was being so unresponsive I decided I had nothing to lose by asking more direct questions.

'Did Tom speak to you last night?' I asked

'I never saw him last night' she said at last with a degree of petulance.

'So you never heard his sad news then?'

'Obviously not.'

She was uncomfortable with my prying questions. Not, I felt, with the nature of them, but with the fact that I was speaking to her at all. Still, I wasn't going to let that put me off.

'So you don't know who died then?' I persisted.

'No' she said. 'So who died?'

A spark of interest. Well that was something.

'I honestly don't know. Tom never told me his name. Just that he was somebody called Sable Wyvern.'

Well that sparked her interest and no mistake. I mean, she didn't twist herself in shock or anything. But she did turn her head towards me.

'You know who that is?' I said, pressing her on it since mention of that heraldic title seemed to have hit a mark.

'Sounds like an officer of the College of Arms,' she said. 'But you already know that since you asked about the College already.'

'Yeah,' I said. 'I know that. I'm just interested because that's who Tom said had died.'

That definitely got a reaction. She didn't say anything right away but I could see and sense the shock.

'How did he die?' she asked and it was the most alive she'd been since we'd left my house the previous night.

'Ruptured blood vessel in his chest' I said. 'Just above his heart.'

I added that last detail in case Toni had any sense of the arrow of Dragon Fire Diana had shot into the chest of the looming black menace that had threatened us in the twenty-seventh Aethyr. I mean, I know we'd had differing subjective experiences in there, but I didn't know how that worked. Maybe she'd have had a sense of what I'd seen so clearly.

'So you did know him then?' I said

'Tom had dealings with him' was all she said.

Fuck she was hard work. I hadn't ever known her to be like this. But I had my horrible suspicions about Sable Wyvern as you can imagine, given that you know I think he was in the twenty-seventh Aethyr with us. Just how that might work I had no idea of course, but there was a lot about this Enochian system of magic that was just a fog to me. Most of it actually.

'How does it work with you and Tom?' I asked, pretending to change the subject. 'I mean, I know that you belong to an Order that Tom isn't part of. But I've seen enough of Tom to know that he's involved with something. Doesn't that cause problems between you? I mean, you having to keep your work secret from each other because of the conflicting oaths you've sworn?'

'How's that any of your business?' Toni was on the defensive. But at least she was engaging in a form of dialogue. Stepping away from the increasing obsession with solitude that had been closing around her.

'Right. None of my business' I conceded.

I didn't want to tell her about Tom's warning. That I was in danger. That she was in danger. Because I suspected that Tom knew the danger we were in through having a more than passing familiarity with the source of that danger. And I hope you can understand how it might be more than awkward – in fact downright difficult - for the two of them to live together. Tom was an Adept. And I'd seen the Temple in the basement; he hadn't followed the path of a shaman to evolve to that exalted state. He was involved with an Ancient and powerful Order.

Something told me that this Order was involved in more than achieving the Great Work. I had a terrible suspicion that whatever Tom was involved with had slipped into arrogance. And hubris. For a reason I couldn't put my finger on I wanted to believe that Tom didn't approve of that. But given the oaths he'd taken he couldn't just walk away.

My head was spinning with suspicions and unprovable conclusions and Toni wasn't in any state to discuss them. Anyway, we were pulling into the professor's road and I parked right outside the house again. I got out and opened the door for Toni, gave her my hand to help her out. She was weak, I could tell. And still cool in all that clothing.

'Come on' I said to her. 'Let's see what they've got to say.'

Toni didn't reply and I had my arm around her as I walked her up the path. I was about to push the doorbell when the door opened. Hesther stood there.

'Come in,' she said.

She seemed cold but not unfriendly. She closed the door behind us then kissed Toni in welcome. And then we stood there, all three of us, in the hall.

'The professor's in his study I suppose?' I said.

Hesther shook her head. 'No,' she said, and she looked away for a moment, then fixed me with those cobalt eyes of hers.

'So where is he?' I asked.

Hesther hesitated, demonstrating a sense of theatre she could have taken directly from Tom then said 'Professor Hanford passed away at three-thirty this morning.'

# The Story Episode # 83 (Moon phase: Day 21)

THERE'S NO SUCH thing as death. Of course there isn't. There's only sloughing of the flesh as spirit-consciousness continues walking the path. Grieving then, is merely self-pity. We all knew that but Hesther reminded us of it all the same. We did repair to the professor's office and Hesther took his place. In his chair. Behind his desk. The symbolism of this wasn't lost on us – not even on Toni who remained distant and physically cold. The King is dead. Long live the Queen.

'How did he die?' I asked.

'His heart stopped beating' Hesther answered.

'And you know this happened at three-thirty' I said.

I wanted her to confirm this because three-thirty was a time that was cropping up more and more often as Tom summoned me to his subterranean meetings. And there's no such thing as coincidence.

'I was sitting with him' Hesther said. 'Watching over him while he slept. So I know the time.'

I was struck with the image of the elderly professor sleeping in his bed while the unimaginably beautiful and much younger Hesther kept a watchful vigil by his bedside. Unable to intervene as the old man's life slipped away.

'It wasn't like that' Hesther said like she'd just read my mind. Again.

'What was it like then?' We both looked at Toni, surprised to hear her speak out in this way.

'Sudden,' Hesther said as though she'd accepted that Toni was as privy to my thoughts as she was herself.

'He didn't look well after the business last night' I said. 'Do you suppose. . ?'

I let my words trail away leaving Hesther to fill in the blanks. I was wondering of course if his death had come as a result of the work he'd done leading the ritual for us last night.

'I really couldn't say, Steven. But in any case you shouldn't burden yourself with guilt. He was there because he couldn't refuse to be there. He loved Helen. We all did. And he felt great compassion for you Steven. You should know that.'

'I'm glad he didn't suffer' I said. And I meant it.

Hesther nodded her acknowledgement. She was taking it all very well, I thought. Then I remembered what she was. An Adept. Beyond the illusion and its programming.

'It's a bad time, I know. But we need to talk about what

happened last night.' I glanced towards Toni because it was her well-being I had in the forefront of my mind.

'Steven we can't. Not at this moment. Given what happened in the night.'

I was about to protest but Hesther, ever the Adept, clearly knew this and stopped me before I could begin.

'I have a lot to do Steven. A lot to arrange. People to contact and so on. And Toni will manage. For the present.'

'I am right here you know. In the same room?' Now this was more like the Toni I knew and I wondered if Hesther had had anything to do with that.

'Yes,' I said. 'We know you are. But you need help. It's why I brought you here.'

'What makes you think I need help?' Toni said with a hint of challenge in her voice.

'Take a look at yourself' I said. 'You're wearing winter clothes on a hot summer day. I don't know about help, I'd say you need sectioning.'

Even Hesther smiled at that, feeble humour though it was.

'So what do we do now then?' I asked Hesther. 'Do we just leave?'

'Yes,' she answered. 'I think you should. For now. I will keep in touch though. I'll be in touch. Soon.'

There was nothing more for it. We'd have to go back to Chelsea. I wondered how Tom would react. He'd insisted I take Toni after all. Toni and I got up to leave and Hesther came with us to see us to the door. Toni walked in front and as I was about to follow her out of the professor's study I felt Hesther's hand on my wrist.

'A moment of your time Steven.'

Toni stopped too, but Hesther dismissed her saying 'I just need a minute alone with Steven' and that was enough. Toni left us and I heard her boots clicking on the tiles of the hallway as she sauntered over towards the front door.

'We will need to talk, Steven' Hesther said quietly. 'Just not now.'

'Yes,' I said. 'You'll call me. You told me. So there's something else.'

'The professor. . .' she said. 'The way he died. I was sitting right beside the bed. He was at peace with his sleep. But he sat bolt upright and his face twisted with what I can only describe as fear. The professor wasn't given to fear. And he fell back on his pillow with that look on his face. Like he'd died of fright.'

'I'm sorry,' I said, unable to think of anything else.

'There's more than that Steven. As he sat bolt upright and before he fell back dead, he called out a name. He called out Helen's name.'

A chill rushed through me at that and momentarily I could feel my immortal beloved Helen as part of me, then it passed.

'So I will call. And we'll talk.'

That left me reeling and once Toni and I were in the car and pulling away from the house, Toni asked what Hesther had wanted.

'She told me to look after you' I lied. I lied because I didn't know what to make of Hesther's revelation.

'Look after me? Like I'm five or something?'

Toni pouted. Like she was indeed five or something. She had though taken off the heavy winter coat and I could sense an improvement in her, a brightening of her spirit.

'You going to turn the heat off?' she said. 'It's boiling in here.'

We drove back to Chelsea with the air conditioning keeping the temperature at a merciful level and once inside the house, Toni told me she was going to go to bed.

'I didn't sleep at all last night' she reminded me. 'I'm

knackered.'

I have to say she seemed altogether more like the old Toni. Not full of her usual sparkle and fizz but light years removed from the woman I'd had to drag out of bed earlier. What the hell had Hesther done? Had Hesther indeed done anything? It was beyond my understanding that was for sure. But I was happy to see her better than she'd been.

For my own part I was tired enough. I'd lain awake until three-thirty waiting for the time when I'd been told to go to the basement. The time when the professor had passed away. And I'd slept only fitfully myself after that strange meeting with Tom. A nap would be in order for me too so I made my way up the stairs to my room. Once there I stripped out of my sweat-soaked clothes and took a cold shower.

Dry, I wandered back into the bedroom in time to hear a couple of taps on the door and see the door open before I could call out. So I stood naked as Rachel came in.

'Whoops, sorry' she said. 'I thought you was out. I just come to throw a duster round the room.'

I made no effort to cover myself because Rachel seeing me naked was getting to be a habit.

'We came back early' I said.

'So I see' Rachel replied tipping a saucy nod at my exposed penis.

She was grinning and I had to smile along with her. She was one of those people you just couldn't take offence at. She had a wonderful personality, she surely did.

'Have you thought on? About the other night? What I told you down in the basement?' She was suddenly serious. Serious for her at any rate.

'What?' I said, surprised. 'Oh, not much. Things have been a bit...'

'Yeah I know. But you gotta give it your time. Earth, air, fire an' water. There's a lotta trouble comin' your way if you don't get nature on your side.'

She wasn't joking, I could see that. 'I know you mean well' I said. 'But I just wouldn't know where to start. Tell you the truth I'm lost.'

'Nah, you ain't lost. That darlin' wife o' yours. She's lost. Nearly.' She narrowed her eyes, examined mine. 'But you carry a piece of her inside you.'

'So what do I do?' I said. 'To get in touch with nature the way you say I should?'

'Didn't I show you the other night? Down in the basement?' she said.

I remembered the sexual experience we'd shared, of course I did. My penis twitched at the memory, began to swell just a little.

'There yer go,' Rachel said, smiling again. 'You do remember.'

'Yeah, I remember that' I said. 'But I can hardly keep calling on you for a quickie every time I want to assimilate an attribute of nature.'

'Oh I don't know' she said. 'An' it weren't all that quick as I recall.'

She'd stepped closer to me and I felt her fingertips slowly stroking my penis, closing around it.

'Your wife is all fire' she whispered and I longed to know where she got this wisdom from. 'Let's quench her. She needs a moist complement.'

She took my hand and guided it beneath her skirt. Her face was so close to mine that I could taste her mint breath. My fingers slid inside her panties right away and as they parted the soft hair to find her soft slit, I felt that she was soaking with arousal.

'See,' she whispered, sliding her fingers along my now-hard shaft. 'I can be water to compliment the fire.'

I undressed her with immodest haste and we kneeled together on the floor. She closed her eyes and held my hands in hers as she chanted words I can't remember. But despite the fact that we were in the middle of the city I felt nature in the air around us.

'Take what I'm givin' yer' she whispered without opening her eyes. 'Do it quick how yer want it, let the fire do what it wants.'

So I enjoyed her. And it seemed that she enjoyed me. We were skin to skin with me deep inside her. Her soft breasts pliant beneath my lips and fingers. Her thighs sliding against mine. Her hands and fingers everywhere until I couldn't stand it any longer and deep inside her, I came with a force and fury, feeling the semen spurting from the tip of my penis and filling her. And for the transcendental moments of orgasm I caught the merest hint of directed fire being a supremely creative force, neither terrifying nor destructive. But It slipped away before I could hold it and analyse it.

For a few seconds we lay together on the carpet. I stayed hard inside her enjoying the soft grip of her soaking vagina as we caught our breath.

'Did you do that?' I asked, breathless as I slid carefully out of her.

I got to my knees and looked down on her lying back with her eyes closed.

'What? Made yer come? I should cocoa darlin''

She opened her eyes and grinned at me. 'You can use those moments to find what you're looking for' she said at last. 'It's part of the way.'

'What way?' I asked.

'The way of the soil and the sky and the sea and the sun. The way of nature, she said. The way you got to learn.'

I understood what she was telling me. I thought I did. Earth magic. Nature magic. I'd forsaken it for an intellectual ideal. And I shouldn't have. But I still wasn't sure how to make a proper start at finding that way. She got to her knees and turned to me.

'You'll find what you need you know' she said. 'There's a lot o' good in you.'

I could see in her eyes that she meant something by that. Something I don't think I'd seen in myself for a very long time. If ever. I was going to say something but she had other ideas.

'Now,' she said. 'Can you remember where yer threw my knickers?'

# The Story Episode # 84
# (Moon phase: Day 21)

TOM WASN'T RATTLED when I saw him that evening. But he was concerned for Toni. Toni hadn't surfaced and Tom told me she was slipping in and out of deep sleep. No longer chilly. Not physically at any rate. But probably freezing deep in the undiscovered realms of consciousness within. I'd told him about the professor passing away and as I say, that didn't rattle him at all.

'So Hesther sent you packing did she?' he said to me after a moment's thought and not an opinion on the professor's passing. I got the feeling again that Tom hadn't held the professor in particularly high esteem.

'Well it wasn't quite like that' I said, feeling the need to jump to Hesther's defense for some reason. 'I mean, she is going to be busy. I got the feeling she was going to have to straighten the professor's affairs. And then of course there's the work. The Order.'

Tom raised an eyebrow at my mention of the Order.

'What?' I said. 'Oh let's not pretend you don't know about the Order. Toni's in it, I was in it, my wife was in it. You know about it so I've given nothing away.'

'Yes, but you and your wife left didn't you? Flouted the rules and the conditions of the sacred oaths you'd sworn and ran away. And how has that worked out for you up to now?'

He had a point. Of course he did. You probably don't know this and even after I've told you, you still won't believe it. That's up to you. I've mentioned before that the truth remains the truth even if *nobody* believes it. Those sacred oaths contain an acceptance of the most terrible consequences if they're breached. Helen and me, we'd breached them. And astonishingly, Tom knew about it.

I think I should say here that you *can* leave a mystical Order, even after swearing sacred oaths that bind you to it. But there are procedures. Formal ways of going about it. And you'll still be bound by the oaths of secrecy. Most mystical Orders will have procedures for leaving in an orderly fashion in this way. Mind you, there are some that will never let you leave peaceably. We'll come to that some other time. But for now, as I said, Tom had a point. Helen and me, we hadn't left our Order in the accepted formal way.

I hung my head. If he was hinting that our actions had resulted in the death of my immortal beloved wife, I couldn't contradict that. Because deep down it was something I believed too. There'd been hints everywhere suggesting that was the case. And Hesther had said that I'd killed my Helen the moment I'd first told her I loved her. Well I was going to give my life and soul to rescue my darling Helen from the confinement she was suffering.

But I wanted to get at the truth. I wanted to learn what was meant by the shadowy hints that kept striking me unexpected like barbed arrows getting under my skin. *They* had killed my Helen, whoever *they* were. *I* had killed my Helen by an expression of love - and this whispered to me by an Adept, a woman who'd been her previous lover. I was no closer right then to understanding what those hints were pointing at. But there, in the living room with Tom, I understood that there was a more pressing consideration.

'Okay' Tom said, 'I didn't intend to hurt you. I know that you have things to discover and that your dead wife needs you. But I need you too.'

'Oh yeah?' I said with more than a trace of cynicism. 'Go right ahead Tom. Tell me just what it is that I can do for you.'

He ignored my disrespectful tone, which in itself spoke volumes for his character and made me feel a little bit smaller in his presence.

'I need you to look after Toni. What happened to her in your house – when she was helping you, remember – it's not going to go away.'

'Yes' I said. 'But Professor Hanford's gone. Hesther will help us but she's busy right now. Just as soon as she's got things sorted she'll help us.'

Tom looked at me like he thought I must be simple. Actually, looking back now, he probably did think that.

'You really believe that do you?' he said.

'Yes' I said. 'Why shouldn't I?

'Tell me what you thought of old Hanford' Tom said, and I could see that this was some kind of test. And possibly a lesson.

'He's a decent man,' I said. 'Was a decent man.'

'And what makes you say that?' Tom prompted.

'For starters, given his background, he'd lost all the traces of snobbery you'd expect to find in a man of his class and intellectual achievement.'

'Not to mention wealth, eh?'

Tom had caught me on that one. Yes, I absolutely was having a dig at him, pointing out positive attributes in Professor Hanford that I implied were lacking in him.

'Do you imagine me to be a snob Steven? Is that how you see me?'

I was about to tell him exactly what I thought he was since he'd asked, but smiling, he stopped me.

'No, don't answer,' he said. 'Put the Salamander back in its box.'

He was right. Hot anger was driving what I'd been about to say. And the salamander did in fact return to its box so to speak. The salamander was Helen inside me. You know that though, don't you? I'm all air, not fire. The salamander is unnatural to me so that when emotional intemperance on my part calls upon its nature, it rises breathing flames. Natural fire personalities often have that side of it under control. For the most part at any rate. Unless something triggers it inside them. Unleashes it so to speak. As had happened with my immortal beloved darling wife. And I will tell you about what happened to her. To us. I promise.

'Look,' I said. 'Hanford's dead. Hesther has her work cut out right now. But she's going to help us. She's promised. Since you can't or won't help Toni yourself that's as good as it's going to get.'

I thought that summed things up nicely but it didn't satisfy Tom.

'I'm not trusting Toni's well-being to Hesther' he said. 'It's as simple as that.'

'You were happy to do that just last night' I reminded him. 'You insisted that I had to take Toni over there. To them. Whether she wanted to go or not. She didn't, by the way. So why the change of heart?'

'Because for all that I considered him to be sometimes feeble through sentimentality, I do share your opinion of old Hanford. To a degree. He was a decent man. With often noble motives. And he'd achieved much. He had, yes. I know you like to throw terms like Adept around, so yes, that's what he was. An Adept.'

'So its Hesther you don't trust,' I said.

'Do you?' Tom shot back at me.

My mind was clouded with Hesther's recent treatment of me. Which had been decent and compassionate. So I asked 'Why shouldn't I?'

'She was your wife's lover' Tom shot back. 'Her *lover*. The relationship was deep. Not a brief fling. Not the spill-over from a schoolgirl crush. Not a series of *ad hoc* sexual encounters. They were lovers.'

'Yeah. So?'

Tom had to fight his exasperation. 'So when did you find out?' he said.

'A couple of days ago,'

'And Toni told you. Accidentally more or less. Why d'you think no one's ever bothered to tell you this before now? Not the saintly professor, not Hesther. And not your wife. Why didn't your wife ever tell you?'

I shrugged. I didn't know.

'Who swore her to secrecy, I wonder? And why?'

'You think that's Hesther's doing don't you?' The penny was beginning to drop. 'But that would mean she'd had to swear an awful lot of people to secrecy. Not just Helen. A lot of people. Including Professor Hanford. Including Toni. But why would they agree. . .' My words trailed off because I couldn't complete this line of reasoning. It was too incredible.

Tom shook his head. 'I really couldn't speculate on that' he said. 'But I won't trust her with Toni.'

'Fine,' I said, wanting to be alone with my thoughts now he'd planted this particular seed of doubt in my mind. 'So what do you want from me? What is it you imagine I can do for Toni?'

'I need you to look after her,' Tom said. 'Take her to see someone who can help her.'

'So there is someone you trust then?' - the salamander poking his head out of his box again.

'Oh yes,' Tom said. 'A shaman. And I want you to take Toni to him.'

'Okay' I said. 'I'll do this for Toni. Because you say it's what she needs.'

'It is,' Tom said.

'So where am I going to find this shaman then?' I asked.

Tom hesitated before telling me. Adding the sense of drama that I knew he loved.

'Berlin' he said at last. 'And I'd like you to take her there tomorrow. Time's an illusion,' he continued. 'But here in *this* illusion it's important to Toni. Go tomorrow.'

'Berlin?' I said, as though I hadn't heard him when clearly I had. 'There's nobody closer I can take her to? Nobody in London?'

'No' Tom said.

'Berlin it is then' I sighed. I really wanted to concentrate on saving my immortal beloved wife. Of course I did. But I owed Toni a debt of obligation. And there was more than that. I felt a close bond with Toni. I don't know if it was Helen deep within me transferring her relationship with Toni to me. I don't know if it was the experiences we'd shared since she'd travelled all that way down to New Zealand to get me. Probably a bit of both.

'You'd better leave the details of this shaman then. Because I'm going out. I need some air.'

Tom didn't speak as I turned to leave, all manner of disparate thoughts careening through my mind. But as I opened the living room door he said 'Oh, Steven. If you are going to make a habit of fucking my housekeeper, do be sure you treat her well won't you? She's not to be treated shabbily. There's a good chap.'


# The Story Episode # 85
# (Moon phase: Day 21)

WALKING EAST ALONG The Embankment I tried to gather my thoughts. I hadn't really had a chance to think much about Professor Hanford's passing. But what would that mean? I'd always seen him as the spiritual, intellectual and hierarchical leader of the Mystical Order that Helen had introduced me to - herself barely introduced to it at that time.

Would the Order fall apart? I doubted it. Hesther would hold it. Seeing her in the professor's chair in his study earlier, I'd realised that Hesther had always been more of a power within the Order than she'd let on.

16. The Tower. A flash of thought that came and went like a lightning bolt. The learned and Adept professor was a figurehead within the Order. Certainly by the time Helen and I became involved he was. Hesther moved things. Hesther was

the guiding focus.

Hesther as High Priestess of the Temple? Yes of course. Always. But Hesther was also 1. The Magician. Hesther as the guiding focus for the Work. The magic wand connecting Heaven and Earth. The embodiment of As It Is Above, So It Is Below. All this came and went in a flash as I say. But it was within me. And it would be assimilated at the levels of consciousness where it would have meaning. Then at some point it would find ways of expressing itself in this level of consciousness. When it was ready or needed or whatever.

Hell of a thought to have. But it did bring a piece of the past to me along with it. More than one actually. In the first part I remembered the Neophyte Grade Ritual that had seen me inducted into that Grade within the Order. I'll not waste your time describing in great detail the layout of the Temple. But I will tell you that it was located in a room within the professor's Hampstead home.

I remember the incense. The altar in the centre of the Temple. The red rose, the red lamp, the wine, the bread, the salt, all placed on the altar along with the red cross and the white triangle. The white and black pillars. The Banner of the East. The Banner of the West. Me in my Black Neophyte robe with the hood over my head and the rope around my neck, red shoes on my feet. The Chemical change representing the magical change of water into blood. Sodium salicylate dissolved in one cup of water, ferric ammonium sulphate dissolved in another. Indiscernible until mixed, when the clear nature of the water becomes deep red to represent the alchemical process of transubstantiation.

I remembered the Officers of the Order present at the ceremony. On the floor of the Temple The Hierus, wearing a black cloak and a lamen and holding a sword. The Hegemon, wearing a white cloak and a lamen and holding a sceptre. The Kerux, with a lamp, a lamen and a wand. The Stolistes wearing a lamen and bearing a cup of lustral water. The Dadouchos, wearing a lamen and carrying the thurible. The Sentinel, who wore a lamen and held a sword.

On the raised dais at the eastern side of the Temple, The Imperator, The Cancellarius, The Past Hierophant – Professor Hanford for my Neophyte Ritual - The Praemonstrator. And the Hierophant in the centre. Hesther as Hierophant, wearing a red cloak over her white robe, also wearing a lamen and bearing a regal sceptre. Inspiring awe.

Now didn't I say that I wasn't going to waste your time describing the layout of the Temple? And you probably think I've done just that. Maybe you're right. But there's a lot more I could tell you. All the same I'm not going to tell you what the names of the Temple Officers mean. I will though explain that a lamen is a magical pendant you wear around your neck so that it sits right over your heart.

I shivered as I remembered Hesther the Hierophant leading the ritual. I saw it clear as day then. I can still see it now. Hesther banging the base of her sceptre once on a side altar next to her on the dais. The Kerux on hearing the knock, going to the north east of the Temple, facing west, and calling out

'*Hekas! Hekas! Este Bebeloi!*'

The Kerux returning to her place (the role was performed by a woman initiate at my ceremony) and Hesther rising majestically, knocking her sceptre once more on the side altar, then beginning the ritual by calling out

'*Fratres et Sorores* of the Phoenix Temple of the Order of the Stella Matutina, assist me to open the Hall of the Neophytes. Frater Kerux, see that the hall is properly guarded.'

I could recall the entire ritual for you, but I won't. It wouldn't serve any purpose. I was just reminded, as I walked along The Embankment, of how powerful and – I'll repeat it here – majestic Hester was. She was beautiful, like a Goddess, yadda yadda yadda. You know all that. What you don't know - and I'll find difficult to express to you - is how she commanded the energy and the very air in that temple. Every element under her confident control. Fuck, you had to be involved in a ceremony or a ritual - or any kind of magical work - with Hesther to get that. And I swear to you you'd be happy to follow her to your death. She had that kind of charismatic aura. Magnetism. During ritual and ceremony more so than ever.

I continued to walk East along The Embankment and by the time I was opposite the National Theatre on the far side of the Thames, or Isis, or whatever you'd now prefer to call that river, another linked memory came back to me. Coming home to the house in Queens Gate Mews to find my beloved Helen alone in the dark, crying.

'What's the matter?' I asked, kneeling down by her side and holding one of her hands.

She wiped the tears from her face with the other hand and composed herself enough to say 'Stevie I can't go any further.'

'What are you talking about?' I said.

'The work we're doing. I've gone as far as I can go.'

I tried to console her, of course I did, but finally I got to see what the issue was.

'I'm all fire Stevie. It blocks everything. Like it's jealous.'

What she meant by that was that her element of fire was so pervasive at all levels of her consciousness and personality that she couldn't equilibrate the other Ancient Elements of Air and Earth and Water within herself. And so much of the Great Work of Alchemy that we were engaged in required you to do just that simply for starters.

I can remember that we talked for a long time about how she'd need to engage the help of Astral and Angelic entities. The moon and her Goddesses as reflections of water to balance the salamander fire. There were many paths we could travel to help my darling Helen overcome this stumbling block and even if it took time to achieve the relationships we needed to form with these Astral entities, I told her I'd be with her and would never move on without her.

I remember thinking that tears and sobbing were so unlike Helen. Representing a petulance that wasn't really in her nature. And then we came to the heart of it.

'Hesther says she knows some people who can help me remove the block. Quickly.'

'Who are these people?' I asked her. 'Does Professor Hanford know about them.'

'It's all very secret Stevie. But Hesther says she'll introduce me. Don't hate me for it Stevie. Please.'

I thought right then that if I'd known of Hesther's and Helen's previous relationship I'd have cautioned against what we subsequently did. But I think I was as much under Hesther's spell back then as Helen was. Ha – spell. I don't mean it like that. Not an intentional act of magic. I mean in the sense of her charisma.

Don't get me wrong, I *was* under her spell. Most people were. And even though I felt that she looked down on me, I admired her. I admit it. And it wasn't just down to her amazing beauty. She carried herself like a Goddess. Then. And always. So events took the turn they did.

And I would have continued wallowing in that memory of my darling Helen but something inside me suggested I look up to the sky. Still blue as evening hadn't yet started to drag the night in but the sun was low behind me. When I tilted my head back,

I saw a horse-hair wisp of cloud high up. I stood and watched it as winds at that altitude, not present at ground level, shaped it. And I gasped out loud as I saw in the white vapour a feminine entity. A Sylph of the Air. My sign, my Ancient Element. High in the sky, taking care of the air we breathe. I turned my head to see if other people were seeing what I was seeing but as ever they were fixed on the terrestrial illusion and missed the wonder of the sky. When I turned to look again the cloud had moved, but was still noticeably her. I felt a connection with her deep in my heart. From me to her, from earth to sky. As it is Above, so it is Below.

'I think you'd better come down from there.'

I looked down and saw two coppers looking up at me. Looking up because I'd climbed one of the lamp posts along the embankment. I'd shinned up it quite a way and I was clinging to it like I was trying to get closer to the Element of my nature, the Sylph. Which clearly I was. But I couldn't for the life of me remember climbing up there.

A few people stopped to watch as I shinned back down and the coppers were actually very good about it when they realised I wasn't drunk or on drugs or anything like that. And the people started to disperse as the coppers gave me the usual health and safety lecture that I had to pretend to be interested in. They finally turned to go and I watched them. And as they passed by a group of tourists I saw one of the group looking at me and I was nearly sick with shock. A tall man. With an unkempt bushy beard. A man I'd last seen burning to death outside my house in New Zealand.

# The Story Episode # 86
# (Moon phase: Day 22)

THE VERY NEXT morning at seven o'clock I was at Heathrow with Toni. Terminal 1. I'd used the laptop they kept at a bench in the kitchen to book our flights. We were scheduled to fly out on Lufthansa LH3373 to Berlin Tegel airport.

Our flight wasn't due to take off until 9.05 am and the departure boards were telling us that it was on time and we'd arrive at 11.50 local time. We'd already checked in and we'd taken only one piece of carry-on luggage with just essential changes of underwear and so on. I didn't expect that we'd be staying long although Tom hadn't given any indication.

When I'd got back to the house the night before, following my encounter with the sylph in the clear sky over London, the place seemed dead to the world. No sign of Tom. No sign of Rachel – who seemed to be there at all manner of odd hours - and no sign of Toni. Toni had been sleeping and I hadn't wanted to disturb her.

When I got to my room I found that a hand-written note had been pushed under my door. It had a name and an address and a telephone number and nothing more. The man we were to see in Berlin, the shaman. It had to be. I wondered if this man would be expecting us, if Tom had been in contact to say we were coming. Maybe Toni would know.

'Do you know this guy we're going to see?' I asked her as we walked through Heathrow.

She didn't answer. She'd become withdrawn again. The brief spark of life that had coursed through her in proximity to Hesther the previous day had faded.

'Have you met him before?' I said.

She turned to me at that, her expression almost vacant. 'Met who?' she said.

'This guy we're going to see. The one Tom's sending us to.'

She shook her head. 'No' she said, not looking at me but absently scanning the crowds around us.

Well I didn't know about Toni but we had a little time to kill and I wanted coffee. So we went to one of the smart looking soulless cafes in the terminal departure lounge. I ordered coffee for both of us and took it to the table where I'd left Toni. A few sips later and she did look a little perkier; sitting up in her seat but still not talkative. I took Tom's note from my wallet and looked at the clear neat handwriting.

*Major Richard Warne*
*Kienitzer Straße 109*
*Neukölln*
*12049 Berlin*
*Germany*

The thing that struck me was that the man we were going to see had an English name. When Tom mentioned a shaman in Germany, I was expecting it to be some peace-nik hippy relic from the German anti-nuclear protest cold-war era. And, you know, the heyday of the Baader-Meinhof Red Army Faction revolutionaries. And maybe that's what we'd get but I really didn't think so. The title Major was used deliberately and suggested something different. So I was thinking British. Military. Potential fruit-cake. And the guy lived in *Neukölln* for fuck's sake.

Now I know Berlin a bit. I've been there a few times but I appreciate that you might not know it. So let me tell you that

*Neukölln* isn't the sort of place where you'd want to be walking the streets at night. Or during the day for much of the time. It's a rough area. I'd like to say it's a rough working-class area but unemployment in *Neukölln* is through the roof.

There's a huge immigrant population, mostly Turks and other middle-eastern nationalities and disaffected riff-raff. There are those who'd like to tell you that *Neukölln* is gentrifying with all manner of artists and associated Bohemians moving in to give it colour and vibrancy. But people who'd tell you that are probably real-estate agents with the urban equivalent of swampland to peddle. I once had someone trying to sell me a small block of apartments there, telling me that it was a low crime area and shoving crime statistics papers in my face. Well don't let that fool you. Crime stats are low because most crime in places like *Neukölln* goes unreported and doesn't show up in the stats. That happens the world over. Gang crime? Who's going to be stupid enough to report that? Muggings? What's the point? Drug crime? Well where do you start? Believe me, stats are meaningless. *Neukölln* wasn't gentrifying. It was rough. And that was where we were going to find Major Richard Warne, shaman.

I put the note back in my wallet and looked around me. Most of the people I saw looked like business travellers. Time was, not so long ago, when I would have been one of them. I felt a brief yearning for those times but it slipped by fast. I'd chosen my path and that path had been the one travelled by my beloved Helen. I wouldn't go back and change that for anything.

I had been wondering whether or not to mention to Toni what I'd seen the night before on the Embankment. Not the Sylph in the sky. But what I'd seen in that crowd of tourists after I'd climbed down from the streetlamp. The bearded man.

My head was a swirling mass of confusion. It *had* been him.

I'd swear to it. But how? He'd been burning like a petrol-soaked rag the last time we'd seen him. And in Auckland he'd been a street vagrant. Here he was with a party of tourists and dressed in nondescript casual clothing just like them. It fucking was him. I know it was. Even though the fire that burned him half a world away and a week ago must have rendered his fat and cooked his tripes. It wasn't just his features. The way he was staring at me. He was connecting with me.

'There's something you should know. Something I saw last night' I said to Toni, my decision made.

Toni looked up at me. She was definitely perkier. 'Yeah?' she said. 'What did you see?'

'That vagrant from Auckland' I said. 'The one we watched burning to death just before we did our runner back here.'

I don't know what kind of reaction I'd expected but Toni didn't react at all really. What she did say was 'We never saw him die.'

I almost gasped at that. She'd seen what I'd seen. 'Are you serious? The way he was burning up. That wasn't just flames licking at the edges of him. It was an inferno.'

Toni shrugged.

'At the very least he'd still be in hospital. And he'd be disfigured like you wouldn't want to see' I said.

'Well whoever it was it couldn't have been the guy from New Zealand then, okay?'

She was exasperated and didn't want to talk about it and I could understand that. Because what she'd just said, that's what I'd say too. Except I'd seen him. I'd looked him in the eye and even from a distance - I'd known. I could swear it.

'You've been to Berlin before haven't you?' Toni said, changing the subject nicely. And it was good to see her brighten up a little.

'Yes' I answered. 'Have you?'

She shook her head. 'No,' she said. 'That's the only reason you've got me coming with you. I hear it's fabulous.'

I felt that this wasn't a good time to describe *Neukölln* to her. 'It has the feel of a new European capital about it' I said.

I didn't want to tell her how much she'd love it, given where we were headed. Maybe we'd find some time to visit the *Ku'damm* once our business was concluded. I looked up at the departure board and saw they'd given the gate number for our flight.

'They're calling us' I said to Toni as I picked up our overnight bag from the seat beside me.

We made our way to the gate, a long long walk - as they all seem to be in Heathrow.

'Why is Tom making you take me to see this guy?' Toni asked as we walked.

I was genuinely surprised by this. I thought he'd have told her.

'Something that happened back at my house. What we did. Tom thinks something happened that still resonates with you.'

Toni laughed, the first time I'd seen her laugh since that night. 'I'm perfectly fine' she said once she'd controlled her fit of the giggles.

I didn't say anything. Because I agreed with Tom.

'You agree with Tom don't you?' Toni said.

'I'm in no position to disagree with him. And I think he might be right, yes.'

'You think he might be right. *You* think he might be right.'

Uh-oh. She clearly thought she was just fine. She wasn't even aware of the change in her personality.

'Look, what can it hurt?' I said. 'We get a trip to Berlin to see this guy, we do as the guy suggests. Then Tom's happy and we can all get on.'

Toni raised an eyebrow at that and seemed to accept it as perfectly reasonable. A few steps later though she said 'Get on with what?'

'With saving Helen' I said, not turning to look at her and not breaking stride.

If anything told me there was something amiss with Toni it was that. Forgetting that Helen needed help. Two weeks ago she'd jetted halfway around the world to get me to come back to do just that. And now she'd forgotten all about it. Toni – the real and true Toni – was being pulled to places that were damaging to her. I just hoped that Major Richard Warne was going to be the palliative Tom seemed convinced he would be.

Not long after, we stood in the queue to board the plane, passports and boarding passes in hand. As we got near to the boarding desk, Toni gripped my hand sharp and tight.

'Look' she hissed.

I turned to look where she was looking and a group of people passed on by. And when they'd gone, nothing.

'What?' I said. 'What am I looking at?

'He was there' Toni said, and suddenly she was cold and distant. And, I suspected, a little afraid.

'Who was?' I said but I felt sure I knew.

'That guy. With the beard. He was there. He was.'

I didn't have time to tell her I believed her – which I did.

'Can I have your passports and boarding passes please?'

I handed our passports and boarding passes to the pleasant woman at the desk who processed us and smiled as she handed our documents back, telling us to have a pleasant flight. Toni and me walked through the security doors towards the jetway connected to the 'plane and Toni never glanced back. I did. But I saw nothing.

# *The Story Episode # 87*
# *(Moon phase: Day 22)*

WE STOOD IN the Arrivals lounge in Berlin Tegel International Airport. We'd cleared customs and immigration quickly, both of us having EU passports, and I had my mobile phone pressed against my ear. This was my second attempt at calling the number on the paper Tom had left me. The name address and telephone number of Major Richard Warne. Again it was just ringing out. No one picking up. No answer machine. Nothing. Normally I'd wonder if I'd been given the correct number but I seriously got the feeling that Tom wouldn't have made a mistake with the detail. The call attempt timed out yet again and I slipped the phone back into my shirt pocket.

'Still no answer?' Toni asked, standing with her hands in her pockets. Listless.

'No' I said.

'So what do we do?' she asked. 'I could call Tom I suppose.'

I couldn't see what purpose that would serve and said so.

'Let's get a taxi and let's go to the address' Toni said.

I was a little hesitant about that. After all, if the guy wasn't there that would leave us in *Neukölln*. Not a terribly pleasant prospect as far as I was concerned. Of course Toni didn't know what *Neukölln* was like. But you know, in the end I agreed because what else could we do? If the guy wasn't there when we got there, *then* we could call Tom.

There were plenty of taxis available at the rank as we stepped out into the sunshine. Our driver was a Turk as most of them seemed to be. I handed him the note with the address on as Toni and I settled into the back seat. The driver studied the address for a second then turned to me.

'English, yes?' he said.

'Yes, English' I answered amazed as ever at how everyone seemed to know some English while most English people couldn't handle a word of a foreign language themselves.

'You sure this is where you want to go?'

'Yeah, sure it's where we want to go. Is there a problem?'

The driver shrugged. 'No problem,' he said. 'Just. . .'

He hesitated, so I prompted him. 'Just what?'

'This district. Is not a business district or a tourist district.'

I knew he wasn't prying and was just looking out for our well-being so I didn't damn him for his impudence.

'We're not here on business' I said. 'And we're not tourists. So I hope the clock's not running. And I hope you're going to start driving sometime soon.'

The driver grinned and handed Tom's note back to me. 'No, the clock isn't running,' he said as he reset it. 'It is now.'

He was still smiling as we pulled out into the airport traffic and headed off towards Berlin and the *Neukölln* district. Tegel airport is to the north west of the city, next to the *Tegeler See*, a large and beautiful lake. *Neukölln* is south East of the city centre, but we didn't have to go sightseeing through the city centre to get to it. We headed south on the *Stadtring*, an orbital motorway circling the city. So Toni didn't get to see the gorgeous and exciting and newly-historic city centre at all as we sped through dormitory suburbs such as *Charlottenburg*, *Grunewald* and *Wilmersdorf*.

Soon enough we were speeding past the southern outskirts of the old *Tempelhofer Feld* airport south of the city centre. If you've ever watched any history documentaries about the rise of the Nazis in Germany in the 1920s and 1930s, this is the airport you'll have seen in those old films of Hitler getting on and off aeroplanes.

After we passed *Tempelhofer Feld* we left the *Stadring* turning left and heading north along *Hermannstraße* into *Neukölln*. It wasn't long before we turned left into the cobbled road paving of *Kienitzer Straße*, where we'd hoped we'd find Major Richard Warne.

The driver stopped right outside 109 and I thanked him and paid him, adding a ten-euro tip, mainly because he hadn't insisted on trying to talk to us.

Toni – who'd been silent the entire trip – turned to me. 'This place isn't so bad' she said.

It didn't look it, truth be told. Drab and homogenous slabs of apartments and very little graffiti but nothing like the horror of Peckham or Broadwater Farm in London. Our driver was quick to put her straight.

'Don't go by how it looks' he said. 'This can be dangerous. So you be careful *fraulein*. And it's bad for you to walk on your own here at night.'

I thanked him for his well-meaning advice and we stood at the side of the road, watching him drive away. We ourselves were watched in silence by three slovenly looking men sitting at a small street table outside what might have been some kind of café opposite. I say some kind, because it was hard to say what the place was. But that was the least of my concerns

'Oh shit' I said as I looked at the grey flat front of number 109. This was a low block of apartments and Tom's note hadn't given an apartment number. 'We don't have an apartment number.'

Toni sighed wearily as I took out my phone and dialled the number again. No bloody answer.

'We're going to have to call Tom' I said to Toni who'd wandered over to the main door and was scanning the bank of intercom buttons.

'What's the name of this guy?' Toni asked.

'Major Richard Warne' I said, walking over to join her. 'Don't tell me you've spotted his name?'

Toni stood back from the door frame and extended her hand with a flourish inviting me to take a look. And there it was, a small card behind clear plastic with the hand-written name 'Warne.' It had to be him. I was about to press the button next to the card when there was a buzzing noise and the door clicked open. Toni and I looked at each other wondering what had just happened. But Toni shrugged and pushed the door open. I followed her inside, letting the door fall closed behind me.

Beyond the dim pool of sunlight washing in through the grimy glass in the door frame, the hallway we found ourselves in was cool and all-concrete gloom. There wasn't a lift but I did spot the broad staircase off to our right. Apartment B7, I remembered. I guessed that 'B' meant that it would be on the next floor up so I headed for the staircase and Toni followed, our footsteps echoing on the concrete floor beneath our feet.

'You know when you were telling us about you and Helen in Paris' Toni said as we climbed, surprising me by speaking at all.

'Yeah' I said.

'Well that guy with the beard who kept turning up in Paris. You don't think. . .'

I stopped in my tracks when she said that. Turned to her. I knew what she was asking and I guess you do too.

'Christ' I said, 'I don't know. That guy was neater. Trimmed beard at any rate. But fuck, how would that even work anyway? How could it be?'

Toni shrugged. 'I don't know' she said. 'I was just wondering that's all.'

We continued up the stairs and onto the next floor landing,

which was even gloomier than the hallway below.

'Number seven' I said out loud, following the row of doors off the landing and looking for the numbers. And there it was at last. Number seven.

I was about to knock when the door opened. The blood drained from me so that I staggered back a step or two, almost fainting. It was him! The bearded man who should be burned to a crisp, big bushy beard and all.

'I've been expecting you' he said. 'Do come on in. I'll make us some tea.'

# The Story Episode # 88
# (Moon phase: Day 22)

THE APARTMENT WAS larger than I'd thought it would be, and lighter - and sparsely furnished. Walls covered with book shelves filled with books. A few slim wooden-framed upholstered chairs that could have come from the 1960s and a sofa of similar vintage. And in a corner of the room an uncovered rustic wooden table. No carpet over bare wooden floorboards. That was it for the living room.

'Sit down' the major said. 'I'll go get us that tea.'

No question that we wouldn't want tea. We were going to get it no matter what.

'What's going on?' Toni whispered to me.

I shrugged. I didn't know. But I was far from comfortable.

The Major came back with a china tea service on a tray and placed it on the table. He poured for us without asking our preference and we took the cups and saucers he gave us. Earl

Grey tea. No milk. No sugar. Just in case you were wondering.

He sat down at one end of the table and he was scrutinizing us as we took our first sips of the hot tea in silence.

'You' he said sharply, looking at Toni. 'You need help. You don't fix that, you're going to fade and drift away. And it won't be pretty. Not at the end.'

He turned to me. 'You have issues but not so pressing. We'll no doubt come back to you.'

Well this came as a shock. What he said and the way he just shot it out at us. Drift away… Won't be pretty… Bile rose in my throat as I remembered the demise of my darling immortal beloved Helen.

He turned to me. 'Yes, that's exactly how it'll be' he said.

Toni and me looked at each other in disbelief.

'Stop' I said to him, 'Stop right now.'

This didn't faze him in the least, but he did stop. Waited for me to continue. And I noticed the serenity about him that was almost blissful.

'What has Tom told you?' I said at last.

He thought about that for a moment then said 'Who's Tom?'

I must have looked at him like I thought he was retarded – which perhaps for a second I did. 'Tom is the man who sent us to you' I explained, turning to nod towards Toni. 'That's his wife. Ring any bells?'

I wondered if he was some kind of hippy relic after all, and was under the influence.

He shook his head. 'No,' he said, calm as a flat lake on a hot still day.

'But you said you were expecting us' Toni piped up. And she was right. He had said that when he'd opened the door to us.

'That's right' he said. 'I've been expecting you since last night. I knew you were coming,'

'But you don't know us' Toni said. 'How can you be expecting us.'

'Stay calm' he said to Toni, and I saw her relax back into her seat. And dammit, I swear I could feel the warm swell of peaceful energy wash over her – and me.

But there was something I just couldn't hold back. 'When were you last in New Zealand?' I asked.

He turned his attention to me. 'I've never been to New Zealand' he said. 'And that's a strange question to ask, given the circumstances.'

Now I didn't believe his answer but paradoxically I couldn't fix him for a liar. I was confused as hell but I still knew somehow that this man sitting right in front of us had burned to death outside my isolated Auckland home about a week ago. It *was* him. For sure. But this wasn't the time to press matters.

'You still haven't answered her question' I said.

'Because I was forced to answer yours,' he replied. 'But really it doesn't matter how I knew you were coming. It's enough that I was expecting you, wouldn't you say?'

'Depends what the welcome's going to be like' I said, as glib as you please.

'I trust you've found the welcome to your liking' he said. 'Even though you're clearly not comfortable. I understand that. Your apprehension will fade though.'

'Will it?' Toni asked. 'Why would my husband send us to you if you don't know him?'

The Major waited a moment then said 'I really don't know. Clearly he understands that you're living with a problem that I can help you with. Wouldn't that be reason enough?'

'You say you don't know him' I said. 'But he knows you. He gave me your name and address. And telephone number.'

'And you called the number. That was you, wasn't it, calling again and again?'

'Why didn't you answer?' I asked, suspicious of him.

'To say what? I knew you were coming. You knew you were coming. And whatever we have to say to each other is best said face to face. Much easier to understand the nature of a person's character face to face wouldn't you say?'

I bet you're thinking he was an irritating character, given to creating riddles where there was no need. And I found him exasperating then too. But actually all he said was perfectly reasonable if you look at it objectively.

One thing that did strike me though was that he wouldn't need to see anyone face to face in order to gauge that person's character. He'd be able to tell you from looking at a holiday snap. Because I knew that we were in the presence of someone so assimilated with the Great Work as to be barely human. I'll no doubt explain that to you some other time. But for now just note that I was still wary of the Major while at the same time knowing that he was more than merely accomplished at manipulating the Astral Light.

'How could Tom – my husband – know your name and address' Toni asked 'if you don't know him?'

'Perhaps it's just a case of him knowing *of* me, without our knowing each other in the social sense that I believe you're implying.'

He looked at me for a moment or two and I was aware of being scrutinized. Then he said. 'Blues and Royals, British Army on The Rhine, several tours from the late 70s through to the late 80s.'

It didn't even surprise me that he'd answered a question running through my head before I'd had time to ask it so I said nothing. And he leaned his head back and laughed so that I grinned and started to laugh with him.

'Understand what the Astral Light is and how it works. If you can find a way to manipulate it everything is possible' he said when the laughter had died down.

'So why do you live like this?' Toni asked. 'In a place like this?'

'You think I should live in a palace with a harem and a fleet of limousines and private jets? Two days ago you wouldn't have even posed such a vulgar question' the Major said. 'I don't think we should delay with you.'

'And what the hell does that mean?' I asked.

'It means there's a woman you should see. It means we should go to *Wedding*.'

'Count me out' Toni said. 'I'm in no mood to go to any fucking *wedding*.'

I corrected her before the Major could. '*Wedding*'s another Berlin district' I explained. 'North of here. That's where we'll find this woman.' I looked to the Major for confirmation and got an affirmative nod for my trouble. And I don't know if a cloud passed over the sun outside but it suddenly became dark in that living room and I could see on the walls what I hadn't seen in the light. Occult symbols, most of which I recognised, glowing gold and silver in the gloom.

# The Story Episode # 89
# (Moon phase: Day 22)

I HADN'T USED public transport since I'd lived in London with Helen. Before our flight to New Zealand. So we were talking a few years. In London I'd used the tube to get about but never the bus. We, of course, went from *Neukölln* to *Wedding* by bus because we were in the hands of Major Richard Warne and he didn't give us an option. He didn't have a car, he told us, and he didn't even offer us the option of taking the *U-bahn*, the Berlin underground rail system, which is probably the cleanest and most sophisticatedly modern in the world.

Actually, going by bus wasn't at all bad. Not the filthy smelly marginally safe transport boxes you get in London where you're crammed together with the great unwashed. Berlin buses were large, roomy, clean, and used by everyone.

For most of the journey our bus was half empty. We had to walk a couple of blocks from Warne's apartment to the bus stop on *Hermann Straße* and we didn't have to wait long for a bus. I paid for our tickets as I had a good supply of Euros in my wallet. Toni was quiet during the journey, which took the best part of an hour, but as we neared the city centre I did strike up something of a conversation with the Major.

'So why Berlin?' I asked as the bus passed *Kottbusser Tor*.

'It's a beautiful city don't you think?'

I could barely believe he'd said that. 'Yeah, it's a beautiful city' I agreed. 'But why *Neukölln*? If beauty's what you're after.'

'*Neukölln* is beautiful' he said in all seriousness. 'You're judging it without experiencing it. And you base your judgment on what others tell you. You believe what you think you have to believe.'

He was right and I surprised myself by feeling a little ashamed. 'You're right' I said. 'And I'll look more closely and make my own mind up.'

He laughed at that. 'Then don't let me influence you either.'

'Rest assured I won't' I shot back.

'Good lad, good lad' he said, and I didn't feel the least bit patronized as perhaps I should have done.

We sat in silence for a while after that. I watched the city go by and I watched Toni watching the city go by. I wondered if she was taking in the sights or if her mind had wandered elsewhere. It was hard to say.

'Beautiful girls in Berlin' the Major said as I looked at the people on the streets going about their business.

'Beautiful girls everywhere' I said. I felt we'd touched on my area of expertise.

The Major smiled. 'You're right of course. But I love German girls. Tall, blonde, shapely. Strapping. And for the most part intelligent. Very well read, I find. Cultured.'

'You ever seen the girls who hang out around *Bahnhof Zoo?*' I asked.

He studied me in that disconcerting manner he had, where you could almost feel the intrusion of those clear blue eyes burning into you. 'Those girls are beautiful' he said. 'I help them when I can.'

I smiled and shook my head but said nothing. I had a picture of the bearded Major stalking *Bahnhof Zoo* like a Victorian missionary. He patted my leg and sat back in his seat. We travelled in silence for a while. But a question came to my mind and I felt I needed to ask him.

'You were described to us as a shaman' I said. 'Is that right? Is that how you see yourself?'

'What's a shaman?' he answered. 'Do these labels matter?'

I shrugged. 'I just wondered about you choosing to live here. Berlin. I thought you had to take yourself off to live a solitary life. Out in a wilderness somewhere to become a shaman. You know, needing solitude to make that journey.'

'Berlin is a wilderness' he said in all seriousness.

I shook my head but he continued, seeming to want to explain.

'To an outsider like me it is. I couldn't be more alone. I don't know anyone – not socially, not even now. When I settled here I didn't speak more than a couple of words of the language. It was the perfect wilderness. And everyone here coming to terms with reunification. Between east and west. Easy to stay lost here.'

I could see his point immediately. I would never have thought it if he hadn't told me but I learned a sharp lesson at that moment. There can be no excuses. You can follow the solitary path of the Great Work, tread the path of the Western Way, in the middle of a great city. You have to find the wilderness that exists everywhere. I remembered the lesson of the twenty-seventh Aethyr that remained fixed within me. Solitude. Solitude as opposed to loneliness.

Turning to look at Toni, I wondered if she was experiencing solitude or loneliness. If solitude, she clearly wasn't experiencing the joy of it, the understanding that solitude was the natural state of the monad. If loneliness, I desperately hoped she'd understand that loneliness is a choice. Hoped that would be a comfort until we could do what we had to do to balance the forces wobbling out of balance within her.

I watched the city go by as we headed, stop at a time, for the district of *Wedding*. I remembered reading that it had always been a tough working class district. A Communist stronghold during the Weimar Republic in the 1920s when politics was conducted on the streets by means of violence. Communist to the point where the district was known as *Red Wedding*. I knew that it remained tough and uncompromising. I wondered at its politics now, now that we were living in times less obviously black and white. Or red.

'*Neukölln*, you know' the Major said as the bus got ever closer to *Wedding*. 'That's a wilderness within the city. For someone like me. Or for you. The demographic. Not our people, most of those people. And you know what I mean by that. Not European. Turks, a good deal of them. Not a language I'm familiar with. But all of us speak German now.'

Another lesson. Solitude in a crowd if you choose the right crowd.

We got to where we were going and the Major indicated that we should leave the bus. It was a short walk through streets tagged with graffiti until we came to another block of state-apartments. We climbed stairs up several floors until we came to a concrete landing. The Major led us through a set of swing doors into a dark and cold corridor. Halfway along we came to a green door with peeling paint.

'This is it' the Major said.

He knocked gently on the door, three times, and after a few seconds the door opened. Standing in the doorway was a terrifically gorgeous flaxen-haired beauty of a woman. I'd say in her early twenties. Fresh faced with no makeup, looking like a hippy-chick in a long burgundy peasant skirt, bare feet beneath and a white cotton smock with eastern European peasant-style embroidery around the edging. Honestly, she was lovely. I noticed her, and the rich fragrance of incense coming from the room behind her.

'Hello Heidi' the Major said.

Heidi's smile lit up the gloomy hallway. 'You' she said to me, not returning the Major's greeting. 'You are English. And you live for sex.' I had no time to comment on that as she said 'Now why don't you all come in. Come in. You are welcome.'

I can't tell you what I thought about that. Honestly, I can't remember. I mean, what could I think about that? What would you think about that?

Anyway I took Toni's hand, not knowing why, and we

stepped inside, leaving the Major to follow us and shut the door behind us. Leaving me, at least, to wonder just who the fuck these people were.

# The Story Episode # 90 (Moon phase: Day 22)

MYRRH IS A perfume associated with burial and death by many people. Because of its association with the death of Jesus in the Bible. But the heavy perfumed fragrance is used in occult circles to inspire a sense of psychic – and physical – protection. The scent is burned as incense to promote a sense of peace and relaxation. And to stimulate sensual love.

The overwhelming scent of incense pervasive in the air of Heidi's apartment was Myrrh and its effect on me was immediate. But within seconds, and even before Heidi could bid us sit down, I detected the scent of Patchouli and Damiana expertly and subtly blended with the myrrh. This blend has a very specific occult use; the stimulation of sexual love. My beloved Helen and me used to mix this very blend to burn on charcoal so that it would hang heavy in the air - like it did in Heidi's apartment - on those weekends that we would give entirely to the heightened pleasure of sex. So the aroma of the room we found ourselves in, Heidi's living room, was heavy with the aura of sex.

Despite the perfumed aroma of the incense, my senses were overwhelmed with an underlying scent stimulating primal and visceral reactions in me. Unmistakable smells of semen and vaginal juices. The aftermath of heightened sexual pleasure and arousal that your stimulated senses continue to enjoy following prolonged and intense sexual activity.

These smells and scents overwhelmed – as I say - my first impressions of the apartment but I did come to notice other aspects of its makeup. In the first place it was dark. Heavy curtains drawn against the bright sunlight. Illumination barely breaking the gloom came from candles, seemingly haphazardly placed, and tea-lights burning in two or three metal and glass occult lamps.

On one wall a cloth hung, blue fabric with stars and crescent moons picked out in embroidered silver thread. On other walls occult symbols, such as the sacred Pentagram and the six pointed star of Solomon.

A table in the centre of the room was draped with a white cloth, and an incense burner stood in the centre, one of three, working to create the scented atmosphere of the room. An upholstered sofa and two matching armchairs were arranged against the walls. And two more upholstered occasional chairs completed the furniture.

'Sit down' Heidi said, 'Please. Make yourselves comfortable.'

The Major sat in one of the armchairs and Toni sat in the other. I was standing close to the sofa so that's where I sat. Heidi looked around the room, then it seemed that she went out of her way to come sit on the sofa with me. Not right next to me but on that sofa nevertheless. She lifted her feet to curl up on the sofa at the opposite end to me so that she was able to give her attention to all of us in the conversation that followed. But her bare feet were only inches from me and I couldn't help but notice them. Because they were perfect. No, seriously they were. Slim without being altogether too narrow, sweetly arched and with lovely straight and even toes. Feet that had never, it seemed to me, been constricted in pinched and awkward high-fashion shoes.

In the sexually charged incense-infused atmosphere of the candlelit room, those perfect feet became a fascination for me. I found myself wanting to caress them. Kiss them. Gently suck the toes. And then I realised that Heidi was watching me. And I sensed her surprise and delight.

'My God' she said, smiling, almost clasping her hands together, 'You are defined by sex. It's true.' She ran the toes of one foot along my thigh. 'Would you mind if I stretched my legs, placed my feet in your lap?'

She laughed, but she did lie back and placed her feet in my lap so that I didn't know what to do with my hands.

'Heidi behave' the Major said.

'Oh but it is just fun' she said. 'An amusement.' She turned to me, wriggled her feet in my lap. 'You don't mind do you?'

How could I answer that? I didn't. I wasn't uncomfortable truth be told. I was enjoying it. As Heidi could plainly see.

'All the same, Steven is at a disadvantage. And he's a guest seeking help. Behave yourself.'

Steven. I picked up on that right away. I hadn't told him my name. I hadn't. But he'd known it. And this wasn't any kind of parlour trick either. It had come naturally to him. He knew my name and he used it. He hadn't been trying to impress.

'Oh,' she said. 'I mean nothing by it. And Steven takes no offence I'm sure.' She waited for my confirmation and I gave it with a thin smile and a shake of the head. Then more serious, she said 'Sex really does define who you are. It is beautiful and you are lucky. But you have a problem because sex controls you and you have no control over it. Would you feel more comfortable for now if we removed our clothes? I don't mind if you need to masturbate. It's very natural and if you need to do it so that you can move on to what you've come here for, then you should do it.'

I dare say you'd be shocked if you were in my place there. But I wasn't. The perfumed air and the dim atmosphere of candle light, and this beautiful temptress had me weighing up whether or not to take her up on it. But the Major took charge.

'We'll come to Steven another time perhaps,' he said. 'But we're here for Toni.'

He turned to nod at Toni who sat listless in her chair but looked up at the sound of her name. 'Toni needs our help' he continued. 'Your help most of all, I'd say.'

Heidi switched her attention to Toni but she was absently stroking my aroused penis through my trousers with her foot at the same time. Doubtless intending to teach me a lesson in self-control. And it was working. Because I didn't unzip my pants, didn't take it out, didn't begin to masturbate over her delightful feet. Even though I wanted to and damn the audience.

After scrutinizing Toni for a few moments, she swung her legs out of my lap and got up from the sofa. She crossed the room and knelt before Toni, taking Toni's hands in her own. She closed her eyes and if you had been watching I bet you'd have laughed her down for a charlatan and a parlour-spiritualist. But I saw right away that she was a talented traveller between altered states of consciousness and while I understood that she didn't necessarily see the raw Astral Light, the way that the Major did, or Hesther did, or Tom did, or the professor had done, she was able to utilize it all the same.

At last she opened her eyes and as she looked at Toni, I felt that for the two of them, the world began and ended with the touch of their hands together. The Major, me, the rest of the world didn't exist.

'You poor, poor darling' Heidi said. 'So cold and so alone and so beautiful.' She spoke to Toni like a mother or a grandmother talks to a small child when it seemed clear to me that she was Toni's junior. In age at least. Like I said earlier, she looked to be in her early twenties.

'She means you no harm, she just wants you to learn. She tries to teach you but you can't learn the lesson. No mind, I know where we can find her. We'll talk to her. Ask her to walk by your side. It will be good, you'll see.'

Heidi turned to the Major then to me. 'We need to go somewhere,' she said. 'But tomorrow. To *der wald* – the forest. We'll go tomorrow. In the evening. When it becomes dark.'

'Tomorrow' I said trusting without doubt that this girl was going to be able to do whatever Toni needed. The confidence just flooded out from her. 'Okay then let's arrange it. And I'll need to organize a hotel for me and Toni.'

'Oh no, that's not necessary' Heidi said. 'Not at all. Toni will be safe with Major Warne.' She turned to the Major looking for confirmation and got it with a discreet nod.

'So what about me?' I asked, wondering what the hell was going on and immediately suspicious but at the same time unafraid.

'Oh I hope you will stay with me. Help me with some work.'

'No' I said, 'No way. My place is with Toni. Where she goes I go. We'll get a hotel. And we'll meet back here tomorrow at whatever time you want.'

Heidi pouted but it was a game to her, nothing serious. 'Oh,' she said, 'But I need that energy so strong in you. That sex energy. Give extra strength to what I need to do. Come on. You'll enjoy it. You'll have fun.'

Something pushed my mind, pushed with a heck of a force. Pushed me in Heidi's direction so that I wanted to stay with her more than anything. I looked over at Toni. She smiled at me. Grinned, actually.

'You'd better stay' she said. 'Because the state you're in I can see it's going to be either her or me. And her need seems greater.'

It was fabulous to see Toni cracking jokes like this – even if you don't see the humour in it – because she'd been listless and silent all afternoon. All the same, leaving her with this Major who neither of us knew and who claimed not to know Tom, I wasn't so far gone as to be happy with that.

'I'm going to be fine' Toni said, and right then a wave of energy washed over and through me. Tingled through me. And with it came an understanding. It could have come from Tom. I felt it had. And it told me that Toni was right. She would be fine with the Major. Safer with him than with me in all probability.

'There' Heidi said, all smiles. 'That's settled then. I'll let you see your friends to the door while I go to make some coffee. You can say *auf wiedersehen*, okay?'

She went to the kitchen and left me to see Toni and the Major to the door. As I opened it for them, Toni took my hand and squeezed it.

'I really will be fine' she said. 'So enjoy it. Go on, knock yourself out.'

I wanted to laugh but I felt more than anything like a cork tossed on the ocean. The Major whispered to me.

'You're wrong about Heidi' he said.

'What do you mean?' I said, knowing I hadn't expressed an opinion about her one way or another.

'I mean she's not the young girl you've imagined' he said. 'She's forty eight years old.' That revelation left me reeling, which I'm sure had been his intention. 'She's looking good don't you think?' He chuckled. 'Early twenties' he said, voicing my mental estimation. 'She'll love you for that. You should tell her.'

With that he took Toni's hand and they stepped out into the hall, the Major pulling the door closed behind him. I turned back to the candlelit, sexually aromatic living room and I'd forgotten about Toni and the Major before I'd even fully removed my shirt.

# The Story Episode # 91 (Moon phase: Day 22)

GENDER ILLUSTRATES THE duad. Male and female. Opposite sides of the same coin. The important thing being that it *is* the same coin. I knew that *intellectually* back then but when I think about it, I hadn't experienced what it meant. Which is like learning to drive a car by reading a book. You could memorize every word in the book, and every illustration but nothing would prepare you for that first time behind the wheel and actually taking a car out onto the road and into traffic.

Occult work is like that. You can learn things on the intellectual level but experience is everything. You *can* become an Adept from experience alone. Which is what a shaman is, I suppose. But you can't become an Adept simply from reading books and learning tables of correspondences. 0. The Fool. Aleph. Bull. Uranus. E Major. Air. You know, that sort of thing.

You could memorize the infinite number of links in existence but merely knowing them wouldn't make you an Adept. Although that's probably a poor analogy since the intense focus and exclusive dedication required to pursue that path would undoubtedly bring about the physical and psychological changes to your body, your ego, spirit, soul, astral body, whatever you want to call it, that would effect the Adept transformation within you.

No matter, you get what I'm saying. So coming back to the point I was making, I knew about gender and its duality but I couldn't claim the knowledge and understanding of it that would combine to grant wisdom. And I was all male as Heidi came back into her living room with a pot of coffee on a tray and two cups and a jar of milk, some sugar and some spoons. I was shirtless and draping the shirt I'd taken off, over the back of a chair at the dining table.

'Oh, so you do want to be naked then' Heidi beamed, placing the tray on the table. 'Go ahead, I'll pour some coffee.'

The heady scent of incense was still overwhelming, joined by the smell of fresh hot coffee. I felt free and I removed the rest of my clothing until, standing naked, I realised that Heidi was watching me. She remained fully clothed.

I made no effort to cover myself – you know me better than that – but smiling she said 'You are embarrassed. Why?'

And she was right. I was standing in the apartment of this woman, this stranger, naked and exposed while she inspected me. So I couldn't answer. Not that it mattered. She answered for me. Not short on confidence was Heidi.

'You thought maybe that I would be naked too. But I do not take off my clothes. I am free to leave on my clothes. As you are free to remove yours.' She stood with her hands on her hips, looking at me. Like Honor Blackman playing Pussy Galore in the movie *Goldfinger*. I almost did try to cover myself up with my hands but resisted it by an act of will.

'You need not worry. You and me, we will be naked together soon, yes? We'll both enjoy that.' She pulled a chair from the table and sat. 'Now we have coffee. Then I think I will take you out. We need to go out from here. It will be cleansing. Go out, get cleansed, come back, get naked. Come on, sit. Have coffee with me.'

So I sat naked at the table with her, and we drank scalding-hot coffee together. Me being extra careful not to spill any of course.

After a minute or two of silence Heidi spoke. 'You know, you should strive to be happy' she said.

I thought that to be a twee little meaningless aphorism and I told her so, barely able to keep the contempt from my voice. She thought about that for a moment.

'Okay,' she said. 'But you do things that do not make you happy. And do you know why?'

'Tell me,' I said in a voice weary with cynicism. Which she ignored.

'You do things where your happiness will depend upon whatever someone else chooses to do.'

Oh God, I thought, here's another one who talks in riddles.

'You took your clothes off. You expected me to take my clothes off. I didn't. And this did not make you happy. In fact it made you unhappy.'

'I wouldn't go as far as to say that' I said, on the defensive without knowing why.

'I would' she said with faultless confidence. 'That is why you were embarrassed when I was looking at you naked. Your embarrassment was a symptom of your unhappiness. People do that all the time. Pin their happiness on their expectations of the behaviour of others. They don't often get exactly what they are expecting. So to a degree they are unhappy. Multiply this by all the expectations a person has over the course of a day, a week, a month, a year. Over many years.'

She was right and I knew it. I hadn't known it, other than intellectually. But she'd given me the experience of it. Taught me with that experience of a few seconds what years of reading about it could never have done.

'So you learn that, yes?' she said, reading my mind, which seemed to be the done thing in Adept circles at that time.

'Yes' I said, suddenly energized. 'Yes I do. Thank you.'

'You needed the lesson,' she said. 'I could see it. And don't you worry. Later when we both are naked, you *will* be happy. I'm sure of it.'

She laughed, smiled, and I was struck by what the Major had told me about her being forty-eight years old. I'd thought early twenties, and as she laughed I swear for a flash of an instant I saw her in her early teens. Temple Maiden. Leading a procession of *Parthenoi*.

'Come on' she said. 'Finish that coffee and put your clothes back on. Let's go out.'

Out meant walking to a café in the *Wedding* district where she lived. Through near-deserted streets in the post-twilight dark. Dark, but not gloom. We could hear the sparkle of the living city to the south beyond the empty canyons of dreary dormitory apartment blocks. And we walked mainly in silence, listening and picking up on the energy. Heidi slipped her warm hand into mine and I knew that she was letting me get to know her, her energy. And she was getting to know mine at the same time.

We ended up in a rather modern, clean yet cosy café-cum-bar-cum-restaurant, the *Auszeit* at *Kiautschoustraße 12a*. The place was half empty – or half full if you prefer - and the dark wood that was a feature of the interior gave it a warm emotional feel. Which was just as well because as we'd neared the place, well, for a couple of blocks or so before we reached it, I'd had the uncomfortable feeling that we were being followed. Heidi must have picked up on it too because as we stepped into the café she whispered to me without turning to look at me.

'Who have you upset?' she said.

'I wouldn't know where to begin telling you' I sighed, and I was only half joking.

She wasn't joking at all when she said 'There's something out there coming for you.'

I didn't know what to make of that but said nothing as she nodded to a couple of the waiting staff she must have been familiar with and led us to a corner table as far from other patrons as possible.

'Well you'll be safe with me' she said smiling, once we were seated.

'And when I'm not with you?' I asked. Because I knew she wasn't joking.

'We'll have to make you safe' she said. But she must have wanted to end the discussion because she changed the subject. 'We should eat. We have a busy night, you and me. But only light food. I prefer salad.'

She picked up a menu and studied it and I did the same. Then she leaned in close and whispered like a conspirator. 'What I want you for tonight, the way you will help me,' she said. 'I have to repay a debt to a Goddess.'

I wondered if she had me in mind as some kind of human sacrifice. And in a sense, she did.

'I repay her with pleasure' she said, in such a way that I became instantly aroused at the sound of her voice. 'Sex. I let her become me. You see what we will do, yes?'

I saw. And this wasn't going to be a case of me simply fucking her. This would be a ritual requiring several shifts of consciousness and careful preparation.

'The Goddess,' I said. 'What do we call her?'

She ran the tip of her tongue along her lips then giggled when she noticed the effect that had on me. 'I draw her down from the moon,' she said. 'And it must be tonight because tomorrow we have business with your friend. And the next day is my time. Menstruation. So you are brought to me today. And tonight I repay my debt through you. It all works out.'

I heard what she was saying but a chill of fear rippled through me on hearing that this was a ritual of the moon.

'What Goddess are we calling down?' I asked again. But I knew. In my heart I knew.'

'Diana,' she said. 'In her aspect as Isis. Different energies, those two. But the one becomes the other and vice versa in the work we do. They both experience what we do for her.' She must have seen my discomfort because she took my hand. 'She hates you, I know. But we can show her how to love you, yes? Kill the two birds with the one stone.'

# The Story Episode # 92
# (Moon phase: Day 23)

AN EXPERIENCE OF moments transcends a lifetime of rote-learning. Are you getting the picture? I mention it often enough and I make no excuses. I'm telling you my story but I'd like to transmit a little understanding too. I owe it to you. To give something back, something valuable even though it's not valued.

So that night with Heidi I experienced something I'd only ever read about and heard spoken about. The Charge of the Goddess.

We came out of the Auszeit at some time before ten o'clock and it was as dark on the streets outside as it can ever be in a city. We'd eaten beautiful organic salad with a light dressing of oil and balsamic vinegar and we'd drank still spring water. We'd talked about my beloved wife, my darling Helen, but we hadn't talked about what had happened to her. To us.

What we did talk about was love and sacrifice and I felt good about it, talking to Heidi. Whatever else she was, she was certainly an empath. I was wary of that at first because an empath can tune into your wavelength without you ever knowing it – if you're unaware – and can steer you in directions according to her will and against your own. This is the mark of sorcery and while I was sure that Heidi was no sorceress I was nevertheless cautious with her at first.

Slowly I loosened up and told myself that I'd controlled that process, that I was beyond any subtle manipulation. I still tell myself that, so we won't take that any further.

Walking back through the quiet streets then we were light and easy in each other's company. Heidi slipped her hand in mine again and I understood her purpose. I'd followed a different path, but before that I'd read a lot of Witchcraft literature.

'We're going to perform a Great Rite then, you and me' I said as we strolled along *Guineastraße*.

Heidi smiled at me. I think she was surprised. 'Yes,' she said. 'You know of it?'

'I've read some' I said, casually understating what I felt I knew. 'But I can't see how it can work. The month long preparation. I haven't done it.'

She squeezed my hand and I liked her doing it. 'The Goddess chose you' she said. 'Sent you to me.' She turned to me as we continued to walk. 'And you don't need to prepare. You are always prepared, yes?' She threw her head back and giggled and she was suddenly young again, a Temple Maiden in my eyes. 'I have prepared' she said, 'knowing you would come.'

So I had to ask. 'You prepared? But how did you know I was coming? A month ago I didn't know I would even be in Europe. I was half a world away.'

'But I knew,' she said. 'I called for you and I knew you would come.'

I accepted that. Because I know and I knew even then how this would work. Her call, the way I'd understand it from an alchemical and *Haute Magie* viewpoint would be to a particular electro-magnetic wavelength; actually a collection of virtually unique specific and subtle electro-magnetic wavelengths. A collection that ended up being me. Magnetic attraction. And it was far removed from sorcery, because she didn't know me as an ego, a personality; she'd just put out a call to attract what she needed. If her need of me had been contrary to a need of my own, I wouldn't have been there. But the fact that Great Intelligences had seen fit to place me there with Heidi did seem to indicate that there was nothing contrary to my interests in what she proposed to do with me as her aid and instrument. Of course, that didn't mean that I was ready for the experience and wouldn't be mentally shredded by it.

'You will be safe' Heidi said like she'd read my thoughts again.

I looked up and the moon was right there between the buildings. A slim crescent in her waning phase. And for the first time in a long time I felt no malevolence directed at me. No affection, true, but an absence of hatred. Which was almost as good.

'See?' Heidi said. 'It will be well.'

In that moment I was acutely aware of her skin touching my skin where she held my hand and it was like an open door. We were like two computers sharing information. She was taking knowledge of what I was and giving herself to me. I felt a sensual love drifting through me like the pulse of a heroin rush, warm and seductive. And silver.

Heidi was the moon. I saw it right there and then. She'd prepared herself to be the moon for the last twenty eight days. So this is a good time to explain a few things. This talk of preparation, the Charge of the Goddess and the Great Rite. Well what we were going to do was an intensely sexual rite.

I think most Witchcraft Covens perform this rite by proxy with material objects representing the masculine and feminine aspects, channels for the energy of libido that the rite demands. For example, a chalice would represent the feminine aspect, so you get the idea.

We were going to perform a natural rite with ourselves as the channels. And preparation is needed as a rule, by inexperienced participants in particular. Because I have to tell you that this sex ritual does not call for us to rut like animals in spring. This is about the control and direction of the libido energy, the most potent creative force available to us. Preparation involves – among other things - daily practice of masturbation. Peaking at the brink of orgasm and not allowing that completion. The idea being to control that slip into an extra realm of consciousness, maintain a focus on it so that the energy created can be applied to the objective of the Great Rite. This takes practice. The longer you can ride and control this unlimited source of power, the greater the effect of the ritual. Both participants should ride the wave together, orgasm together. The Great Rite itself I'll describe shortly, but for now understand that it's the creation of balance between male and female sexual energy with the intention of directing the resulting creative force to work upon a known and desired objective. Under the approving watch of universal intelligences.

Typically, the way I saw it, one of the participants in the rite would take the lead role and the leader would bring extra power to the ritual by assimilating the form of an appropriate God or Goddess. And I mentioned earlier something called the Charge of the Goddess. Well that's what Heidi was going to do. She was going to Draw Down The Moon, that is to say, perform the Charge of the Goddess prior to our practice of the Great Rite.

'You don't need to practice' she said to me breaking the silence of our walk. 'You know tantra.'

'Do I?' I said, knowing full well that I did.

'A man like you, it's almost all you know.'

You perhaps think I could have taken offence at that but I didn't. I knew what she meant. She wasn't saying that I didn't know anything other than sex. But that my knowledge – born of experience – of matters sexual was so much greater than my knowledge of other aspects of the truth. And she was right.

'Come on' she said unexpectedly picking up the pace. 'We're almost there.'

Nothing in the energy I experienced through her touch indicated any disquiet but I sensed it anyway because it transmitted itself to me. I found myself looking round. Seeing darker and deeper shadows in the doorways. Hearing footfalls on the pavement where there were none. I was being followed. Something was after me. I shuddered and kept pace with Heidi. Soon enough we were back at her apartment building. We hurried up to her apartment and she closed the door behind us with a smack of finality.

'There' she said. 'Go sit down for a minute.'

I sat at the table and watched as she took a piece of white chalk and took great care while drawing a pentagram on the floor just inside the door. The bottom two points of the pentagram faced the door. A barrier then.

'There' she said again, standing and facing me. 'Now we won't be disturbed, eh?'

I knew what she meant by that and I'm sure you know it too.

She got me to clear the living room of furniture and roll up the rug. She took a huge rug from one of the bedrooms and together we unrolled it on the floor. It took up most of the floor space in that living room. It was a black, thick-pile woollen carpet and dominating it was a huge silver circle with a pentagram design in the centre. At least we wouldn't be performing the Great Rite on the cold floor.

She stood in the centre of the circle and called me over in a whisper. 'Come to me' she commanded. And I obeyed. 'Undress me' she breathed, her lips almost touching mine. And I'm not being flip here when I tell you that I did as I was commanded. I undressed the Goddess. And I realised that the ritual had begun.

# The Story Episode # 93
# (Moon phase: Day 23)

UNDRESSING HEIDI WAS as much a part of the ritual as all that followed. I knew it right away as we stood in the silver circle in her living room. Candles and occult lamps the only light in the room, incense burners making the air heavy with mind-altering scents.

I took my time with each item of her clothing. Barely touching the fabric, never touching her, as I slipped the garments from her smooth and beautifully shaped form. And I stood as a supplicant before a Goddess as she performed the same ritual on me. Our clothes we folded carefully then placed them outside our circle of silver.

We knelt in the centre of the circle, in the centre of the sacred pentagram. Facing each other. Barely – but not quite – touching. We explored each other with our fingertips and our lips. Every inch of each other, gentle touching and stroking and breathing until we were familiar with every contour of each other's body.

My breathing was held regular and slow as her fingertips trailed across my pubic hair, prompting an almost painfully hard erection. I held my focus and controlled my heart rate and my soaring libido along with my breathing as she caressed the swollen head of my penis with her lips.

When she lay back on the carpet for me to press my lips against the swollen labia hidden among the blonde curls between her legs she maintained the same balance of breathing and heart rate and control as me. And you might think that this is difficult to maintain but it's not as difficult as you'd imagine. The practice of tantric yoga helps you learn this degree of control. And Heidi had been preparing with a month-long daily ritual of masturbation during which she'd practiced the art of holding herself for prolonged periods at the point just prior to orgasm – Riding the Dragon – before releasing her explosive pleasure to the Goddess. Yes, even the acts of preparation are dedicated to the Goddess.

'Kneel with me' she whispered, her mouth so close to mine that I could taste her breath.

We knelt together in the circle and she put her lips against mine. Just touching, barely pressing. Gently using her tongue to ensure that our mouths were open, forming a channel from her to me and from me to her. And we began a process of shared breathing; her breathing in slowly through her nostrils as I inhaled the air from her mouth. Then we'd reverse the process. And this continued for some minutes until we'd established a shared intimacy of breath as intense as any more overtly sexual contact.

She reached down between us and with a gentle and respectful touch she took my engorged penis in her fingers and guided it between her thighs so that her slit rested against the top of the shaft, soaking it with her aromatic juice. I was merely following her lead in all this and she took my hands in hers, held our hands out to the side, then slid her palms down mine until only our fingertips were in contact. And then she removed that physical contact, our fingertips just a whisker apart but the energy coursing between us real and tingling and luscious and warm and flowing.

Pulling her lips from mine she tilted her head back. Her eyes closed and even as I watched I experienced a shift in our collective consciousness. The ceiling of the room became open to me so that I could see the vast black infinity of the universe. No punctuating silver stars. . . but the moon. A glittering crescent more beautiful than anything I'd ever experienced in my life. Powerful. Unforgiving. Nurturing. Healing. Everything. But not hatred. I loved her. And I wanted her to love me.

Heidi gently pressed her thighs tighter around my penis and began the chant to call down the Goddess with a whisper. She was Drawing Down The Moon, and the words were the words of the Goddess. The words of Isis. Of Diana. The Goddess invited, becoming her, accepting her. And the Goddess spoke words of promise.

*'Whenever ye have need of anything,*
*once in the month and better it be when the moon is full,*
*then shall ye assemble in some secret place,*
*and adore the spirit of me,*
*who am Queen of all who live in wisdom.*

*There shall ye assemble,*

*ye who are fain to learn all knowledge of craft,*
*yet have not won its deepest secrets;*
*to these will I teach all things that are as yet unknown.*

*And ye shall be free from slavery;*
*and as a sign that ye be truly free,*
*you shall be naked in your rites;*
*and ye shall dance, sing, feast, make music and love,*
*all in my praise.*
*For mine is the ecstasy of the spirit,*
*and mine also is joy on earth;*
*for my law is love unto all beings.*

*Keep pure your highest ideals;*
*strive ever towards them,*
*let nothing stop you or turn you aside.*
*For mine is the secret door which*
*opens upon the Land of Youth,*
*and mine is the cup of the wine of life,*
*and the Cauldron of Cerridwen,*
*which is the Holy Vessel of Immortality.*
*I am the gracious Goddess,*
*who gives the gift of joy unto the heart of man.*

*Upon earth,*
*I give the knowledge of the spirit eternal;*
*and beyond death,*
*I give peace, and freedom,*
*and reunion with those who have gone before.*

*Nor do I demand sacrifice;*
*for behold, I am the Mother of all living,*

*and my love is poured out upon the Earth.*

*I am the beauty of the green earth,*
*and the white moon among the stars,*
*and the mystery of the waters,*
*and the desire of the heart of man.*

*Call unto thy soul, arise, and come unto me.*
*For I am the soul of Nature,*
*who gives life to the Universe.*
*From me all things proceed,*
*and unto me all things must return;*
*and before my face, beloved of Gods and of men,*
*let thine innermost divine self be enfolded,*
*in the rapture of the infinite.*

*Let my worship be within the heart that rejoicest,*
*for behold, all acts of love and pleasure are my rituals.*
*Therefore, let there be beauty and strength,*
*power and compassion, honor and humility,*
*mirth and reverence within you.*

*And thou who thinketh to seek for me,*
*know thy seeking and yearning shall avail thee not,*
*unless thou knoweth the mystery;*
*that if that which thou seekest thou findest not within thee,*
*thou wilt never find it without thee.*

*For behold, I have been with thee from the beginning;*
*and I am that which is attained at the end of desire.'*

A tingling of dragon-fire energy buzzing through my flesh as

Heidi's voice rose to a vibrating crescendo approaching those final verses of the Charge. But by then the voice was no longer Heidi's. It was the voice of the Goddess!

She pulled gently from me and I felt an ache of longing at losing just a few inches of the closeness I was sharing with the her. She arched back., spreading her thighs, exposing her glistening vulva to my eager eyes as she slid to prostrate herself on her back, in the form of the pentagram woven into the carpet. Her arms and legs spread to map the points of the sacred star. I knelt between her legs, my penis aching with desire and burning with the flow of energy I shared with her. And in the heavy, perfumed, candle-lit atmosphere as I looked down upon her waiting and receptive naked form, I saw the Goddess as the Maiden of the Temple. Saw her in the flower of unsullied youth, untouched and perfect and pure and unafraid.

Raising her hips, she invited me to come to her, to penetrate her. To be her. This impossibly beautiful and impossibly young girl. And as her fingers reached up to close around my penis, to pull me down to her, she transformed before my eyes. I lay above her, supporting my weight on my hands not wanting to crush the youthful perfect beauty and as the tip of my penis touched and began to part her soft pubic wisps of hair, she became a woman. Not Heidi, still the Goddess. But mature and fecund and nurturing. Knowledgeable on all matters concerning love and sex and pleasure.

She stroked my penis, pulling the skin back tight at the base as she guided the tip to her hot, open, inviting vagina. I closed my eyes and tilted my head back needing to exercise control as she brought me to the brink of love-pleasure. And when I opened them, beneath me and before me, I saw a wrinkled ancient crone. Grey creased skin and dark eyes, a display of all the unfair wretchedness of time. And while I hesitated for a moment, appalled at the sight of her creased parchment skin and withered features, at once I felt a wave of sexual desire. So I pressed my lips against hers and slid my tongue into her ancient mouth as I slid my penis into her dry but welcoming vagina. And as my penis slid deep inside her I experienced a shift of consciousness so intense and so explosive that it may have pushed me close to the point of insanity.

Awareness flickering at the edge of consciousness of the infinite scope of the universe, silver stars bursting and seeding new stars that grew and bulged with fecund energy before bursting to seed ever more stars. And all this fast like bubbles forming and bursting on the surface of water boiling in a cauldron. Then when sight came back to my eyes, there was the Goddess beneath me, accepting my gift of love and sex and pleasure. The Maiden and the Mother somehow mixed.

The Goddess and I, we gave and took pleasure, sharing it, playing with it. Teasing. Delight. Abandoned and uninhibited. Holding each other on the brink of explosion, Riding the Dragon together. And at one point, the strangest experience of rapture and reversal. The Goddess became Helen. And the love coursing between us intensified. I felt myself deep inside her, held by her, soft and warm and wet. We lay still together, the deep penetration all we'd ever wanted or needed. Riding the Dragon together for eternity, it seemed. Helen, the Goddess, granting me a gift even though my purpose was to give to her.

My eyes closed and I became intensely aware of being no longer flesh and blood but the pure truth of Astral Light. Vibrating at a frequency so similar to that of the Goddess, of Helen, that we became indiscernible. She became me. I became her. Then for a moment that seemed an age, realization of the illusion of flesh. But I was still her and she was still me. So that I experienced, with amazement and delight, the unbearable pleasure of penetration given with love and respect. I understood for just that moment in the illusion of time, what it was to have a vagina, to feel the stretch of penetration, to understand what was given when a woman gave that gift to a man.

And then another loss of consciousness, another burst of stars. An awareness that all this experience was not mine alone. The Goddess was sharing it with me. As the stars burst and died and formed and burst and died, we shared an orgasm of the most intense pleasure so that the feminine aspect of experience granted to me by the Goddess could feel the hot thick semen spurting deep inside, pulse after pulse.

After that, I don't know how long it was before consciousness of Heidi's apartment returned. But at some point I opened my eyes and the candle-lit gloom presented itself and the heavy aroma of incense surrounded me. I was lying in the circle on the rug with Heidi. My penis still hard and deep inside her. I could feel my semen trickling out, soaking us as Heidi stroked my hair and kissed me.

'I think we make the Goddess happy' she whispered. 'Don't you think?'

I shook my head. 'I don't know' I said.

Heidi was gentle with me. 'Yes you do. She let you see. Let you feel it. What it's like to be a woman experiencing love. I won't ask you what your thoughts are. That is private. A gift for you. A great honour I'd say.'

I kissed her. Just a gentle kiss on her lips as we lay on our sides, me still deep inside her, her making no effort to do anything about that.

'We should sleep a little' she said. 'I'd like to sleep here. Is that okay?'

I knew she meant right there, on the rug. So I nodded to say yes. And she wrapped her arms around me, pulled me close to her and rested her head on my shoulder. And with me still enjoying the post-orgasm pleasure of remaining deep inside her, we drifted off into a deep and dreamless slumber. Because I wasn't dreaming when I opened my eyes sometime later and in the gloom saw a shadowy form in the corner of the room, shifting and fidgeting. But unable to penetrate the sanctuary of our sacred circle.

# *The Story Episode # 94*
# *(Moon phase: Day 23)*

WHAT CANNOT TOUCH you cannot hurt you. This is true provided you understand that touch is not purely physical. You can be touched mentally and emotionally. But I knew this and I knew that whatever lurked within Heidi's living room, our Temple, couldn't penetrate the protective silver circle where we lay entwined.

If you didn't have experience of this sort of thing you'd have been gibbering in terror at knowing about the black shadow sharing the room with you. I'll say two things about that. Firstly, you're probably a liar if you try to claim that you wouldn't be scared. Secondly, if you are one of those people – those very few people – who *wouldn't* be scared, unless you were an Adept, then you'd be in a mental institution, or dead - probably within days but sooner or later - most definitely. Certainly one or the other at some point. Because being unafraid, you'd no doubt break the circle to investigate or confront the nature of that shadow. And then you'd be fucked. Because you wouldn't even notice it assimilating itself within you.

You'd notice the effects of it though. Hours, days, weeks, and sometimes even months later. At the very least – and I mean *very* least – the manifestation would take the form of an unshakeable depression. No treatment would shake it. I can't tell you how much I sneer with contempt at the products of the pharmaceutical industry. Particularly when it comes to drugs that will supposedly control the mind. The drugs don't work. They never have. But you go on believing in Big Pharma since I know how much of a false comfort that is to you. You're wedded to the Illusion and I can't help you with that. I'm not inclined to help you either. I'm just telling my story. But the point is, I wasn't afraid because I knew what was keeping me safe so I simply snuggled closer to Heidi and fell into a deep sleep again.

We both drifted awake at around the same time, although thinking about it Heidi probably woke before me and it was her gentle stroking of my penis that roused me. I remember that a chink of early sunlight suggested itself to us in the form of a narrow band of light streaming beneath the long curtains to play upon the floor. The first thing I noticed was the scent of the room. A lingering residue of the incense we'd burned and the overwhelming alkaline smell of spent semen. Heidi must have noticed that too.

'Your gift to the Goddess' she said. 'A generous gift. We pleased her, I think.'

She'd said that to me earlier. That she thought we'd pleased the Goddess. There was no need for her to reinforce that view. I wasn't a nervous amateur needing reassurance. But she meant no harm by it and I slipped my fingers between her legs to feel her still-soaking hair and the warm slit hiding within.

'Do you think she'd like more of the gift? Or was that

enough?'

Heidi took my fingers from between her legs and sucked them, tasting the residue of her juices and my semen.

'I think we let her enjoy the gift we gave her already for now' she said.

And believe it or not, although I was aroused and hard, I felt no sense of disappointment. And in realising that, I shivered through to my core with the wonder of it.

'There, you see? The Goddess gives and does not just take. That mathematical, scientific path you follow, it's not the only way. And now you see.'

I saw. I saw that I'd just experienced a natural and subconscious control of my libido. The Dragon Fire flowing through me not diminished but directed. At that moment I felt I could do anything.

'We need to complete what we started' I said. 'We need to clean this space.'

Heidi knew exactly what I meant. 'A banishing rite, yes' she said. 'Something came here. Followed the path illuminated by the Goddess.' She got to her knees, slowly scanned the room. 'It remains,' she said. 'So we say goodbye to the Goddess, right? Then we banish whatever has come for you.'

'Come for me?' I repeated, shocked.

'Don't pretend to be surprised' Heidi said. 'This black shadow follows you. It has been with you for a long time.'

I didn't argue or ask questions. 'Then let's banish it' I said.

'It's strong,' Heidi said with a shrug. 'We can banish it from my home. To send it from you will take a lot more work. It clings to you. You understand me?'

I understood. What Heidi had described was almost a form of possession. But not by any demon the way you'd see it in a stupid Hollywood film. An intelligence. Targeting me specifically. Coming after me and manipulating the Astral Light to do it.

'Okay' Heidi said. 'You understand. So come. Let us say our goodbyes to the Goddess and send whatever has come for you out of here.'

And that's what we did. Two banishing rituals. One a gentle thank you and farewell to the Goddess. The other a call to the Gods to pull whatever wasn't welcome out of Heidi's Temple, her home, and stand temporary guardian against a quick return.

Satisfied that the banishing rituals had worked – and strangely I felt that a light had returned to the room at their completion - Heidi rose and went to open the curtains. She stood naked before the open windows and threw up her arms in a welcome to the sun and the new day. She was staggeringly beautiful in silhouette like that and I wanted her. Kneeling on the rug, watching her, I wanted to take her, to spend the whole of the sunlit day fucking her on that rug in that room, surrounded by the stale scent of my spunk and her cunt and I wanted her like a fucking animal ruts in season. I wanted to take her. Take her. Until she turned to me.

'Maybe you should know me better first, eh?' she said. 'And if it's meant to be you can fuck me however you want to whenever you want to. In any place.'

Well that put me back in my box. And she was right. So I smiled and said 'In any place? Are you sure?'

She laughed. 'Sure I'm sure' she said. 'Fuck me however you want, wherever you want. I smile as they take us to their prison, yes?'

I found that I loved it when passion took hold of her and her English became less precise. What poker players call a *tell* showing me when she was abandoning emotional control.

'But what a way to go' I said.

She came back to the centre of the rug and knelt beside me where she couldn't help but feel the sexual energy flooding through and around me in my arousal. She stroked my penis somewhat absently with the tips of her fingers. 'Maybe the universe will bring us close together in that way some day. But it's not right for us together. Not right now' she said.

I understood the truth of it. Because a million thoughts rushed through me, stimulated by her words. And most of them had my beautiful immortal beloved darling wife Helen at their core so that I couldn't help but cry. And Heidi held me and stroked my hair, comforting me as she crushed me gently to her. The nurturing Goddess. And no sign of hatred. Nor of contemptuous pity. I cried for a minute or two and Heidi didn't say a word, just let me release it from my system.

Finally, after my sobbing had stopped, she said 'If it happens, ever, you know that I'd love that. For us to enjoy each other. Even if it was only for a brief while.'

All I could do was nod in acceptance and thanks. Because I was supposed to have been helping her, and perhaps I had, but the way it had turned out I felt that I'd been the recipient and that great gifts had been bestowed upon me.

So we showered and dressed and cleaned the room, transformed it from Temple to living room once again. I turned on my mobile phone to see if there had been any messages from Toni. But there were none.

'That shadow that comes for you,' Heidi said. 'You know who it is. Who is it?'

'Sable Wyvern' I said straight out without thinking. And fuck knew where that had come from. I'd never even met this Sable Wyvern. And just why would an officer of the secretive and impenetrable College of Arms, whom I'd never heard of until a few days ago when Toni's husband Tom – with whom I'd only just become acquainted - told me he was dead? As though I'd care. Maybe I should have cared.

Things didn't make sense but I felt that pieces of a complex jigsaw were falling into place. All the same, why did I believe that the dead Sable Wyvern was coming after me? What the fuck was that about?

'You are surprised that you know? Or surprised that it is him?' Heidi asked, clearly noticing my state of confusion.

'Both,' I said.

Then my phone rang cutting the conversation dead.

'Hello' I said, answering it.

'Steven is that you? I've been wondering where you've got to. I've been looking for you.'

Hesther calling from London. Hesther the Adept, so I didn't even have to wonder how she'd got my unlisted New Zealand mobile phone number. Hesther the Adept. Hesther the Goddess.

# *The Story Episode # 95 (Moon phase: Day 23)*

SHE KNEW I wasn't in London. Hesther I mean. I mean, she never said it and she pretended to be surprised when I told her I was in Berlin. Even more surprised to hear that I was there with Toni. That was the kicker for me. Hesther wouldn't have been surprised that I was with Toni wherever she'd found me. Toni was my guide and companion for this part of whatever journey I was undertaking. Hell, you know yourself; she was the initiator if anything. And Hesther would have all of Toni's contact details. She'd have made every effort to contact Toni before contacting me. Probably. So why the act?

I did get a feeling that Hesther was irritated that we'd left London without telling her. And I couldn't really understand why that would be. I suppose I'd have liked to have sat down for a while and tried to think that through. But I was with Heidi. And I'm going to try to explain what that was like, being around Heidi right then.

Heidi was beautiful. Not the porcelain untouchable classical effortless beauty of Hesther. But in a way, more like Toni. Simply gorgeous and with an infectious sense of fun. Maybe I haven't shown you a great deal of that side of Toni but you can rest assured it was a large part of her charisma.

Heidi had it too, but with it an almost intangible and difficult to describe earthy confidence. I mean, Toni wasn't lacking in confidence but a lot of Heidi's confidence came from a direct link she seemed to have with nature. Every moment I spent with her reminded me of what I'd constantly been told by everyone – not least by Rachel back at Toni's house in London – that I needed to attune myself to the Ancient Elements. Earth. Fire. Water. Air. That I needed to balance their essence and attributes within me. That I needed to find a path through the labyrinth via nature. You got that sense of nature with Heidi. You just absolutely did. She was the Dancer in the forest, wearing a tiara of leaves and twigs. Holly. I saw her wearing a crown of Holly and dancing naked through the trees wearing nothing but that crown and the joy of freedom. Heidi as a free spirit, a natural Adept.

Let me tell you, I'd never met anyone with an aura remotely approaching hers and I couldn't help but love her. Yes, love her. In all her aspects of Maiden Mother and Crone.

You probably think I fall in love easily, and maybe I do.

Except I know for the most part it's just lust that I wrap in the kind of emotional sensitivity I think a woman needs to feel; I give it to her with words I think she needs to hear. Is that disingenuous? I don't know. Men and women all play these games where love and sex are concerned. Women usually play the game that I play. Men rarely do. That gives me an edge. Gave me an edge.

But the way I felt about Heidi, that was love. Not the burning, consuming passion I feel for my darling beautiful immortal beloved Helen. But a persistent love burning with a gentler heat. I felt that in particular as we walked an hour later holding hands along the *Kastanienallee* about a couple of miles from *Wedding* and just on the western edge of the *Prenzlauer Berg* district. Heidi was taking me for coffee and bread rolls at her favourite coffee shop, Morning Glory. Yes, I did get the connection. Morning Glory being slang for the wake-up erection a lot of men experience each day.

We walked because the sun was spreading blessings from a perfect azure sky on all who would accept them, and because the *Kastanienallee* was only about a couple of miles away.

Heidi may have been a spirit of nature but in the city she was metropolitan chic. Moschino from head to toe. Gorgeous narrow-brimmed soft red hat over long free-flowing blonde tresses. Off-grey bolero jacket with muted turquoise trim at the cuffs and front edges. Beneath the jacket a sweet little slip-over silk top, mostly grey with a discreet abstract white pattern and a just-above-the-knee silk skirt, printed with almost tie-dye abstraction in a riot of colours – pink, blues, turquoise, red. On her feet, broad yellow sandals and she carried a turquoise day-bag that perfectly matched colours in the print of her skirt. As I say, every piece by Moschino and everything matching so you'd think she'd hired a stylist to put the whole look together.

Happy to walk through Berlin hand in hand with Heidi? You bet your fucking life I was. I loved her. And yes, I still wanted to enjoy endless sex with her but I had that under control. I could feel the creative Dragon-Fire sexual energy running through me, fuelled by lust, but it was not an all-consuming passion. I could control it and I felt that I could direct it towards a creative purpose should the need arise. This was new to me. I think Heidi understood that as she squeezed my hand and turned to me, smiling.

'That phone call' she said. 'Hesther. What does she want with you? You don't have to say if you can't or don't want to.'

'No,' I said. 'It's fine. You know, there are things I can't say. I just can't. You understand?'

'Sure. I understand. Sacred oaths.'

I didn't answer that. I couldn't. To say anything would be to give away something. Heidi laughed and I was coming to find her little bursts of laughter exquisitely charming.

'It's okay' she said. 'You say nothing. But that tells me what you try to hide.' She laughed again. 'So this Hesther belongs to a mystical Order. And so do you. And I am guessing, so does Toni. Am I right?'

I didn't answer. She laughed again. An almost shy giggle so delightful that I just  wanted to push her against the wall and kiss her.

'Okay, she does' Heidi said, knowing she was right.

We wandered along for a while saying nothing more, then Heidi said 'And Helen? Your wife?'

I shook my head. I couldn't say anything. Heidi kissed me on the cheek, gentle and lingering so that I could feel her breath and it took all the control I had not to break down and cry. Instead I said 'Hesther just called to find out where I was. We left without telling her.'

'And you have to tell her?' Heidi asked.

'She has a difficult time ahead' was all that I would say.

Heidi nodded, understanding. 'Yes,' she said. 'A death. She deals with the fallout.'

'Something like that' I said, not even remotely amazed that she seemed to know what I didn't think she could have been told.

'Well she will have to wait,' Heidi said. 'We have work to do. To free your friend, Toni. Hesther cannot have you until then.' She giggled again, squeezed my hand like I was a toddler needing constant reassurance and love – which I suppose I did – then said 'Ah, here we are.'

There's no point in telling you what happened in the Morning Glory coffee shop because nothing happened. Nothing worth mentioning. We talked for half an hour had some incredibly good coffee and fabulous warm fresh pastries. But what happened when we left is something I do have to tell you, so let's move on to that.

We were walking together down a narrow street not far from Heidi's apartment block in *Wedding*. Virtually nobody on that street at that early hour. And we passed a doorway. And the next thing I remember was that we were jumped from behind by a number of men. A few but I can't say exactly how many. I was knocked unconscious and my last memory was of a dirty old white van screeching up alongside us and Heidi and me being bundled in through a sliding door in the side.

# *The Story Episode # 96*
# *(Moon phase: Day 24)*

I LOST A day. Because the Major eventually found me and that's how I found out. I was sitting on a bench near *Bahnhof Zoo*. I was alright except that the back of my head was sore where I'd been hit with a cosh. But the skin wasn't broken and there was no bleeding. Funny thing is, I can't remember anything until the Major came up to me. Stood before me.

'Alright Steven' he said. 'You can come with me now. Come along, there's a good chap.'

As I looked up to see him standing there with his bushy beard and otherwise neat appearance, it was like I suddenly woke up. I'd been sitting on that bench totally unaware of myself or my surroundings. But seeing the Major brought everything back. Not the events following my abduction, but certainly everything up to then.

'Heidi. . .' I began, taking the Major's hand and letting him pull me to my feet.

'We'll find her,' the Major said. 'But let's deal with you first.'

I noticed Toni standing behind him then. Her eyes seemed dead and she didn't speak. Not right away at any rate. So we went back to the Major's apartment - public transport of course – and when we got there the Major asked me what had happened.

It turned out that by mid-morning on the previous day, when the Major and Toni hadn't heard from us, they'd tried calling and got no response. I reached for my pocket and my mobile phone when the Major mentioned that and was surprised to find it still there. I looked at it and saw that I'd missed several calls from the Major and Toni. I reached for my other pocket expecting my wallet to be missing but it was there, and when I took it out I found all the cash and my credit cards.

You'd think I'd be pleased about this but I wasn't. You see my immediate concern was for Heidi. Whoever had attacked and abducted us hadn't had money as a motive. The Major picked up on this too.

'Someone was after *you*' he said, looking at me. 'This isn't about Heidi.'

'Why did they let him go then?' This was Toni.

'It's someone who knows what Heidi is,' the Major said. 'Stop Heidi helping you stops you helping Steven.' He paused for a moment. 'Then Steven here is theirs for the taking.'

'Who says I'm helping Steven?' Toni asked, and I was becoming increasingly concerned about the lack of her natural spark.

The Major laughed. 'You went to New Zealand to fetch him. You're his wife's best friend, -'

'My wife's dead' I said, interrupting.

The Major took my hand intending the gesture, I think, to be a comfort.

'Death is an illusion' he said. 'You don't know much but you know enough to know that.'

He did that Adept thing, silently scrutinizing me like I was a lab specimen then said 'You're still together, you and your wife. She's part of you and you're part of her. That happened the day you first told her you loved her.'

Christ! And you know what I was thinking when he said that, of course you do. Hesther. Hesther the Adept. Hesther. Ishtar. Istar. Isis. *That* Hesther.

Hesther had said that I'd killed my darling beautiful immortal beloved Helen the day I first told her I loved her. There's no such thing as coincidence, I bloody knew *that* for certain.

'You're right,' the Major said. 'There's no such thing as coincidence.'

I said nothing. I was becoming accustomed to having Adepts prying into my private thoughts. As if there's any such thing as privacy really.

'There's something special about your wife' the Major said absently as though thinking out loud. 'Something that somebody – perhaps it's a group of somebodies – has a use for. Has a need for.'

I bowed my head, sad. 'She's a special girl' was all I could say.

Toni came to sit beside me. She put a hand on my arm. 'She'll always be special,' she said.

The Major paced the room for a few moments like Sherlock Holmes pondering a clue. 'Who's following you?' he said suddenly.

'If I knew that we could just go straight to the police. I don't know what you're talking about.'

'I'm not talking about the people who took you and Heidi. They're a different bunch. Agents. And like as not dead now.'

That shocked me I have to say. All this intrigue and the possibility of murder. It was all getting a bit James Bond and I said so. What the fuck would that world have to do with me anyway? I wondered if the Major, Adept or not, was a bit off his trolley.

'Come on' The Major said. 'You know someone was following you. You'll have talked about it with Heidi. If I can sense it she would have.'

I wasn't holding anything back on purpose but I realised that it wouldn't hurt to tell him about the ritual I'd helped Heidi with when I'd stayed behind with her. The repayment of the debt to the Goddess Diana. And I told of the black shadowy presence in the room held back by our silver circle. A presence that we'd banished. From the room at any rate.

'You banished it from Heidi's apartment' the Major said when I'd finished telling the story. But not from you. It pursues you from a distance. Waiting for the chance to take you.'

'Why would anyone want to take me? Take me where?'

'They want to take you because you stand between them and your wife.'

I still didn't understand. Not really. 'So what do they want with Helen?' I asked.

'I don't know' the Major said. 'But I'm going to find out. I think it's dangerous.' He looked at me again, digging deep within my consciousness. 'You know who it was in Hcidi's apartment don't you? You know.'

I'd forgotten. But he was right. I did know. 'Sable Wyvern' I blurted out.

You couldn't see anything physical but I knew that the Major had frozen on hearing that name.

'The College of Arms,' he said. 'Oh.'

'Oh?' I said. 'Is that it?'

'You're swimming in dangerous waters' he said, unhelpfully from my point of view. 'And I think, so is Heidi.'

'So you think Heidi's still alive then?' Toni said, reminding us she was still with us.

'I would say so' the Major said. 'She's not who they're after and she might be more of a thorn in their side dead than alive. She's an incredible and special intelligence is Heidi.'

'The same way my Helen's special?' I asked, reminded of how he'd described my immortal beloved wife earlier.

'Not exactly' the Major said. 'What's special about your wife is impenetrable. Deep. I can't see what it is exactly. I couldn't see. But I knew it was there.'

He was building up to some sort of revelation and both Toni and me could sense it. All eyes focused on him.

'Yes,' he continued after a suitably dramatic pause and fixing his eyes on me. 'I knew it. Knew it from the moment I first set eyes on her. With you. In Paris.'

# The Story Episode # 97
# (Moon phase: Day 23)

KNOW THYSELF. IT'S good advice. The advice given to all would-be initiates. Inscribed or carved before the entrance to all esoteric Temples of the Mysteries going back through antiquity. And yes, I could write you an essay telling you exactly what's meant by that and why it's important and yadda yadda yadda. But always, *always*, experience trumps intellectual voyeurism every single time.

We all of us have to learn this lesson. Sometimes we learn it the hard way. So when I went for the Major after he'd mentioned that he was the bearded man my beautiful darling immortal beloved Helen had encountered in Paris, it was a lesson waiting to be taught.

I didn't have to wait long to learn it. Know thyself. Well what I should have known in the first place was that I wasn't a fighting man. Not in my nature. Not a coward but not someone interested in physical combat. In the second place, I should have known that I knew nothing about the Major. In the third place that title of his, that military background and the fact that he looked as lean and tight as rope ought to have cautioned me.

Yeah, know thyself. And act accordingly. So I was up out of

my chair and swinging punches and kicking out and quickly found myself thrown against a wall and slipping down to the floor with a few sharp aches and pains making themselves known. Whatever the Major's military background, I guessed too late that it was probably active. The Major hadn't been concerned with a desk-bound logistical role.

Toni was quickly by my side, then seeing that I was okay – or at least still alive – she put herself rather smartly between me and the Major. The Major was calm as you please as he took a step towards me and I swear that Toni was prepared to take him on to protect me. And no, I didn't feel emasculated by that. Toni and me, we were friends and we were close and we'd both of us risk everything to protect the other. I felt that then.

'Step aside' the Major said to Toni. 'There's no harm done and really, I'm on your side. I am.'

Now this wasn't one of those stupid Star Wars moments with the Major as a Jedi giving it one of those "these are not the droids you're looking for" hypnotic effects. Because what the Major was saying represented the truth and he had a way of speaking and projecting his personality so that we could understand. Had to understand.

So Toni stepped to one side and the Major reached down to offer me his hand. I didn't hesitate to take it either, and he helped me to my feet again.

'Sorry about that old chap,' he said to me.

I must have looked more than a little sheepish. 'Yeah, well that's okay. My own damn fault.'

'I know. But I hurt you in protecting myself. And that's a pity. Still, let's put that behind us and let me accept that you may have a question or two that I ought to answer. To the best of my ability.'

My anger had subsided but I was fucking suspicious of this

man and had my guard up, so to speak. 'What were you doing following us in Paris?' was my first question.

'I wasn't' the Major replied, raising his hands palms forward to forestall my skeptical objection. 'I wasn't at first,' he added. 'I was still on active service then, bear in mind. But you know the path I was following. And even back then had been following for quite a number of years.'

'You mind if I sit down?' I asked. I was feeling tired as well as bruised.

'I think it might be good for all of us to sit and relax' the Major said.

I glanced over at Toni and she came to sit on the sofa with me. We held hands. And that was a great comfort. To me at least.

The Major took a seat opposite. And he told us how he'd been researching the Western Way, the Path Through the Labyrinth or whatever we wanted to call it. A solitary path for him. And he'd taken leave in Paris because Paris is. . . well, Paris as a location is a fantastic mediator of the Astral Light. I mean, every occultist should know that. You can access unlimited levels of consciousness in Paris, easier than most places in Europe. And the centre of it? Well, take a wild guess what the deciding factor was when they were searching for a place to build the super-giant gothic cathedral of Notre Dame? Get it now? London is another such centre, but not to the same degree that Paris is. Most other places that mediate the Astral Light to that degree tend to be sacred wilderness sites. Places like Stonehenge, for example. And the most powerful and versatile location in all of Europe and maybe the whole world, Glastonbury in Wiltshire. Glastonbury Tor being the Heart-Chakra of the Earth. Yes, the planet, not the Ancient Alchemical Element.

But anyway, the Major had gone to Paris to experience altered states of consciousness. Dimwits claim that it's no different than using mind-altering drugs, but you know as well as I do that those pitiful idiots are simply using *that* as an excuse for their self-obsessed and self-destructive behaviour. The intelligences responsible for our part of the universe have opened the channels of the Astral Light in these centres precisely so we can discover them and use them to access the wisdom and understanding needed to gain knowledge and there's no need of external stimulants and depressants or psychotropic agents. I'll say no more about that here other than to say only cowards and weaklings and the terminally lazy make use of recreational drugs and they are not true travellers on the occult path. Never have been. Never will be. And what becomes of them really serves them right. Drug users, whether pseudo-occultists or the merely profane, are disgusting. Some shamanic cultures use them, mostly in south and middle America. But that vast majority of shamanic cultures don't use them. The vast majority. But I digress when I should be moving on with the story I'm telling you.

'I could tell you here that I spotted your wife by accident' the Major said. 'But we both know that there are no accidents any more than there are coincidences.'

'So you'd been placed there. Why do you think that was?' I was playing along because I knew what he was saying and I knew that it was a possible truth.

'To see her and warn her. Warn you, when I found you there with her. That's what I'd say. Wouldn't you?'

'Warn her about what?' This was Toni. Beating me to the question I was about to ask.

'About what I saw as black shadows. Following her –' he turned to me '- and you. I don't know how many. Could have been one, could have been a dozen. Flickering in and out of the realm of experience. From my perspective at any rate. And I dare guess you experienced them to.'

I remembered that night-time walk back to our hotel, that first time darling Helen and me had been to Paris. Down the narrow street, feeling the shadows in the doorways. Behind us. Then in front. Flickering I suppose, just as the Major had described.

'So who were they?' I asked. 'What were they? What did they want with Helen and me?'

'Oh I don't know what they are,' he said, 'much less who they are. But since you mentioned Sable Wyvern just now some bells have started ringing.'

I turned to look at Toni. She'd sunk back into the sofa and she looked suddenly grey and tired. And I remembered that we were only in Berlin to help her.

'The College of Arms,' the Major said absently. 'What the hell is going on. . ?' he turned to us then, to Toni and me, all business-like. 'I haven't forgotten that you need help' he said, addressing Toni, then turning to me. 'But we must see to Heidi first of all. Come on, we need to go to her apartment.'

'She won't be there' I protested, rising to my feet with the Major and pulling Toni up behind me. 'She was taken along with me. That much I do remember.'

The Major ignored me.

'Come on' he said and we didn't have a choice but to follow him out of the apartment block and onto the street.

I grabbed his arm to stop him striding off down the road. 'We'll get a cab' I said, and I already had my mobile phone at hand searching the web for a taxi company.

I called and my pitiful German was met with passable English. Five minutes later we were in the taxi heading for *Wedding*. When we got there I paid the driver and gave him a good tip because he'd been quick and again, thankfully quiet.

The Major knew the code to get into the building and we hurried up the stairs. We soon found ourselves outside Heidi's apartment door. It was shut of course and I was agitated as the Major knocked and waited I don't know how many times. Finally he took a key-ring from his pocket and I watched as he used a couple of narrow metal rods in the lock. Seconds later the door clicked open.

The Major turned to me, smiling. 'A little skill left over from the eighties' he said by way of an explanation I hadn't demanded. 'East German border crossings' he added, winking at me as though I'd know what that meant.

He was right though. I did know. Thought I knew at any rate. Special forces. Whatever branch I couldn't say. But I was thinking SAS, and I suppose you are too.

'Come on' The Major said, stepping through the door and into the hallway. 'Close the door behind you' he added without turning back.

Toni clicked the door shut and followed me following him. I was only a step behind him as he opened the living room door, the living room that had served as a Temple for Heidi and me. He stopped dead so that I almost walked into him. He didn't say anything but stepped carefully into the room and to one side so that I could see.

What I saw was shocking. To me it was shocking. The room was stripped bare. Only bare floorboards. Not a stick of furniture, not an ornament. Just occult symbols and words written in occult angelic alphabets and runes. Covering the walls. But that was the least of it. Because huddled and gibbering wide-eyed in a far corner, defiled and covered with the vomit and excrement lying in smeared piles all around her, I saw Heidi.

# The Story Episode # 98
# (Moon phase: Day 23)

SHRIEKING AND KICKING and screaming. It took all three of us to get Heidi to the bathroom and into the shower. Her doing the shrieking kicking and screaming. Not us. But we did it and we were covered in filth by the time we got her into that shower stall. We stank of her vomit and excrement. Over our clothes. In Toni's hair. In the Major's beard. But as I say, we got her there and we turned on the powerful jet of water.

Amazingly the water calmed her. The Major stood in front of the shower stall and he reached in with a broom to scrape the worst of the filth from Heidi. Then he took off his clothes and joined her in the shower stall, using the water and soap to clean himself then carefully holding her and washing her gently all over using soap and a flannel. He even washed her hair using the Treseme shampoo and conditioner stored in the shower stall.

I watched as Toni cleaned herself the best she could in the wash basin. But my attention was drawn to the shower stall. The Major was so careful and so compassionate in his treatment of Heidi I could have sworn that they were lovers. Not just a man and a woman sharing casual sexual experiences or even ritual sex the way Heidi and me had shared them a couple of nights earlier. It seemed deep, especially when the Major held Heidi close to him once they were both clean.

Yes, I watched them then under the hot stream of water and they were oblivious to me. I saw Heidi's face where she leaned her head on the Major's shoulder. Even through the spray of shower water I could swear I saw tears running down that beautiful face. Watching them in the shower like that tore at my heart because there was sadness there. An incredibly beautiful moment. But an incredibly sad one.

I thought of the sex that I'd shared with Heidi. How she'd said that if it was meant to be she'd love to have endless sex with me. Yes, waves of guilt pulsed through me. I felt Toni standing next to me, just behind my left shoulder.

'That's beautiful' she whispered, seeing what I was seeing. 'I didn't know they were lovers.'

Lovers. 6. Zain. D Major. Sword. Gemini. That stung, hearing her say it like that, lovers. But I let it pass then turned to her. She'd cleaned the vomit and shit from her hands face and hair. Pretty much she had. But there were still smears of it on her clothing. Wet patches where she'd tried to sponge it off. I could still smell it on her. And to a lesser extent me. It was on my hands and some smears on one shirt sleeve but beyond that I'd escaped unscathed. This reminded me that Toni wasn't herself. That she was the reason I was here in Berlin in the first place. To do whatever Tom had felt necessary to fix her. The real Toni would have had scathing and sarcastic and belittling comments to make about that. Delivered in an amusing way of course and not meant to be hurtful. But that Toni was held in a place somewhere dark and secure.

'The wash basin's free' was all she said.

I used a scrubbing brush to get the filth out of my shirt sleeve as best I could, cleaned myself as best I could. And while I was doing this, the Major and Heidi stepped out of the shower. Toni handed them some towels but the Major made no effort to dry Heidi in the crowded bathroom. Instead he took her to her bedroom. Toni and me, we didn't follow. Instead I stripped out of my clothes. It had been a couple of days since I'd enjoyed a hot shower.

'Wanna join me?' I said to Toni as I stepped into the shower stall.

I watched Toni undress as the hot water sprayed down over me from the monsoon shower head. I've told you before how gorgeous Toni was and I felt the familiar stirring in my groin, the twitch of my penis as she slid her panties down to her ankles and stepped out of them. But as I took her hand to help her safely into the shower stall with me, I instinctively knew how to control this energy, this Dragon Fire within me. It was still there, flowing around me but I knew that I could release it to the universe by means of breathing and relaxation techniques or I could channel it and use it. A lesson Heidi had taught me.

Now I should say here that it's not as easy as I make it sound in the telling of it. I mean, it wasn't back then. Heidi had shown me that it could be managed and what I'd need to do to manage it. Like all things though, it would take practice. And this was my first experience of trying to do just that. Not altogether successful in as much as my penis remained hard and ready for action. And yes my conscious mind wanted Toni, urged me to put moves on her that I felt certain would have us fucking under that hot running water. But I was able to find the means to control that. So that in the end I didn't even make the effort. It doesn't sound much but I'm going to tell you that I marked that down as a victory. Yes, victory. 7. The Chariot. Cheth. D – Sharp.

And no, I didn't have the experience of a monk in that shower. But I'm blaming Toni even though I know that everything that happens to me is my responsibility. Go on, laugh. Because I'm laughing. It's a joke. I know that what happened is something I could and maybe should have stopped. But I didn't. We were cleaning each other all over with soapy flannels, and when Toni came to rub her flannel over my still-hard penis she looked up at me with mischief in her eyes and I didn't make any effort to resist. So that a few minutes later I was cleaning thick creamy white globs of my semen from her belly and breasts and letting my flannel rub between her legs. Until she stopped me. Laughing at her own demonstration of self-control where I'd lost mine. Another lesson learned. I still had a way to go before I was master of the Dragon Fire.

'I'm getting all wrinkly' Toni said at last once we were squeaky-clean.

We stepped out of the shower and turned off the stream of running water, which saddened me briefly. Then we towelled each other dry – and it was gentle and beautiful and in no way sexual. Anyway, once we were dry I dressed myself but Toni remained naked. She looked down at the pile of her clothes in disgust.

'I can't wear them' she said, her voice soft and sad and distant.

I was thinking of what to say when the Major – still naked himself - appeared in the doorway to take charge. Good old military leadership training eh?

'Steven, your clothes are the cleanest and I dare say you have credit cards and access to funds and so forth. Why don't you get dressed and go buy some clothes for all of us to change into. Just casual, nothing fancy. Something we could wear to go hiking.'

Hiking. No, I didn't ask and neither should you. Just wait.

'Fine' I said. 'And where do you suggest I go?'

'Someone like you, I'd have thought you carried a list of outfitters around in your head' he said and I suppose he had a point since I've always been a clothes horse and a fashionista and he'd obviously sensed that. 'Use that phone you have to call a cab. Tell the driver to take you to KaDeWe on *Tauentzienstraße*. We'll wait here for you.'

So what happened was that I took a cab to *KaDeWe* to buy us all clothes and it didn't matter that I hadn't asked what size Toni, Heidi and the Major would need because I'd sized that up in an instant. A lifelong obsession with women will give you that skill if you're smart about it. And I had been. So I went off to *KaDeWe* and on the way in the taxi I called Avis and booked a rental car. No more messing about.

I think I had it easy. Because while I went shopping, I left my naked companions cleaning shit and puke from the floors and walls of Heidi's flat. And as I tripped down the stairs to go meet the taxi I heard Heidi over my echoing footfalls. Shrieking kicking and screaming.

# The Story Episode # 99
# (Moon phase: Day 23)

LATER. NO LONGER shrieking and kicking and screaming, Heidi sat in the back of the rented Mercedes E300. Silver in case you're wondering, which was the only colour Avis had available. Not that I cared about the colour anyway.

The Major sat with Heidi and Toni sat in the front next to me. Heidi and Toni were two rather subdued women at this point but for the first few minutes, especially as we made our way through the Berlin streets, I remained on edge.

'Where are we headed?' I asked the Major as we crossed the ring road circling the city.

He'd only given me a vague instruction to head west and he'd concerned himself with comforting Heidi. The clothes I'd bought for us all fitted perfectly by the way. I just thought I'd mention that. And while I'd been to several places to get them, you'll understand how we looked if you imagine we'd all been outfitted by The Gap.

'We're going to the Harz Mountains' the Major told me. 'Head for *Magdeburg*.'

He gave me more detailed instructions of course. And said he'd supplement them as needed. So we cruised past *Charlottenburg*, then past *Potsdam* on the E26, heading west towards *Magdeburg*, first on the E51 then the E30. But I'm getting ahead of myself.

We learned more about the Major on that journey. And about Heidi. I mentioned to the Major that he obviously hadn't known *Magdeburg* during his army days, stationed in what was then West Germany. He'd have been stationed in the British Zone of Occupation the way I saw it, and I said I knew that *Magdeburg* and the Harz Mountains were in the Soviet Zone of Occupation. Looking up at the mirror I saw him smile at that. He didn't say anything more, but when I pressed him on the matter he opened up and told me. Perhaps not everything but an interesting enough story nevertheless.

'I can see you smiling' I told him. 'So what does that mean? I'm wrong and you were involved in illegal border crossings back in those days?'

'Maybe' he said. After a pause he sighed and said 'I don't suppose it matters much now.'

'So you're SAS' I said making sure not to sound too eager and worshipful and gushing as so many do these days.

'No' he said. 'They're not the only unit to have fun. They just have that great PR machine.'

We drove in silence for a while after that until I realised he wasn't going to say any more. So I said 'Well? Are you going to tell me who you were with?'

I think he realised that I needed the company on the drive and since Heidi and Toni seemed disinclined or unable - or both - to provide it, it would be down to him.

'Intelligence Corps' he said and I thought back to how easily he'd disposed of me when I'd gone for him.

'So it really is a James Bond existence' I said.

I saw him shake his head. 'No, not at all. Not for the most part. Some do get that extra training though. For field operations.'

And after that he told me. Not everything I'm sure, but enough to keep my interest as we drove carefully along the clear German roads heading west. He'd made border crossings with SAS units. Intelligence gathering operations. And he'd been responsible for making personal contacts with dissident military personnel within what was then the German Democratic Republic, or DDR. East Germany if you prefer the simpler description.

Then he told me a story that started to tie things together, even if it was a tiny bit startling. So I'll get the startling bit over with first. And I'll begin by saying that the Major looked young but I'd had him figured for a man in his early fifties. Which would have allowed him to be operational in occupied Germany during the last decade of the cold war, the 1980s. Now you need to understand that he looked younger than a man in his fifties, but he's an Adept and I'd learned to let things like that slide. I might come on to explain more about that some other time. But what was startling to me was that the story he told me took place in the 1970s. Which would make the Major a decade older than I'd imagined him to be. Which is absolutely crazy.

Anyway, let me tell you what he told me. He'd been inserted – that's the terminology he used – into the DDR by an SAS unit sometime in 1975. His mission was to make contact with a dissident army officer based in *Magdeburg*. It was delicate because you couldn't move around easily in the DDR and in a country where people would routinely spy on and report their neighbours and members of their own families, strangers were always at risk. So he'd been met in a quiet location not far from the town by a girl of thirteen, the daughter of the officer he was to make contact with. The girl would make it look like he was a visiting relative or something. People would be suspicious, but less so than if he'd been alone. Look, I'm not going to prolong this story. During the course of that year, the Major made several incursions into the DDR to meet with this dissident officer. And in the end, the Major's assessment had been that the officer was genuine and an asset worth bringing to the west because of the information he'd bring with him.

The Major told me that the preference would have been to run him as an asset within the DDR, but the officer was having none of it. He was married with two daughters and he wanted his family safe in the west. That was the deal. And it was agreed. But on one incursion, the officer had told the Major that he didn't have much time. That the *Stasi* – East German Secret Police – were on to him. His elder daughter had been taken, along with his wife. The young girl who'd always accompanied the Major and given him his cover would be next. They probably had less than twenty four hours. The officer had begged the Major to take his young daughter to the west. And reluctantly the Major had agreed. You doubtless guessed a while back that this young girl was Heidi, right? Anyway, it was. And they'd lied to her, telling her that her father and her mother and sister would be following her soon. So he'd taken a tearful Heidi back to the west with him.

Less than twenty four hours later all contact with the East German officer was lost. Clearly he'd been taken. He'd told

Heidi the truth of what had happened. He'd done that personally. The authorities tried to foster Heidi because she had no family whatsoever in the west but she would never settle. And she ended up living in care until her eighteenth birthday when she'd taken her steps out into the world on her own. Well not quite on her own. The Major had stayed in constant contact during those five years. I don't know the full nature of the relationship but after hearing the Major tell the story I was no longer so certain that his relationship with Heidi was or ever had been sexual. The bond of love that Toni and me had witnessed could just have been something deeper and more beautiful than that.

Now I'm not going to tell you anything more of the Major's story – or Heidi's – at this point because the Major didn't tell me any more than that on our drive. And I've only given you the barest outline of what the Major told me because the detail is something that doesn't affect my story, the one I'm telling you. I only give you the background so that you have a better understanding of the relationship. Or the way I thought it to be at that time.

Anyway, for the last half hour we drove in silence to *Magdeburg*. And a few miles west of the city we came to a relatively isolated house in a large section of land. Not quite an agricultural small holding, but a very large area for a house. We pulled into the drive which was long and lined with trees, and eventually I parked the car in front of the house. The house wasn't exactly shabby but it was rustic rather than smart. And although large it had a homely feel to it. We all got out and before the Major could knock on the black wooden door, the door flew open and out stepped a woman with a heart of purest gold to greet us with smiles and warmth. This, I was to learn, was Elke. And I'll describe her because I always do and you're expecting me to.

She was flaxen-haired, and wore her hair partially braided with wild flowers forming a tiara around her head. A traditional white Saxon smock and a rich green skirt hanging from her hips to her ankles completed the ensemble so far as I could see. Although she did have a band of silver loose around one ankle. She didn't wear shoes. Of course she didn't. I'd have pegged her age at around the mid-thirties but I was learning not to set much store by my estimates. I was learning that age was irrelevant anyway. I was constantly learning lessons of incredible value and was starting to understand that. I'm only telling you she looked to be in her thirties so that you can paint a picture. Blue eyes as you'd expect, and the figure of a Goddess rather than a catwalk-model stick. A hint of soft curves beneath her clothes, and yes, even though you're rolling your eyes, I might as well admit that I was immediately sexually attracted to her. And this forms part of another lesson I needed to learn and that Elke would play a part in teaching me.

Anyway, she greeted us all smiles and hugs until she came to Heidi. She placed her hands on Heidi's shoulders and stood at arm's length, inspecting her. Until at last she put an arm around Heidi's shoulder and said 'I know exactly what to do poor darling. Come with me. We'll make it right.'

She said this in German of course but I'm translating it for you. The Major turned to me as we all followed Elke and Heidi into the house.

'That's Elke' he said. 'And she's ten thousand years old.'

# The Story Episode # 100
# (Moon phase: Day 23)

TEN THOUSAND YEARS is meaningless set against infinity. The singular monad of existence is infinite in scope. Both infinitely large and infinitely small. So that existence is both everything and nothing. Which I believe I've mentioned before. But it's also infinitely old and infinitely new. Meaning that time is an illusion granted to us to allow us to assimilate and analyse experience.

There's really no such thing as time. I knew that. But at the same time it allowed me to understand what the Major meant when he described Elke as being ten thousand years old. He was describing an intelligence that could call upon the memory and analysis of ten thousand years of experience. Perhaps it's best we should just understand that she was wise.

Inside the house as we filed in following Elke and Heidi, I couldn't help noticing the gloom. Not oppressive because the *atmosphere* was anything but gloomy. Just the lighting. The house seemed almost medieval in that respect. White rustic walls and ceilings with exposed dark wooden beams. Dark wooden floors polished smooth by the footsteps of several hundred years. I loved the place immediately.

The smell of ylang ylang incense lay sweet in the air and brought to the forefront of my emotion thoughts of my beautiful darling immortal beloved wife Helen and the depth of our love. Visions of her stumbling in the dark and me just unable to reach her across a black abyss of infinite depth.

'Stevie. . .' This was Toni's voice and I opened my eyes to find myself slumped in a wide hallway with faces peering down at me. Toni's face closest since she was kneeling next to me. But there was the Major and Elke, and Heidi standing next to Elke, and a naked teenage girl who I didn't recognise, and two naked young men who I didn't recognise, and an older bearded man that I didn't recognise who was – you've guessed it – naked.

I was still sobbing when Elke turned to the Major. 'You bring such damaged goods' she said, smiling and waving a hand to indicate me and Toni – but of course meaning Heidi too. 'You think perhaps we are a repair shop?'

'Well you are' the Major answered. 'Among other things.'

At that point the light faded and died so that I felt I was in absolute darkness. Yet I could still perceive the people staring down at me, if you can imagine that. Worse, behind them and looming was a black shadow. Black on black, hooded and louring so that I cowered back against the wall and whimpered with fear. I can't tell you because you read this in comfort but this was a terrifying experience.

Elke turned to look over her shoulder and it seemed that she could see what I was seeing, when she held her left hand before her eyes and made a sign with her fingers that I couldn't quite make out. But the black shadow seemed to hesitate and falter, confused. Elke turned her attention back to me.

'Your companion isn't welcome I'm afraid' she said and I'm guessing this was meant as a joke. 'Here' she said, kneeling in front of me.

She leaned forward and carefully pressed her lips against mine. I could see the smile in those blue eyes right in front of me as she blew a soft warm steady stream of breath into my mouth. I knew that I had to inhale it, that she was giving me more than just her fragrant breath.

Stars exploding around me all silver and gold sparkles. The cycle of birth life and death in a continuous flow with me at the heart. Fire and plasma burning in the black infinite. White light brighter than a billion suns. I was given a glimpse of the mechanics of existence and experience while I remained still and unmoving. Seeing everything in all directions.

Later I'd understand that this was a lesson but at the time I didn't understand that. The sheer scale of what was happening around and about me is something that I can't describe. I mean, how can you describe standing next to a star? Something as vast as that. How can you describe being in the heart of a supernova? It really isn't worth me trying to describe it. But those of you who are ho-humming my attempts here, really you should Google stars and supernovas and stuff and try to imagine what it might be like to stand next to something as large as that as hot as that as bright as that as violent as that.

Time is an illusion. Have I mentioned that before? Ha ha – of course I have. And I mention it again now because I was witnessing the birth and life and death of stars in the time it takes for bubbles to burst on the surface of boiling pan of water. I marvelled at it and revelled in it. Until the thought occurred to me that I was in a dangerous place. These things so large were altogether frightening to me. Me. That was the key. This horrid insipid little thought represented the return of ego. The return of awareness of the illusion. I think I must have screamed. Because when I opened my eyes I was crushed back against that wall, struggling on the dark wooden floor with Elke holding me close, my face pressed against her soft breasts. Toni holding my hand and everyone else looking down with expressions of concern. Except Heidi. Heidi with the thousand yard stare. Poor, poor, beautiful Heidi.

The Major reached out a hand for me to hold. 'Come on,' he said. 'Try to stand.'

I did as he suggested and I remember thinking that he was a bastard because I was comfortable wrapped in Elke's arms with

Toni by my side. But once I stood I realised that he'd grounded me back in the illusion. No sign of the looming shadow. The house altogether brighter. And while this sort of thing never bothered me in the slightest, I did smile at the situation. I mean, there was me recovering from a touch of the vapours; there was Heidi like a beautiful zombie. There was Toni with inner demons we hadn't really investigated, spitting and popping in and out of her consciousness so you couldn't tell if she was Arthur or Martha from one minute to the next. And there was Elke the earth Goddess and the stunning naked teenage girl and the two guys who I could now see were rather beautiful themselves in their unashamed nakedness and the older naked bearded man. I mean, you'd laugh wouldn't you?

Picture it. This wide hallway with exposed beams and dark hardwood floor and white plaster walls and the group as I've just described them. It could have been an eighteenth century madhouse, though I was about to discover it was anything but.

Another reason to laugh was the absence of that dark looming shadowy presence. We were going to have to deal with that though. Whatever it was.

Elke leaned in close to me, whispered in my ear. 'You're going to have to tell me about Sable Wyvern' she said. And before I could reply she was all smiles. 'I'll introduce you to everyone in good time, but could we go to the hall please?'

She indicated a set of double wooden doors at the far end of the hallway. Doors made of oak as dark as the beams framing the house and those forming the floor. And this strange band – meaning us as described above – made its way down to the hall beyond them.

I didn't know what to expect but I experienced love and peace and light as the naked teenage girl pushed those doors open. I was at the front of the group so I had an uninterrupted view inside. A massive open space for a house, maybe forty feet by forty feet. A circle and a pentagram inlaid into the floor, and I was to learn that they were made of silver-plated nickel. Signs representing astrological houses and other corresponding alchemical and musical symbols were similarly inlaid into the floor. Now all of these were on concealed runners. So that the pentagram could be turned to face any direction. So could the astrological symbols, the constellations and so on. A simple but unexpected and fascinating work of engineering and I could immediately see the value of it. Scatter cushions everywhere but no furniture. Rugs spread haphazardly outside the circle. The ylang ylang incense hanging sweet in the air. I won't describe all the craftwork ornaments and decorations because it would take too long. But I will say that stepping into that hall as I did, following the naked teenage girl, it felt like stepping into the heart of nature. Yes it really did. So much peace and joy.

My mind filled with the first movement of Beethoven's sixth symphony. Until my hearing was shredded by a most appalling scream that momentarily chilled my blood.

I turned to see Heidi screaming and kicking and not wanting to enter the hall, and the Major holding her and Elke attempting to calm her and Heidi puking all over them and herself. And Heidi's eyes bulging wide seeing something invisible to us but terrifying to her. Heidi shaking violently. Until she dropped down seemingly dead to the hardwood floor.

# *The Story Episode # 101*
# *(Moon phase: Day 23)*

THERE'S NO SUCH thing as death. I've said that before, I know; but it's worth saying it again now. Death is a symptom of the illusion and fear of death is a programmed reaction instilled in the greater part of humanity over thousands of years. But more so over the last few hundred years.

You'd be surprised to hear that fear of death is a relatively new phenomenon. Back in the ancient world, and even in the middle ages, death - while not actively sought - wasn't feared. Everyone understood that death is part of the natural cycle. People were more in touch with the nature of the universe and existence itself. People *en masse* may not have known the scientific rational basis of existence and the illusion that allows us to experience it, but they were aware deep down that it was all natural and not to be feared.

This programming of fear that has taken an ever-increasing hold since the middle ages, is engineered. It's not an accident. This is true and I'm not joking. Plant fear into people and understand for yourself how to manage and manipulate that fear, then you can, to a large extent, control the people who live in the fear you planted. I'm going to say no more about that for now though. Just stop worrying about death. You won't escape it and it's perfectly natural. What I just told you is a gift from me to you. But I suppose you won't value it. Nevertheless I give it to you. Make of it what you will.

I'm talking about death because I mentioned just now that Heidi dropped seemingly dead to the hardwood floor of Elke's house. I said seemingly because there was no sign of her breathing. No sense of a heartbeat. But she wasn't dead the way you imagine death while you're wedded to the illusion.

'Carry her into the hall' the naked young teenage girl said.

The Major Toni and I looked briefly at each other, and before we could react the naked young men had taken the lifeless form of Heidi and carried her effortlessly into the hall. They laid her carefully down in the centre of the pentagram and I immediately had flashbacks to the ritual I'd performed with Heidi in her apartment just a couple of nights previously.

'Now remove her clothes.' This again from the teenage girl who seemed to be taking charge.

The two naked young men kneeled beside Heidi and began the process of undressing her but the Major stopped them. 'No' he said, 'we'll do it.'

He looked to me clearly wanting me to assist him.

I need to tell you something here. For my part I was sure that Heidi was dead. It seemed that way. But no one was rushing to telephone for the emergency services.

We undressed Heidi quickly but with a care almost approaching reverence. We handed her clothes to Toni who folded them slowly and neatly and placed them in a pile in a corner of the room. We arranged Heidi face up on the silver pentagram on the floor. And I found myself starting to cry but the lovely naked teenage girl noticed me and put a finger to her lips, stopping me dead.

The older bearded man appeared with a silver bowl of water and two white flannel cloths. He knelt by Heidi's head and looked up at the Major then to me and it was clear that he was inviting us to perform a ritual cleansing of Heidi's body. We accepted his invitation and each of us dipped a flannel in the water.

The Major began with Heidi's face and I moved to kneel at

her feet. Both of us went about the process of ritual cleansing.

I saw the Major begin by wiping the vomit from around Heidi's mouth and I started with her lovely feet, wiping the flannel around each toe, between her toes, almost caressing her soft skin with the damp cloth. By the time I'd reached the top of her thighs, I met the Major who'd been cleansing her from her head down. I moved aside to let the Major complete the ritual, watching without embarrassment or shame as he carefully cleansed between Heidi's legs with the cloth, making sure that no part of her vulva escaped the cleansing, seeming to know that this was important. I felt that it was important.

I keep saying that this cleansing was a ritual. Well that's how it seemed and that's what it was. Because as the Major and I had been cleansing Heidi, the two beautiful naked young men had lit a number of candles and occult lamps in this huge hall and had drawn heavy drapes across the windows. They'd also begun burning Myrrh in a number of large burners so that the atmosphere had become charged with the scent of it by the time we'd finished cleansing Heidi. This was a ritual and one of incredible occult antiquity.

I had no idea what would happen next or what the purpose was. But I was feeling a charge of energy building and flowing over and through me as it filled the room. The naked bearded man took the silver bowl of water and the two flannels that the Major and I had draped over the sides and held it above his head as he took it from the room. The Major and Toni and I watched him go as the naked teenage girl stood at the top of the silver pentagram above Heidi's head, facing her feet. The two naked young men stood either side of Heidi's head, facing each other. I know that I was fascinated and not at all concerned that Heidi had died, and I know that sounds terrible. But I think that there was a reason for this. Something that I knew at a subconscious level. Toni had come to stand beside me, close enough for her arm to press against mine.

'Please, take off your clothes' Elke said from behind us.

It wasn't a request, despite the polite form of the words. We all turned to see that Elke was naked and I know that the Major and Toni experienced what I did. Elke was a Goddess in the room with us. Calm. Majestic. Powerful. And I mean powerful in a sense that transcended human charisma. Beautiful. Tall. Fecund. Sexual. Unapproachable. This was Elke, not *representing* a Goddess, but *as* a Goddess. If you ever experience an occult ritual like this – unlikely as that is - you'll understand.

So we undressed slowly and folded our clothes as we placed them next to Heidi's in a corner of the hall. Which was now a Temple.

Elke went to stand beneath Heidi's left arm, next to her left breast. And - it wasn't lost on me - next to her heart. The naked bearded man returned and knelt by the silver circle, pushing it on its hidden runners so that the point of the pentagram faced east. Don't ask how I know what was east, because I just did know. I can always tell you the cardinal points of the compass. Occult training gives you that and it's important, even if you can't perhaps see why.

Anyway, let me describe the scene in the Temple for you before I continue to tell you what happened. Heidi's head was pointing to the east. The naked teenage girl stood above her head, her arms outstretched, eyes closed, breathing slow and shallow, meditating down to an altered state of consciousness. The naked young men were in a similar condition of consciousness. Elke, in her position next to Heidi's heart knelt on the floor and closed her eyes, adjusted her breathing. The older bearded man knelt between Heidi's legs and closed his eyes, adjusted his breathing to match Elke's. This was clearly visible.

The Major took Toni's hand and my hand and he walked us to a place within the silver circle facing Elke. Clearly he was familiar with the ritual and what was required. He positioned us so that we stood behind Elke where she knelt facing Heidi. The Major and me stood next to each other and Toni stood between us but in front of us.

I felt the room begin to darken. Nothing had changed. The lighting remained as it had been. But I got a clear impression that the naked teenage girl was manipulating the energy within that Temple. I sensed the Major and Toni adjusting their breathing and very soon we were all breathing in slow shallow synchronisation with the teenage girl. She was the mediator between the worlds, Priestess of this ceremony where she controlled the energy swirling around us. Incredible. Just incredible.

Then, with her eyes still closed, she began to chant. Resonating the words within and beyond the Temple and us, out into the infinite regions of existence. I'd normally give you a form of the words she chanted to call upon the Gods but it was a language I'd never heard before. I can tell you that it was an Angelic language but it was totally alien to me. I can only tell you that without knowing the words, they were having a deep effect on my state of consciousness. Same for all of us. She was leading us.

I watched the two beautiful naked young men move so that they stood one to each side of the teenage Priestess, facing her. And then the strangest thing. I watched one of the naked young men, the one nearest us, stand on his hands. His posture, upside down, was as straight and precise as that of a gymnast. And he maintained that posture as the chant of the Priestess rose in intensity, pulling a particular energy into the Temple to buzz and fizz around and through us. And as she reached the climax of the chant, I felt my penis become aroused. Charged with the energy that the Priestess had called into the Temple. I noticed that the energy was having the same effect on the two naked young men. Even the one standing on his hands. The Priestess reached out and took a penis in each hand. I watched her slide the foreskins back as she gripped them at the base, keeping them as hard as steel and exposing the swollen glistening heads. I know that the energy called into the Temple was having the same effect on the Major too. I know because he took my hand and placed it on his fiercely hard erection. Instinctively I pulled his foreskin gently back and gripped his penis at the base, the way the teenage Priestess was holding the naked young men next to her. I almost gasped as the Major's fingers found my own erect penis and rolled back my foreskin so that I was almost painfully hard.

All the time our teenage Priestess continued a steady rhythmic chant in this language that was unknown yet hypnotic. Holding the energy she'd called into the Temple in a constant state of spiral motion. I felt it flow from the Major's fingers to my penis, flood through me, then flow out from my fingers to the Major's penis.

The chant guided our breathing. Managed our heart rates. Managed the sex energy pulsing within us. I watched as Elke kneeled towards Heidi. She placed a hand on Heidi's left breast. Holding it gently, Heidi's nipple exposed between the first and second fingers. Then Elke placed her lips on Heidi's. This wasn't an erotic sexual or affectionate kiss. Elke was breathing her charged life force into Heidi the way she'd done for me. The sight of Elke leaning over Heidi, all smooth exposed curves aroused me beyond pleasure to the point, almost, of pain.

I watched Heidi's breasts rise and fall in time with our

breathing. The whole Temple in synchronisation, held there by the rhythmic chant of the teenage Priestess. And once this was established, I noticed for the first time, the older bearded man between Heidi's legs. He knelt there, and I could clearly see his huge erection as he lifted Heidi's hips. And he manoeuvred himself so that he could slide his penis deep inside Heidi's vagina.

Yes I know she was dead. Yes I can sense your disgust. Your disgust wasn't mirrored by mine though. I felt no disgust whatsoever. There's no such thing as death.

The older man didn't move inside her. Just held himself there. His breathing and our breathing still in perfect synchronisation. I can't tell you how long this went on for. Because my consciousness became lost in the magic of it. The myrrh, the dim lighting, the chanting, the energy, the sexuality in balance. The Dragon Fire controlled by the teenage Priestess.

But after a while I could sense a change in the energy. A subtle change in the chanting of our teenage Priestess. Was it getting faster? I think it got faster. Certainly there was a shift in intensity. I became increasingly aware of my penis held in the Major's fingers. I felt his own begin to twitch and throb in my fingers. And the intensity increased. And increased. And increased. Until. . . Heidi coughed and spluttered and opened her eyes suddenly as Elke threw herself back in abandoned ecstasy while my penis exploded in spurt after spurt of hot thick semen, more than I'd ever produced, as all of us in that Temple shared the most electric of orgasms. All of us sharing a simultaneous orgasm of enormous intensity that lasted at least a whole minute.

As the energy subsided and the Major and I let go of each other, I was able to take in the scene in the temple. Elke was cradling Heidi who still spluttered and coughed. I watched the older bearded man slide his large and still erect penis out of Heidi, slowly and with great care. I saw his semen dribble from Heidi while it continued to dribble from his the tip of his penis. The beautiful naked young men stepped back from our Priestess and I could see that she was absolutely drenched with white thick semen that the young men must have pulsed all over her. I have never – and I mean never – seen so much semen. You would have thought that maybe half a dozen men had ejaculated on her. It was dribbling down her.

I saw Heidi open her eyes and look at the Major. She seemed to be in a trance but I could feel the love in that look.

'Everyone ground yourselves in the way best beloved of your Gods,' Elke said, bringing us all back into the realm of illusion.

I felt the eyes of the teenage Priestess upon me. 'Come with me to the shower,' she said in English. 'Cleanse me. And I will cleanse you.'

She held out a hand and I walked over to her to take it. Her fingers were sticky with semen and as I let her lead me from the Temple, I turned to look at Toni. Toni was fine. But in the corner of the Temple where we'd folded our clothes, I saw something that made my heart lurch. I saw, neatly folded on top of Toni's clothes, a satin nightie that we certainly hadn't placed there. And anyway, I knew it couldn't belong to any of us. Because it had once belonged to my dead immortal beloved wife, Helen.

# The Story Episode # 102
# (Moon phase: Day 23)

DEATH IS AN illusion. I'm just reminding you that I knew that. Because it didn't stop me turning on all of them and saying 'You'll have to fucking kill me first.'

You see what had happened is that I'd rushed over to our pile of clothes and I'd taken that nightie from the top of the pile. And I knew it was my immortal beloved darling Helen's nightie right away as soon as my fingers touched the satin. As soon as the silver sheen of the fabric glimmered before my eyes. I knew.

The older bearded guy reacted first. 'Nein,' he said, rising quickly from where he still knelt between Heidi's legs and reaching out to take the nightie from me.

I stepped sharply back and I could feel hot fire burn through me manifesting as aggression. The bearded man must have sensed it, felt it, seen it in my eyes. I won't say he was frightened of me but he did hesitate and didn't step any closer.

So picture the scene in that Temple room, lit by candles and occult lamps with the fragrance of Myrrh heavy in the air. Me backed into a corner with Helen's nightie held behind my back in one hand and my other hand held out in front of me to ward them off. *Them* being this bearded guy, the Major, Toni, the two beautiful young men and the teenage girl, our Priestess. And all of us naked. Elke remained in the consecrated circle where she tended to Heidi, cradling her in her arms. Toni looking at me, and seeming shocked at what she saw. The two beautiful young men not moving, observing and not approving. The teenage Priestess taking slow careful ballet-dancer's steps towards me and holding out a hand with an open palm.

'Come on. You must hand it over' she said and I think she knew exactly what she was doing. I think she had the measure of me.

And this is when I said – meaning for it to resonate with all of them – that they'd have to fucking kill me first. Kill me before I'd hand over this physical link with my darling immortal beloved beautiful wife.

Now I said that our teenage Priestess had the measure of me. And I said that because I could tell that everything about her was speaking directly to me. Others could see her and hear her words but every single other detail of her posture, movement, tone and a million other aspects beside were designed with a focus that would resonate with me alone.

Right then I wanted her, just as she'd known I would. Still can't believe how quickly she'd been able to find exactly the resonances that would hold me. Visions fizzing and flashing and flickering at the forefront of my consciousness. Me holding her naked in the darkness. Feeling her soft flesh next to mine, feeling her warmth, tasting her sweet breath. Feeling her hands and feet and arms and legs and fingers and tongue exploring me. Wanting her soul to wrap around mine. She'd managed all of that in an instant of sizing me up. She'd looked at me and she'd known me. Known what I was at my core. What everyone seemed to want to tell me. A man obsessed by sex.

There was more though; she'd seen even deeper than that. She'd seen in an instant that with me it wasn't *just* sex. Nothing purely mechanical. She'd seen my need, my longing to associate sex with romance. To connect sex with a spiritual dimension that took the experience beyond mere physical pleasure.

This was a power I'd rarely experienced before. A power that perhaps I'd only ever seen in Hesther prior to this. And it would have worked. At any other time and for any other purpose she'd have gently imposed her will on me. But something inside me was beyond her ability to fathom. The bond that I maintained with my beautiful darling wife Helen. My immortal beloved Helen. Helen whose essence resonated so closely with my own that we'd been a single spiritual entity from the moment we'd first met. The Priestess hadn't been able to see Helen within me, as a part of me. And my darling Helen gave me the will to resist.

'Nobody's going to kill anybody Steven.'

We all looked to Elke on the floor cradling a sobbing Heidi. Elke the Goddess in this her Temple. Not angry but not prepared to have us profane the sacred space. You could feel the tension dissipate. But we still had a stand-off. We all watched each other in silence for a few moments and it was like a scene from a Sergio Leone spaghetti western. Apart from the nakedness. Then the Major strode over to the window nearest him and drew the drapes sharply back. Brilliant sunlight flooded the room in an instant, breaking the spell and grounding the Temple. And us. For the briefest instant I swear I saw them all as creatures of golden light. Made of the same substance as the sun. Which of course is the truth. But I marvelled at being given such a glimpse of that truth and it seemed to me that a vast intelligence was communicating with me.

'Give it to them Stevie' a voice said, and I could tell that it was Heidi's voice, half sobbing, even as I blinked to get used to the brightness.

Heidi back from the dead and I couldn't refuse her. So reluctantly I pulled my hand from behind my back and held it out to the young Priestess. But when I looked, my hand was empty. The silver nightie of my immortal beloved wife was gone.

I whimpered and almost sobbed. But the lovely naked teenage girl – no longer a Priestess now the Temple had been grounded

– stepped over to me and took my hand. Her fingers were still sticky with semen and semen still glistened where it covered the soft white skin of her breasts, belly and thighs.

'No need to cry,' she said. 'Nothing has changed.'

She smiled at me and I could feel her giving comfort to me where her sticky fingers wrapped around mine.

'Come on,' she said, seeing that she'd calmed me. 'Let's go take that shower.'

I turned as I walked with her to see that all eyes were upon us and I felt ashamed at how I'd behaved.

'Steven' Heidi said, now on her knees and kneeling beside Elke.

We stopped in our tracks, waiting to see what Heidi wanted. She looked sad and weary as Elke held her close.

'It wasn't there Steven,' Heidi explained. 'Just a projection of your love strong enough for us to see.'

She meant the nightie of course. A symbol of my darling immortal beloved. And I immediately realised that Heidi was right. A symbol. And maybe you're wondering what the hell that could possibly mean. So I should remind you in case you've forgotten, that intelligence does not communicate using verbal language. It uses symbols or tones or colours or temperatures or any of an infinite number of other attributes. Human language allows us to explain our experiences and desires to each other within the illusion. But the truth of existence and the intelligence that governs existence doesn't acknowledge the verbal human language of the illusion.

Let me explain the business of the nightie to you because after hearing Heidi I understood it immediately. The nightie was symbolically telling me that Helen was communicating with me. The essence of my darling immortal beloved wife. The satin nightie that I loved her to wear for me sometimes. A code letting me know it was her. Silver to tell me I should focus on the moon. Silver reminding me to maintain a focus on making my peace with the lunar intelligence and power. Lilith. Astarte. Isis. Diana.

A warm glow tingled and sparkled through me at the realization and the teenage girl holding my hand turned to me and said 'Good. Now come on. To the shower with me before I start to feel all yucky.'

I was astonished by that. It was the sort of thing a child would say and as I turned to her I suddenly saw her as much younger than I'd thought previously. Mid-teens rather than late teens. Making her knowledge and wisdom and power and her ability to manage the Temple as Ceremonial Priestess utterly astonishing.

'I'm old for my years' she said, having read my thoughts and starting to pull me along towards the Temple's rear exit.

'Just you be gentle with that young girl' I heard Elke call out after us and I turned, mortified. Surely she didn't think I intended to fuck our young Priestess? Christ, what kind of debauched monster did she see in me? But as I turned I saw that Elke was grinning. It was her idea of a joke.

'Chill out Steven' she said and it sounded bizarre somehow, coming from her. 'Go take your shower. And when you're all cleaned up and you've had a rest, I think we all need to have a talk.' She glanced over at Toni. 'Tomorrow night we go up into the mountains to fix your friend.'

# The Story Episode # 103
# (Moon phase: Day 24)

WAKING FROM SLEEP is like coming back from a journey. In spiritual terms it is. You should never forget that your spiritual experiences while sleeping – including your dreams – are every bit as real as the illusion you find yourself in while you're awake. You'd profit well to go over that again and again and really think about it. But I'll leave it at that for now. I just mention it because I woke up to find the bedroom in darkness.

The teenage girl had taken me to a bedroom with an en-suite bathroom where we'd showered together, taken great care to cleanse every inch of each other and then towel each other dry. We were both tired beyond words when we were finished and she'd suggested we lie together on the bed in the adjoining bedroom to sleep.

You may wonder why we were so tired but that's because you've never taken part in a ritual like that. Or maybe you've played at it. But when it's done for real, the way that resurrection ritual had been done, you're altering incredibly powerful currents of energy and astral light. Think of the effort it would take to alter the direction of a fast-flowing river. It's the best analogy I can give you. Of course it's a mental and spiritual weariness I'm talking about, but you get the picture.

At any rate, I went to draw the curtains and block out much of the sunlight then I joined the beautiful young girl on the bed. She still appeared young despite the fact that she was easily as tall as me and mature curls of blonde hair grew between her legs. But I didn't even need to apply the lessons I'd learned from Heidi to control my instinctive sexual urges. She was so very young it didn't bear thinking about. She was lying on her back staring at the ceiling with her innocent blue eyes and I lay on my back beside her, staring up at the ceiling with her. She rolled onto her side and propped up on one elbow, she smiled down at me.

'How old do you think I am?' She asked.

I was starting to get used to this question now. It was being asked often enough for me to realise that I was being given a lesson to learn. 'About fourteen' I said. 'I don't know – maybe fifteen.'

She laughed at that and my heart lurched because it was a sweet innocent laugh and I could swear that I heard in it, faint echoes of the bell-tinkle laugh of my darling immortal beloved wife.

'So you, a grown man, you happily lie naked on a bed with a child' she said, smiling and almost laughing with delight at the terrible thought. 'Whatever would people say? I think maybe Elke should call the police.'

She laughed some more and was more like a child than ever. I was horrified at her suggestion but she continued through her giggles. 'Never mind. Just a few hundred years ago I would have been married by now. Surrounded by dirty peasant children.'

Then she laughed some more. Not laughing at me. Not laughing vainly at her own jokes. Laughing with delight and nothing more. She rolled closer to me and wrapped her arms and legs around me and I'm telling you truthfully here that while you think that this is a prelude to some appalling sexual behaviour on my part I remained beyond sexual arousal. I didn't even have to work at it.

Yes, feeling her close to me like that, her skin pressed next to mine like that was beautiful almost beyond my ability to describe. But the beauty came from a spiritual closeness that I felt for this girl and that she was transmitting to me and perhaps taking from me.

I rolled onto my side to face her and wrapped my own arms and legs around her, pulling her close. And that's how we'd drifted into sleep together. And you know, at that point I still didn't even know her name. She hadn't offered it and I hadn't asked. But waking in the darkness I found us lying side by side on our backs on that bed. Not touching. Not even holding hands. I looked across at her and she was as peaceful as a baby. Sleeping beauty. I smiled when that thought popped into my mind. A smile wiped from my face when Snow White replaced her there.

I got off the bed without disturbing her and of course I had no clothing. My clothes had been left down in the large hall, the Temple of our ritual. So that's where I'd go to collect them. I had no problem with wandering naked around the house and I'm sure you understand that by now. I was already at a state of spiritual evolution way beyond being ashamed of the body that the illusion clothed me in.

Wandering through the huge maze of a house in the dark I encountered Elke before I ever reached the hall. She was as naked as I was and that didn't surprise me at all.

'You slept well?' Elke asked

I nodded. 'I think I needed it. I hadn't intended to sleep so long.'

She took my hand and started to lead me through the house and back up the stairs. 'Yes,' she said. 'I could see that you were tired.'

We continued in total darkness along a narrow passageway with doors to either side. 'Did you sleep alone?' she asked. I looked at her sharply and she smiled, ever the joker. 'No, she kept you company and looked after you in your sleep. And you were the perfect gentleman.'

I didn't ask what Elke meant in saying that the girl had looked after me in my sleep because I could imagine it meaning any number of things. But I did get a flash of an image of the girl as Snow White again, lying dead but beautiful. Dead but dreaming. As she waited for her Prince to come.

We came to the end of the passageway and to a door with dim yellow light spilling out from underneath. Elke opened it and led me into a large enough room with tapestries on the walls, green carpet and large scatter cushions on the floor. And everywhere craft symbols and amulets. Cotton dollies with white cloth skin and black button eyes. Wooden twig-men. Pentacles and pantacles, symbols and sigils, clusters of dried herbs hanging from hooks on the walls. All lit by candles with a scent of Frankincense hanging in the air giving the atmosphere an immediate magical charge.

Elke lowered herself onto some cushions and reclined like Cleopatra waiting for someone to peel her a grape. She invited me to sit so I sat cross legged before her. She inspected me for a few moments, something else I was getting accustomed to.

'The girl you just slept with,' she said. 'Do you know her name?'

I shook my head. I wasn't about to offer up Sleeping Beauty or Snow White as suggestions.

Elke smiled. 'No,' she said. 'When you give someone your name you give them a means to have power over you. She's wise not to give it, perhaps.'

Now I knew this to be true. It *is* true. You might not know it. You might not believe it. I am absolutely sure that if you *are* giving this any thought whatsoever you're dismissing the idea and wondering how we could possibly live in societies without knowing what to call each other. And you'd be right. But only up to a point. You see, we've lost a wisdom that was common knowledge to our ancient ancestors. The certainty that your name becomes a sort of pantacle, containing and representing every aspect of your personality and spiritual essence. It represents everything that you are. Once you know someone's name you can exercise control or power over that person. For good or for ill, if you are seduced by the terrible and dark arts of sorcery.

Now you may scoff at this, reasonably suggesting that millions of people share the same name so that performing sorcery focused on a name would have an effect on all the people sharing that name. But if you *do* think that, you haven't thought it through. It's the combination of you and your name that becomes the sorcerer's focus. Think of it like this. If you use a computer, you often have to provide a username and password to access certain information. If I want to access your information, I have to have your username and password. Having just one isn't enough. I need the combination. Millions of people could have the same password as you. But I can't access any information with just the password alone. And I am limited to accessing your information only, even if I do have your username and password. That's how it works, you see. If I know your name, I can focus on you, on a mental image of you and use your name associated with that image to focus my sorcerer's intention. If I've never seen you but have a personal representation of you, that would work just as well as an image. The more personal the representation the better. Nail clippings or snippets of hair are perfect. And if I incorporate them into a doll that I make to represent you and become a physical focus for my sorcery, so much the better. This is exactly how sticking pins in a voodoo doll works, to give you an example you're probably aware of. And if you think that voodoo is just a load of hokum, just Google it to find loads of scientifically attested – though often scientifically unexplained – examples of voodoo working.

Right. I should make this clearer. So I'm going to tell you something that maybe you don't know. Just about everyone involved in occult study and practice has a secret, magical name. There's the name used in society at large and there's the name kept very secret, told to no one. Once you adopt a magical name, you transfer your essence to that secret name. Your given name becomes a label for society to understand you by, a name that you can give to strangers with impunity.

You only have to go back a few hundred years to find a time where people wouldn't readily give their names to strangers. A stranger would have to have a good reason for needing to know your name before you would grant it. You should read perhaps the medieval work by Thomas Mallory, *Le Morte d'Arthur*. This work concerns the life and deeds of King Arthur and the knights of the Table Round, and I'm suggesting it because time and time again when knights encounter each other they refuse to give their names. They will only do so when it's considered safe to do so. Wow, so that was a long digression. But I think it's important that you should know why we need to protect our names.

Now, getting back to me sitting in that dim and candlelit room with Elke.

'But she knows my name' I said, meaning the teenage girl, 'Remember, Heidi called it out to the whole room.'

Elke simply laughed at that. 'Just the name you give to the world' she said. 'Not the one that counts.'

She had me there, as I've just explained, so I smiled back at her.

She sat upright, arranged herself in a lotus position facing me.

'Your friend Toni' she said. 'Tomorrow night we are going up onto the mountain, into the forests. We go to fix her the way Heidi was going to fix her. Mother earth. Father sky. Let nature care for her child. Richard told me all about your friend but I have seen it in her anyway. Still, we fix her. Tomorrow is a good night for it.'

I didn't wonder about the Major's name being Richard. He'd have a secret name the same as the rest of us. But I did wonder about Heidi.

'What about Heidi?' I asked. 'Is she okay? Everything good with her?'

Elke shook her head. 'No,' she said. 'Not good. But she is safe. Among people who know what to do. It's going to take time.'

She must have seen sorrow and concern in my eyes because she said 'Don't you worry. We will make her good.'

I did feel reassured about that but said nothing.

'You care about her,' Elke said. 'Is it because she is beautiful? Because she gives you good sex?'

I could see why she'd think that. I can see why you'd think that. But I looked away feeling sad. Sad because of Heidi. Sad because I realised that Elke seemed to regard me as being altogether shallow.

'Hey,' she said, clearly picking up on my sadness, 'Come on. I was teasing you. You care about her because you know she suffers and suffers because of you. It's beautiful that you are like that.'

Her words went some way towards comforting me but not all the way. I still had much to learn and I knew it. Elke stretched out a foot and stroked my leg. Spoke softly to me. 'We concentrate on what we must do tomorrow. For your friend Toni' she said. 'But after, you should talk to me. Tell me about Sable Wyvern. Tell me about your wife.'

I was about to speak but she stopped me by putting a finger to her lips. 'Shhh,' she said. 'We talk about these things after tomorrow. I can see your sadness. And I see what you need. Let me help you. After tomorrow.'

I couldn't help thinking of what Elke had said to the Major when we'd first arrived, about her house being a repair shop and the Major bringing her damaged goods. Well she'd been right about that. Heidi, Toni and me, we were damaged alright and in need of more than a mere oil change.

Just then the door clicked open and Elke and me, we both turned to see the beautiful teenage girl I'd left naked on the bed step into the room. Somehow the candlelight seemed to grow a touch brighter at her entry like it was responding to her beauty, however fanciful that sounds.

She was no longer naked. She wore a beautiful soft silk dress that came down to just above her knees, midnight blue or maybe even black, flowing with fabulous large paisley print patterns. Over it she wore a light-weight jacket embellished with sequins and Persian embroidery. Barefoot of course, and she came to sit with us on the cushions in the middle of the floor. I couldn't help noticing, as she crossed her legs to sit down, that she wasn't wearing any panties beneath the dress. I tried to look away but she'd seen that I'd been looking.

'No, no underwear,' she said smiling. 'It ruins the lines of the dress.'

I had to smile at that.

She shrugged. 'I'm a girl,' she said. 'I'm allowed a little vanity.'

I had to agree with that. How could I disagree? And she did look spectacular in that dress and that jacket contrasting with the nakedness of Elke and me. Elke turned to her.

'You didn't tell Steven your name,' she said.

'No' the girl said, unconcerned. 'He never asked.'

Well she was right of course. I hadn't asked. And I really got the feeling that I should have. That I'd been mistaken not to. Another lesson learned. I looked at the girl but said nothing. I couldn't tell if it was the dress and the jacket doing it, but somehow she seemed older than she had earlier. When she'd been giving me the hint of a lesson concerning the appearance of age.

'Let me put you out of your misery' she said. 'I'm nineteen.'

Elke felt the need to explain further. 'You'd never have guessed it. She has a gift. Up to a point, she can make you see whatever age she wants you to see. People have been known to think of her as just entering her teens. And her as tall as a baby giraffe. A gift, like I say. But she should learn not to play with it.'

As admonishments go it was as mild as could be and the girl wasn't hurt by it.

'Anyway' Elke continued, 'Perhaps it's time I introduced you, since the two of you seem too shy to make acquaintance.' She turned to me, indicated towards the girl and said 'Steven, you should meet Brunhilde.'

Not Snow White then, which was a relief. The girl smiled and cocked her head to one side. In the candlelight right then I'd have put her in her early twenties. I took the hand she held out to me, leaned forward and bringing her soft fingers to my lips, I gently kissed the fingers of a Valkyrie.

# The Story Episode # 104
# (Moon phase: Day 25)

HIGH IN THE Harz Mountains taking a seldom-trod path through the dense pine forest, I was transported back to New Zealand where all this had begun. The pine forest was far removed from the sub-tropical New Zealand bush but the atmosphere in the dark of night was familiar enough. I suppose that forests everywhere share this.

We were all wearing hiking gear. Boots, shorts, thick button up shirts of uniform colour and manufacture so that I couldn't help thinking that we must have resembled a troop of *Hitler Jugend* on a night-time exercise. It was all I could do not to sing *The Happy Wanderer*. You know the one – *I love to go, a-wandering, along the mountain track, and as I go, I love to sing, my knapsack on my back, Val-deri! Val-dera! Val-deri! Val-dera ha ha ha ha ha! Val-deri! Val-dera! My knapsack on my back. . .* There. I wish I'd never remembered that. I won't be able to get that out of my head for ages now. Goddammit. And actually, I remember thinking that if we'd been marching up through the *Bayerischer Schwarzwald* – that's the Bavarian Black Forest to you – I wouldn't have been able to help belting the ludicrously cheerful ditty out to the world.

There was something about the Harz Mountains though that made you want to keep bloody quiet. Like the whole place was a *do not disturb* notice. In New Zealand, the Maori would have called the entire Harz Mountain forest *tapu*, or sacred and forbidden. The forest was haunted all right. Not just the ghosts of dead ancestors either. This was clearly a place where other states of consciousness drifted nervously close to our own plane of illusion.

Many of the stories set down by the Brothers Grimm were collected in the Harz Mountains. That thought had me looking back at Brunhilde following close behind me on the narrow overgrown track. She smiled at me but I couldn't help thinking of how Snow White had come to my mind as I'd watched her sleeping. It sent a chill through me and although I was in the middle of our group, marching in single-file silence, I glanced nervously about me seeing shadows moving and hiding among the sinister-black trees surrounding us.

I suppose I ought to mention who we were, marching ever higher on the *Brockenberg*. Leading our group was the older bearded man from Elke's house. He'd been introduced to me as Jurgen earlier in the day and he clearly knew his way around the forest and the mountains. He was guiding us where paths were invisible if they existed at all. Elke followed close behind him and behind her Gerhard, one of the beautiful young men, marched in step like a guardsman. Toni came next and I was right behind her with Brunhilde behind me, as I've already said. Karl, the other beautiful young man followed a few steps behind Brunhilde and I was glad to know that the Major was covering our backs at the rear of our column. Heidi wasn't with us. She'd been left back at Elke's house and Elke had called in a friend, a woman living in nearby *Magdeberg*, to sit with Heidi and look after her.

I'd expected Heidi to object to this but she hadn't. She'd seemed tired and listless all day. High up on the mountain in the pitch dark, I was glad she hadn't come with us. I'm going to tell you something here. In the middle of that marching column, dwarfed by the black pine trees looming over us and blotting out the inky star-spangled sky, I was afraid. I anticipated the wicked crone of the Snow White story stepping out from behind every tree, shiny red apple in hand. I fancied we were being stalked by shades of other-wordly menace. A werewolf perhaps. Shapes without names. From time to time I could have sworn I heard the moans of dying soldiers. Romans from the Legions of Quintillius Varrus, decimated in the *Teutoburg* Forest by the Germanic tribes in rebellion. That this wasn't necessarily the *Teutoburg* didn't seem to matter. But then again, maybe it was that ill-fated place. The exact location of that ancient killing ground has never been satisfactorily identified.

Toni turned to smile nervously at me. I could see that the atmospheric energy of this forest and this mountain were having a profound effect on her. I smiled back, trying to look encouraging but my smile must have appeared sardonic because she turned quickly away. I wasn't fooling anyone.

Little Red Riding Hood wending through the forest alongside us. The wolf tracking her. I saw Hansel and Gretel in the stones along our lesser-trodden path. I was spooked. And I tripped, falling heavily onto my bare knees as I trod on my own bootlace. I cried out in pain because sharp stones buried into my skin and I cursed. The whole column came to a halt and all eyes were upon me. But this was good because it brought me to my senses and the thoughts that had been creeping me out just disappeared.

'Go on,' I said to them, 'Keep going. I'll just tie this lace and I'll catch up.'

Jurgen at the head of the column needed no encouragement. He simply nodded and continued on his way. The others had no option really but to follow him and leave me there. Let's face it, it was no big deal. A few seconds to tie my lace and I'd be right back with them taking my place behind Toni.

As I dusted myself down I became aware of the Major standing next to me. 'I'll stay with you,' he said and I was a little offended that he'd seen me as such a feeble frightened lightweight.

As it was, he had my measure, let's make no mistake about that. Especially when I had cause to look to the sky and found a break in the dense high tree canopy. And found *her* staring down at me. Silver. Disapproving. The moon. Appropriate that she was silver. For as it is above, so it is below. And there were seams of silver in the rock beneath our feet in these mountains. One of the Titanic elements bound to mother earth.

I concentrated on tying my lace and had just finished when I heard the clear sound of furtive footsteps coming from behind. I turned as my blood ran cold and I could have sworn I saw a cloaked figure dart behind a tree. I looked up to the sky and the moon had gone.

'Shit, let's get out of here' I said, turning to the Major. But fuck me, he already had.

I was all alone in that haunted forest on that haunted mountain in the dark. I was adrenaline-scared right then and I ran but there was no sign of the Major and no sign of our group even though I couldn't have been more than a few seconds behind them. Something touched the top of my head and while I didn't scream I gasped out loud and I started to run aimlessly faster. Which, when you think of it, was a stupid thing to do since I hadn't a clue where I was or which way to head. I was lost and still running. Running and not daring to scream, too scared to break the silence of the haunted place. Until I was stopped dead in my tracks. A black figure stepped from behind a tree directly ahead of me, maybe twenty yards in front. A man. Tall and slender and wearing a black overcoat. Black leather gloves on his hands. A man. Except this man had a face I recognised. White. Tight black-lipped smile. Black soul-less eyes. Malevolent. *Her.* But a man.

A hand suddenly on my shoulder and I turned whimpering, nearly screaming, almost fainting.

'Steady boy' the Major said, because it was his hand. So I steadied, just as he'd commanded.

'Come on now, let's go catch up with the others' he said, dead calm.

He held me by the wrist and almost pulled me along after him. I kept looking back but he just pulled me along until at last we came to an eerie rock formation rising up out of the mountain among the trees. We stopped there and when I caught my breath, I realised that the rest of our crew were there.

'Sit down' the Major ordered, and I sank in a heap on the floor next to Brunhilde who leaned over and kissed my cheek, giggling. Nothing fazed her at all. Valkyrie.

'Who was it?' Elke asked.

I was about to ask who was who but the Major stopped me dead answering with unimpeachable certainty. And his answer didn't fill me with comfort and joy.

'Sable Wyvern' he said. 'Sable Wyvern.'

It was all I could do to maintain control of my bowels.


# The Story Episode # 105
# (Moon phase: Day 26)


EXISTENCE IS AN illusion so that everything we see is subjective. When I look at something, the image I perceive is not the same as the image you perceive. Suppose that when I look at something red, I see what you perceive to be blue. In other words we both *see* different colours. But we might never know that if our personal experiences remain consistent. In other words, it doesn't matter if the colour I see in my head doesn't match the colour you see in yours. Provided we both agree to call *that* colour red, neither of us are any the wiser, and we can both co-exist without confusing each other. The term *red* is merely an artificial label used to describe an attribute. If I see a red rose, the colour red is merely an attribute of the rose. If you look at the same rose and agree to label the colour of the rose red, the same as me, it doesn't matter if the image in my head doesn't match the image you see in your head. So long as we both agree that when we look at that same rose we both see a *red* rose, there is no confusion.

This is actually how it works. There are loads of academic psychological research study results that demonstrate without doubt that our individual experiences of the universe, the illusion, are utterly subjective. I have given a particularly abstract and inflexible example, but the common phrase *beauty is in the eye of the beholder* explains it rather more simply, even if it's not entirely satisfactory.

You wonder why I'm gibbering on about this I suppose, and you think it's stupid and you don't believe it or you don't see the point. Well that's up to you. But the reason I mention it is because of the rock formation we'd stopped at as we climbed through the forest on the *Brockenberg Tor*. The area seemed to be carpeted with dark flat-topped slate rocks, but rising up from their midst was a tower of this same rock maybe ten or twelve feet high. And here's the point about this rock. It consisted of stratified layers of what I considered to be inert stone, but as I looked upon it in the darkness I swear that its appearance changed.

It didn't morph its shape exactly, because I didn't perceive motion. But it did manage to confuse me. The first time I looked upon it I could have sworn that it resembled a giant head with the features of a head – ears, nose, mouth and so on. But after I'd turned my attention to look at my companions resting in silence at its base, I looked up at it again. And then it appeared to resemble a giant, towering above us. Not merely a giant head, but the whole damn thing. A giant that just might stride out after us and smash us to death against the side of the mountain if it so wished.

Something made me turn to look at Elke as this chilling thought washed through me. She was observing me, understanding something. But she turned back to the Major.

'Sable Wyvern' she said. 'This name keeps cropping up.' She looked at me again. 'Probably too late for you to be telling me about this Sable Wyvern' she said. 'Another time. For now I don't like him. I am right not to like him, I think.' She turned back to the Major. 'We have come here to commune with nature. Sable Wyvern will not interfere. We have ways.'

I must say I believed her and I was comforted by her words.

'Should we move on?' I asked. 'How far do we have to go?'

Elke smiled. 'We can rest here' she said. 'We do not have to hurry now.'

I looked at Toni sitting on a slate outcrop next to Brunhilde and seeming altogether weary. She must have sensed me looking because she turned to me and smiled, although smiling seemed to be an effort for her. I suppose I knew how she felt because I was a wreck after hiking halfway up the bloody mountain. All the same, I understood that Toni's weariness was more than merely physical.

Elke came over to stand beside me. 'The rock' she said, pointing to the tall outcrop. 'Tell me what you see.'

I studied the rock as silver moonlight fell across the face nearest to us.

'I don't know' I said, shaking my head. 'I guess it's an outcrop of stratified rock, but I'm no geologist so I can't describe it properly for you.'

Elke smiled and shook her head. 'You know that's not what I mean. I saw you just now. Tell me what you saw.'

'I think I'm just tired. I thought it looked like a giant head when I first saw it. Probably just the shadows here.'

Elke waited and when I didn't continue she said 'There's more.'

I was reluctant to tell her but she had this way of using silence so that I felt the need to fill it. She'd have made a great interrogator. In the end I told her. Told her how the second time I'd looked at it, it seemed to resemble a tall powerful giant.

'Like the guardian of the mountain' I said in the end.

Elke took my hand and squeezed it at that. 'Not *the* guardian of the mountain' she said. 'But one of them.' We both stood looking up at the guardian, admiring the reflected silver sheen of its smooth surfaces and the shadows that defined it. 'Why do you imagine that you see it in two different ways?' Elke asked.

I could only shake my head. I knew the answer wouldn't be obvious and that I was about to learn something.

'You see exactly what it presents to you' Elke explained, and it was like a flash of lightning before my eyes as I realised just a hint of what she meant. 16. The Tower. C Major. Peh. Mouth. Mars. Iron. The rock was intelligent. Communicated through imagery. And it had spoken to me.

'See, you get it' Elke said, seeming delighted for me. 'The guardian shows you his head to symbolize his intelligence. He wants you to know that.'

'Do you see that?' I asked. 'A giant head?'

Elke shook her own head. 'I see only what he shows me.'

'He gets to choose?' I asked.

Elke stepped back from me to regard me with some surprise. 'Of course,' she said. 'Don't you? You can appear happy or sad or welcoming or unapproachable. It's the same thing.'

'Does he have a name?' I asked.

'We all have names,' Elke said. 'But a name is a source of power as you know. Up to him to tell you or not.'

'So what do you suppose he *is* telling me?' I asked.

Elke didn't answer my question. Just posed another one. 'What do you feel he's telling you?'

I couldn't begin to imagine, not tired, not frightened as I was. And yes, I was still frightened. Apprehensive at any rate.

'He shows you his head to tell you that he sees and understands.' This was Brunhilde. 'He knows why you come to him. He tells you that you are not alone while you are here.'

Elke and I had both looked over at Brunhilde. I turned to Elke for confirmation and got it in her nod and her smile. Brunhilde rose, came to stand with us and the three of us looked back at the rock.

'He shows you the giant to let you know that he is a guardian of this place. He expects you to come in a spirit of unity and respect and with an open mind.'

'And if I don't?' I asked.

'I think he already showed you' Brunhilde said with a shrug.

I shuddered, remembering the thought I'd had of the terrible dark giant smashing unresisting bodies of flesh and blood against the mountainside.

'Don't imagine him coming to life like some sort of Judaic Golem. His power is administered on the astral planes of consciousness. Mentally. You feel his wrath maybe right away but maybe also in days or weeks or months.'

I didn't have time to ponder this or ask any of the million questions I think might have come to me because everyone stood and we could see their faces as they did so. Toni, the Major, Jurgen, Gerhard and Karl. We turned to look at what they could obviously see. And as I describe it to you now, it won't seem much. But up there on that dark moonlit mountain, shrouded by an imposing dense black pine forest and in the presence of the living rock guardian, I can tell you it shook me out of any comfort zone I might have created for myself.

There were four of them and they appeared from the four cardinal points, North South East and West. Surrounding us and equidistant from the living rock guardian. Four silent black-robed figures, their faces obscured by deep hoods. And you'd like to say that they appeared from where they'd been hiding, behind trees. *I'd* like to say that. But that's not how it appeared to me at the time, even though I learned later that that's exactly what had happened.

You see, the way it appeared to me, these four figures materialized from the matter of the living trees themselves. I swear that's how it appeared. And for some reason as they approached, I looked up at the living rock guardian. And the lips in that giant head seemed for all the world to be smiling.

# The Story Episode # 106
# (Moon phase: Day 26)

SOMETIMES YOU THINK you're on the cusp between worlds. Like you have one foot in the illusion and another foot in a different projection of it. Yes that's right, it's all an illusion. Some half-baked tossers talk about other realms of consciousness like they're the reality we're all supposed to be seeking. But here's the way it is. All of these altered states, they're all illusions. There's only one reality. And we should be striving to get back to it – in the end, that is. Deluding ourselves that other states of consciousness are in some way better than the illusion here in this projection of existence actually stunts spiritual progress. Actually stops it dead. Without telling you. So you could imagine it's laughing at you. Because some of us are here with a purpose. And we'd do better to awaken to what that purpose is and who and what we are, rather than go chasing the blessing of the Holy Grail. Some of us – and this I know is barely credible, given the horror that this world is – have even volunteered to be here, to live in human form, tasked to help in an infinite multitude of ways, to put it right. So when some New agers smugly try to make you feel inferior because your inner voice is telling you that their reach for Nirvana isn't for you, you should not despair. You are doubtless here for another reason. And their smug know-it all attitude to others not sharing their vision ought to tell you everything you need to know about them. They are far from being enlightened, no matter their grandiose claims. You'll never persuade them of that truth and you shouldn't waste your time trying. You could, maybe, pity them.

Anyway, I felt that I was on the cusp between two worlds up there on the *Brockenberg Tor* in the darkness and moonlight with these hooded figures seeming to emerge from living black trees of the forest surrounding us. They came gliding in, it seemed to me, not taking steps. I heard no pine needles crunching beneath their feet, no impression of footsteps at all. I instinctively moved to stand next to Toni. Probably for protection if I'm honest. Because I will be honest now and say that I was afraid at first. And I was glad that the Major came to stand with us. With Toni and me. But before these figures reached us, I became aware that the rest of our group - Elke and her people - were not in the least concerned. In fact they were all smiles and open-armed welcomes.

I relaxed when the Major did, and as the four figures reached us in the rock-clearing they threw back their hoods. Two men and two women, and Elke and the others knew them well because there were hugs and greetings all round.

Eventually we were introduced. Elke telling the four newcomers who we were and telling us who they were. Not magical names of course. Just the common labels used in the everyday world. Ulrike and Karin, Andreas and Uwe. Once things had settled, Karin looked at me and spoke to Elke.

'This man Stevie. We come together to fix him?' she said.

Elke shook her head. 'Uh-uh,' she said, taking Toni's hand. 'This one. She needs the help.'

Karin nodded in acceptance, but couldn't help looking back over at me. 'We fix the poor little girl,' she said. 'But this one. He's in trouble too.'

Well you can imagine I was far from comforted by that. Nevertheless, we'd come to Germany to help Toni. It seemed a million years since Tom had told me to take Toni to Berlin. But it had only been a few days. At least now I felt that we were among people who could put Toni back together again. Give us the old Toni back. I realised I'd kind of lost track of all that. But I remembered it then and it pleased me no end.

Ulrike and Andreas had taken Toni in hand. Literally. I watched them undress her so that her white skin seemed to shimmer in the moonlit clearing. They took a black robe from the backpack Toni had carried up the mountain with her. We'd all carried them. I noticed the others taking the robes from their own backpacks so I followed their lead. Soon enough we were all wearing the black robes. I knew what was coming. I was used to the preparation for ceremony, for ritual. I've described some of the ceremonial rituals I was used to. The technical Temple rituals with all the appropriate Officers present. The geometry of the symbols being mathematically precise. Angelic language more precise than mathematics used to call down powers and open gateways and so on. Enochian Magic. Qabalism. Gemutria. Stuff I haven't even mentioned to you yet. Lots more. But this was mighty different.

The terrifying restrictions were altogether missing. Just being on the mountain rather than in a Temple was liberating. I could feel the connection with the earth beneath my bare feet and the air and the sky above us. Sister Moon in the indigo sky. Titanic elements, the offspring of Mother Earth given up from the soil. The guardian of the mountain, the giant rock, was smiling. Laughing. Because there was the joy of celebration.

Uwe placed his hands on Toni's shoulders. Looked her in the eye.

'Twenty-seventh Aethyr' he said, and I wondered just how he could know we'd been there.

'You bring a little of it back with you, yes? You leave in a hurry. Don't take the time to take off your boots and change them for running shoes, eh?'

He laughed at that like he'd made a great joke. I was about to ask him how he knew we'd been to the twenty-seventh Aethyr but a look from Elke stopped me.

'You shouldn't be playing around with that Enochian stuff. It's dangerous' Uwe said.

I really did want to protest at that but the Major grabbed my wrist. He was right to do so. I mean, these people didn't mean any harm. I realised they were just making conversation.

'Now,' Andreas said to Toni like the rest of us weren't even there. 'You've learned the lesson of the twenty-seventh Aethyr, yes? The difference between loneliness and solitude? Well no need to keep living it. We bring you home now.'

I looked at the Major and then at Elke, wondering just who these people were but I got a stonewall poker face from the Major and an encouraging smile from Elke. Ulrike sidled over to me.

'You want to know how we fix your friend?'

'Yeah,' I said.

Ulrike laughed. 'We don't' she said. 'We let nature take care of her children. Mother Earth. Father Sky. Brother Sun. Sister Moon.'

'It's night. . .' I began to say, but Ulrike smiled at me and it shut me up.

'Brother Sun,' she said. 'He made us and he guides us. You think he's not with us because you do not see him?' I knew better than to answer. 'In the middle of the day you may turn your back on him. You cannot see him. Your face is in shadow. But you feel him on your back. Nourishing you. Comforting you. Feeding you life. Now you understand?'

I understood. Brother Sun always shining on Mother Earth. Nourishing her. And her children. Brother Sun. Fire. Mother Earth. Earth. Father Sky. Air. Sister Moon. Water. The four Ancient Elements. Anything that could be worked could be worked with them. The ancient roots of everything in our world of illusion. Intelligences that make the illusion all that it is. And compared to working with *Haute Magie*, the technical world of Ceremonial Magic, it all seems so simple. Brother Sun. Sister Moon. Mother Earth. Father Sky. All so very simple. And it is. Except that to commune with elementals and work in harmony with them while getting them to work with you takes a monumental effort. I'll be going into that in more detail later, have no fear.

For now all I can tell you is that there were twelve of us robed on that mountain. And a giant guardian in our midst. And Uwe had us all holding hands in a circle. Me between Toni on my left and Brunhilde on my right. And all smiles and joy, Uwe led us in a dance around the guardian of the mountain. Our bare feet skipping along over the rocks and pine needles. Our robes flowing and flapping. The rock-guardian smiling in the reflective waters of Sister Moon. Us dancing and skipping faster as Ulrike and Uwe and Andreas and Karin began to sing in German, a song I didn't recognise and words I couldn't translate.

Faster and faster we circled the giant rock, the singing and chanting beautiful in our ears until I found myself singing along, as we all did. Me not knowing what the words meant but singing them anyway. Faster. Dancing Faster. Singing. Dancing faster, circling the rock-guardian, circling, circling, singing, chanting. Until none of it made sense. I lost track of who I was and what I was and what I was doing. Lost all sense of ego and Sister Moon spinning above and Mother Earth beneath my feet. Just the laughing smiling guardian of the mountain, guardian of the forest smiling and nodding in time with the song. The trees all one black mass. Then darkness becoming light. Bright. Bright yellow. Bright white. Getting brighter and brighter until it exploded. And when the light faded I found myself alone on the mountain in the lee of the giant guardian.

As I picked myself up off the ground I became aware of the black pine trees of the forest surrounding me. I caught movement behind a tree to the west of me. I became all of a sudden apprehensive. With good reason. The figure stepping from behind that tree was familiar. White face, black eyes, tight black-lipped smile. Black overcoat, black gloves. It was *her*. But it was also Sable Wyvern. Now advancing on me. Slowly. But I couldn't move. Like a dream where you need to escape but you just can't seem to run fast enough.'

I *was* moving though. Down. Down that fucking cursed mountain. Cursing in my mind that my so-called companions had left me alone up there. Sable Wyvern following me. Slow paced. Even, malevolent smile. And no matter how fast I ran, no matter how even-paced Sable Wyvern's pursuit, I never got any further ahead. In fact I was being caught. My heart beating beyond endurance. Me careering into trees, bouncing off like a pinball. Falling and rolling. Looking behind me to see a hand reaching out and nearly upon me. And I turned and smashed into. . . someone.

I looked up, whimpering. And it was Tom. I didn't scream just turned, and Sable Wyvern was almost touching me. So I turned back to Tom but Tom was gone. I could only run, so head down, I ran. And I tripped and fell. I rolled over onto my back, scrambled away from my pursuer who was reaching down with white-skinned hands and nearly grabbing my throat until I managed to scramble back away, gaining a few feet of distance, transfixed by that black, tight-lipped smile.

I got to my feet and turned and this time I did run, gaining pace down the mountain through the trees. Faster and faster and faster and – bang! I hit a giant black pine trunk and it took the wind from me, threw me to the ground. In agony and unable to breathe, I looked for my pursuer. No sign of Sable Wyvern but the pain was horrific in my ribs so that I cried. Until I heard a voice almost whisper to me.

'Don't cry Stevie. Please don't cry.'

I looked up because I wanted to look up. But I didn't have to look up. I knew that voice. It was Helen. My Helen. My darling beautiful immortal beloved wife. And I saw her not a couple of feet away as I cried out her name. Then passed out into the infinite blackness.

# *The Story Episode # 107*
# *(Moon phase: Day 26)*

STILL ON THE mountain. Hadn't moved a beat. Still on the *Brockenberg Tor*. Lying on my back in the lee of the rock-guardian, the Titan-offspring of Mother Earth. And when I opened my eyes I saw the faces peering down at me. Elke kneeling by my side. The Major leaning close in over her shoulder, all concern. In fact all of them standing in a circle looking down at me seemed concerned, so that I did a quick check to make sure I had all my limbs and no broken bones.

'Keep still' Elke said softly, stroking my face. 'Just rest for a little while. Get your bearings. You're among friends.'

That reassured me as you can imagine. Because although I recognised where I was, I still had this feeling of disorientation. Possibly because I was lying flat on my back. Possibly because I was staring up through a gap in the canopy of impossibly tall black pine trees at the carpet of silver stars. *Probably* because *she* was up there leering down at me. Lilith. Astarte. Isis. Diana. The Moon. Sister Moon. Looking like no sister of mine.

'No family lives in harmony all the time.' Brunhilde, the lovely teenage girl wise beyond reckoning had come to stand over me. 'You never shouted at your sister?' she asked, removing her robe so that her pale skin glowed with a silver translucence in the moonlight. She knelt and draped her robe over me, even though I wasn't in the least bit cold. When she stood I saw her as a Goddess of the forest. As. . . I hesitated, but the name that came to mind was. . . Diana.

'I never had a sister' I said in answer and it sounded feeble.

'Just as well' said a voice I recognised. 'He'd have fucked her into oblivion.' I recognised that voice and I recognised that tone. Toni. And all eyes on her. She feigned a mild outrage at their questioning looks. 'Oh come on' she said. 'You know what he's like.'

Elke laughed and the Major smiled at that. Even I smiled. Because I could take the ribbing. What was important was that this was the old Toni. Feisty, gobby, confident. Gorgeous. Whatever had happened up there on the *Brockenberg Tor*, it had worked.

'You think he wants to fuck *me*?' This was Brunhilde, and I saw her standing above me, striking poses like a series of marble statues. Beautifully naked. Beautifully proportioned. The golden mean. As close as dammit in her proportions and the angles she formed with her thighs, her arms, her elbows, her knees, her ankles, her feet. From the edges of her shoulders to a point down in her navel.

Needless to say, I didn't say anything. In answer to her question I mean. I didn't have to did I? I'm guessing you know that I'd have loved to have spread her over one of the flat rocks right there, even in front of everyone, and fucked her like we were animals. Just for starters.

'He wants to fuck you, yes,' Elke said, rubbing her palm over the erection barely concealed by my robe. 'See?' she said, grabbing my shaft through the rough cloth and laughing.

'Do you think he can last a whole weekend? Give a girl what she needs?' Brunhilde asked this, her foot placed on a raised rock so that I could see the slit between her legs where it nestled between the wispy curls of soft blonde hair.

'We better ask Heidi that wouldn't you say, Major Warne?'

Elke was still laughing so that not for the first time I had to remind myself that different cultures found amusement in different things.

'No need,' Toni chimed in again. 'In the last couple of weeks he's fucked me, more than once, fucked my cleaner, fucked who knows who else while he's been staying in my house. I think I can vouch for him if you can't wait to get the verdict from Heidi.'

I should tell you here that Toni wasn't being at all nasty. She was just sliding into the mood of jovial banter. Even I was getting in the spirit of it because I propped myself up on my elbows and laughed along with them.

'Just as well we came to Germany when we did,' I said. 'Any longer at your place and I'd have probably been having a pop at Tom.'

Toni didn't laugh at that though. She merely shrugged and turned away.

'Tom would probably have let you' she said. 'He can be versatile. But he's happier when he's a top than a bottom. I can vouch for that.'

I winced inwardly at that, remembering Tom's huge penis. I should, perhaps, explain the terminology. Some of you will know, but some of you won't. The terminology refers to anal sex. Homosexual anal sex, really. A 'top' is someone who likes to do the penetrating, a 'bottom' is someone who likes to receive. Versatile refers to someone who can enjoy either. So now you know why I winced, thinking of Toni saying she could vouch for Tom liking to be a 'top.' We'll say no more about it.

Anyway the mood had changed. Everyone was stripping out of their robes and getting back into their clothes. In the case of the four newcomers this meant a variety of outdoor casual clothing. For our group – meaning Elke's people plus Toni, the

Major and me - it meant a return to our *Hitler Jugend* uniform. I did wonder about Elke because of that, but I had to laugh as I pulled on the shorts. And it struck me right then that there was humour in the air. The atmosphere of the mountain had changed. Changed since our whirling singing chanting dance. No longer oppressive, no longer the domain of werewolves. Nor of crones in search of Snow White. Nor of Sable Wyverns. Now it was, even in the pitch dark of night and by the light of the silvery moon, a place of ringing joy. I saw glittering silver shine on the flat faces of the rocks on the ground, almost a reflection of the constellations of stars way up in the indigo sky.

'Now you see, eh?' Elke put a hand on my shoulder. 'We go down the mountain in joy, right?'

I had to agree with her. Because I could feel it. The way the mountain presented itself to us. We had changed. The ritual dance had changed us. And the change in us meant a change in the way the mountain appeared to us.

Let me explain. If you stand to the left of a mirror and look at the glass, you see a reflection of the world to the right of the mirror. Stand on the right and you see a reflection of the world to the left of the mirror. Same mirror, but it appears different because *you* have changed insofar as you are standing in a different position. Same with the mountain. The ritual had changed us, altered our consciousness and that changed how the mountain appeared to us. It was beautiful beyond description. So I won't try to describe it.

'Things you saw. Only you. Can you remember them?' Elke asking me but the Major standing close by, interested.

I nodded. I could remember most of it. And on my own it would have chilled me to remember. But not there. Not with those people.

'Who was the girl?' This was Ulrike who'd wandered over to

us, hands in the pockets of her jeans.

'What girl?' the Major asked.

'There was a girl' Ulrike gently insisted. 'I didn't see her. But he did.'

I knew who she meant. Helen. My immortal beloved and beautiful wife.

Elke didn't allow the atmosphere to change with the question as it so easily could. 'Come on,' she said. 'Let's get down the mountain. We talk through everything back at the house. Maybe tomorrow is best. It's been a good night, no?'

I had to admit that it had.

'Perhaps Brunhilde lets you sleep in her bed?'

Brunhilde turned to us and smiled. 'Not bloody likely,' she said, imitating my English accent.

'Don't worry,' Elke said. 'You can sleep in mine.'

# The Story Episode # 108
# (Moon phase: Day 26)

A NEW MORNING and as the sun – Brother Sun – appeared over the horizon to spread light and love and life, I awakened to find myself in Elke's bed. Alone. As I had been all night. Elke had given me her bed as she'd promised but I hadn't shared it with her. She, it turned out, had shared Brunhilde's bed. Yes I did speculate about that. I'm a guy and a sexual obsessive and yadda yadda yadda. But that's as far as I can go because I'm not going to deal in idle speculation. For all I know it could have been perfectly innocent. Probably was.

Anyway, moving on. I woke with the dawn, seeing the light

grow in the curtainless bedroom and hearing the dawn chorus of birds in the trees outside. This was bliss and beauty. I lay there staring at the timber-framed ceiling and the white plaster between the timbers.

First thing I considered was Toni. Mission accomplished there. Whatever remnant of the twenty-seventh Aethyr had stayed with her was gone. I imagined it spinning away as the circularity of our dance had gathered pace. The dance had sent me into a trance and transported me to an altered state of consciousness. I could only imagine that it had done this for all the others of our group. The dance, the movements, the circularity, the increasing speed, the singing and chanting of Karin, Uwe, Ulrike and Andreas leading us. I understood in that moment as I lay there, the purpose of the dance of the African Dervishes. The trance-inducing spin following the course of nature's existence. All motion is spiral. *All* motion. It is, whether you accept that or not. In this story I'm telling you what I *know*, and know empirically at that. Whether you have the capacity to understand it or believe it is neither here nor there to me. And that's not me being harsh. Just a reminder that virtually everyone is wedded to the illusion.

One of the ways in which certain self-interested groups of intelligence have manipulated the illusion is to make the truth seem so unlikely as to have it rejected by just about everyone it's presented to. This is how the illusion works. If I tell you that just a handful of people control the illusion of the world through a selfish desire to exercise control over it - and all of us - you laugh at me. You think it's fanciful at best. You immediately put a label on me. Conspiracy Theorist you say. And you say it in a way that demonstrates your derision and disbelief. I mean, *Illuminati*. It's just too fanciful for words. It's impossible. And every time you think that way, every time you say that and deride it, their power increases because they have effectively closed down an avenue of valid inquisition. If I say that part of their aim involves enslavement and population control, you find the details of this so monstrous that you reject it out of hand. Thus they can bring these plans to fruition without meaningful opposition. I'm going to leave it there, because this is not part of the story I'm relating to you. I just went off on a tangent. Thanks for indulging me. I'll move along now.

I was talking about the dance up on the mountain though. The dance that had, as we'd progressed with it, brought us into a state of communion with our surroundings. I'd definitely felt that. That giant rock, that Titan borne of Mother Earth, had become one of us. As much a part of the dance as any of us. And while we didn't communicate in human language, we exchanged an emotion. That of joy. The Titan experienced our joy and shared his own with us. The giant black pine trees of the forest surrounding us were happy spectators, encouraging us on in our communion with all of nature and truth and beauty.

Mother Earth below, Father Sky above, Sister Moon approving. Brother Sun overseeing, unperceived by us. Yet I couldn't help dwelling on the other things. Sable Wyvern pursuing me in that altered state. How the devil had he found me? What did he want with me? I couldn't understand that at all. I'd never heard of the bastard until Tom had mentioned him, telling me that he'd died.

I made a note to question Tom further when we got back to England. There were plenty of pieces of the jigsaw missing and Tom most certainly held this one in his pocket. I'd make him show me. And of course there was Helen. I didn't have to guess how she'd found me. She'd never really left me. And I'd never left her.

Sliding out of bed, I stood and wandered over to the window. Looked out upon the lawns breaking into forest not far beyond. Gazed on the mountain rising beyond the trees in the distance. I turned as the door clicked open. Elke entered, and she was wrapped in an oyster-coloured silk robe.

'I knew you'd be awake' she said as she walked over to sit on the bed.

I was naked of course. And I was getting used to having women walk in on me in that state. With Toni's cleaner Rachel it had become a bloody habit.

'Come,' Elke said. 'Sit next to me. Let us talk.'

I slid onto the bed and lay on my back, looking up at the ceiling once more. Elke lifted her legs onto the top covers and lay next to me. Both of us staring up at that ceiling with just the birds chirping away outside. We lay like that for a while, in silence.

'So what do you want to talk about?' I asked in the end.

'You,' she said. 'You are in danger. Are you aware of that?'

Well that surprised me. I mean, I was concerned by the appearance of Sable Wyvern even though I didn't know anything about him other than that his absurd name was actually the official title he'd used in his capacity as an officer of the College of Arms in London. But what was Elke referring to?

'Who is Sable Wyvern?' she asked me, damn near answering my question for me.

'An officer of the College of Arms in London' I told her. 'I'd never heard of him until Toni's husband Tom told me he'd died.'

'And why did he tell you that? If you don't know him?'

'I don't know' I said. 'That's something I'm going to be asking him when we get back to London.'

'You shouldn't go back to London' she said, rubbing her foot against mine.

'Why not?' I asked, moving my foot away. Not because I didn't like what she was doing but because I knew where it would lead. Where it would lead me, at any rate.

Elke laughed. 'My, Heidi did teach you some tricks, didn't she?'

'I'm sure I don't know what you mean' I said, then laughed along with her.

She held my hand. Hers was warm and soft. 'We can you know. If you want to.'

'I want to,' I told her. 'But we won't. Because we shouldn't. I shouldn't.'

'It's not because you find me unattractive then?' she said.

We looked at each other for a second then burst out laughing.

'Actually,' I said, 'I'll be in the shower having a wank the moment you leave. And I'll be thinking of you.'

'Then maybe I should stay and watch' she said.

But I was having none of it. She was teasing me. Testing me. Tempting me. And I knew it.

'Why shouldn't I go back to London?' I asked her, suddenly serious again.

'Somebody's setting traps. For you. You're not ready.'

'Why the fuck would anyone be interested in me?' I asked in exasperation. 'What would anyone want with me?'

'You know that already' Elke said. 'It's your wife. Everything that happens, it's to do with your wife. She's still part of you and you are part of her. And you are on the edge of the precipice, you know?'

I didn't know and said so.

'You think *she* hates you,' Elke said. 'The Moon.'

I was astonished by that. Because it was true as you know.

'And in a way, *she* does,' Elke continued. 'But maybe hatred is a form of love, don't you understand that?'

'I'm tired. I'm confused. So spare me the riddles.' I said this because just for once I wanted straight talking. You can understand that, right? Of course you can.

'*She* hates you because you act in a certain way. *She* pursues you because she hates you. Because the way you act hurts *her*. Change the way you act and you no longer hurt her. And when you choose to no longer hurt her, you get to see the other side of hatred. . .'

'Which is love,' I said. 'But what is it that I'm doing? Christ, what have I done wrong?'

Elke shrugged. 'This is all to do with your wife, like I say. It's all I know. All I can tell you.'

This was actually very upsetting. I don't expect you to understand that but it was. I'd do anything, anything to make things right. But I had to know *what* to do before I could do it.

'If I can't go back to London then, where should I go?'

'You need to balance nature' Elke said, not answering directly. But I listened to her and didn't interrupt, because this wasn't the first time I'd been told this. 'The magic we made up on the mountain last night. You need to find that. Earth, Air, Water. And Fire. You find them. And you learn how to balance them. As it is above, so it is below.'

'You're not the first person to tell me that' I said.

Elke shrugged. 'I make no claim to unique wisdom' she said. 'And if you keep getting told this then you should be listening.'

'I haven't had a chance to act on it yet' I said. 'That's all. Not that I'd know how.'

'You made a good start last night I'd say,' Elke said, squeezing my hand. 'Leave that Temple magic for a while. Put your hand in the soil. Reach up to the sky. Learn to love everything in between.'

'Easy to say,' I said.

'Listen, before you go I give you something. Someone to see. Somewhere to go. But first you will go back to Berlin. With Toni and the Major. Leave us to look after Heidi, yes?'

I could only agree as she slid off the bed.

'I'm going to see Heidi now' she said. 'Shall I give her your love?'

'Of course' I answered, surprised at being asked.

'Yes,' Elke said. 'Heidi is in need of love. Much love. Now, you go for your shower, and for your – what did you call it?'

'Wank,' I said.

'Yes, your wank. Think of me if you like. Or perhaps if you prefer, Brunhilde.'

She didn't give me time to come back with a remark because she laughed and was out the door before I could react. So I wandered over to the bathroom and stepped into the shower stall with the water on full blast and nicely warm. And I wanked myself silly. Thinking of both of them, as it happens.

# The Story Episode # 109
# (Moon phase: Day 26)

THE HARZ MOUNTAINS stay with you. That's all I can say. We left that same afternoon, the day after we came down from the mountain. No point wasting time and nothing we could do for Heidi anyway. So it was just Toni the Major and me driving back to Berlin. Me driving the hire car. None of us saying much. And it was already dark by the time we got to *Charlottenburg* in the western outskirts of Berlin. Even there, the Harz Mountains were with us. Not clinging. Just the dark and sparkling hint of the memory.

A piece of paper folded in my pocket, slipped there by Elke as we'd hugged and kissed goodbye. Just as she'd promised. I guessed she'd written contact details of a place I should go to, a person I should seek out. Something like that. Anything other than a return to London.

I couldn't help dwelling on the thought of what she'd told me. Traps being laid for me in London. Me the centre of something that didn't bear thinking about. Because of Helen. Because of my beautiful immortal beloved wife who remained a part of me as I would always be a part of her. I let that thought slide.

Instead I pondered on that strange commune of Elke's. A loose group of people well-travelled on the path of Mystery. Nothing formal. Each of them working their own way. Sharing their experiences. Helping each other with rituals that they created for themselves. Yes that's right. Created for themselves. Elke's place was like a research academy in a way. And while I'd been connected to the earth by them, I realised during the day as we'd all talked and wound down, that these were people steeped in the technical macroscopic aspects of the Mysteries. Familiar with the Enochian Angelic language and magic. Steeped in the Tarot. Steeped in the Qabalah. And more that I'm not inclined to list at this point in the story because it doesn't help move us along.

There was something I did want to know though, so I broke the silence. 'So what happened last night?' I said, turning to Toni in the passenger seat next to me.

'What do you mean?' she said. 'You were there. You know what happened.'

She wasn't being sharp or waspish. I just hadn't made myself clear. So I tried again. 'No, I know about the dance. I know the experience I had. But it must have been different for you. The work it did for you. I just wondered if it was something you could put into words.'

'Yeah, I can try to tell you. Don't know what you'll get out of it though. It was pretty straightforward the way it presented to me.' She turned as much as she could in her seat like she was trying to face me. Like she wanted my full attention. She got it even though I kept my eyes on the road ahead.

'I suppose I did what you did,' she continued. 'Controlled breathing through the dance. Focus on the steps and the motion. You know, letting the dizziness grow until it became all-consuming. Did you do that?'

'Sure I did,' I said.

She knew that without me saying it. The techniques for accessing altered states of consciousness are a common human experience. Relaxation, breathing, allowing the clutter and chatter of your thoughts to drift away. I won't go into much more detail here. The fact that it's possible to manage that while you're engaged in an intricate and ever-faster circular dance while chanting what amounts to a mantra of song is what takes some practice. Toni and I, like everyone else up there on the mountain, were practiced enough to do it without effort. Which is the only way to do it actually. Because the moment it becomes an effort is when you're already preventing the shift in consciousness from happening. But back to how it was with Toni.

'They took me back there. To the twenty-seventh Aethyr. I can't say I wasn't apprehensive about finding myself there. Black. Cold. Empty. You know what it's like. Alone. But not lonely. All the same, not wanting to be alone because it wasn't my choice. That's what it's been like for me. That feeling slipping in and out of my earthly consciousness. Ever since we. . . well you know, did what we did back at your house.'

Yes I knew. I'd never forget it. I didn't say anything though. Just waited for Toni to continue.

'So the way it was' she said, 'I was surrounded by the cold darkness. And it was spinning. I mean, there was nothing to see. But it was spinning around me, like I was the hub of a wheel. So I was the centre and the circumference of a circle at the same time, you know what I mean?

'Yeah,' I said.

She was describing one of the great occult paradoxes. That all points were simultaneously at the centre and the circumference of a spherical or at least curved, universe. Which is itself a paradox because the universe is infinite in extent. So how can it be infinite and at the same time spherical? I'll just smile and leave that one with you.

Back to Toni though - the twenty-seventh Aethyr was spinning around her but she herself was part of that circular motion with the rest of us as we all danced the circular dance around the Titan rock-guardian of the *Brockenberg Tor*.

'So what happened then?' I prompted, knowing that Toni had more to say. I was surprised that she wasn't full of sassy smart-arsed remarks. Whatever had happened had really made an impression on her.

'The moon happened then,' she said. 'In the total spinning darkness the silver moon came. I mean, I didn't see her in the black sky. Just a whirling silver mass. And you know that silver light you see when you're out in the countryside under a full moon? It was like that. So I could tell that there was ground beneath me. And grass growing but shining silver in that silver light. And flowers and trees growing up out of the ground around me in the dark, lit only by the moon. And the funny thing is, as these things grew, fed by the silver moonlight, it all became like an enchanted forest and I was in the middle of it. You had to be there. And I couldn't see them but I wasn't on my own in that forest. I don't know who or how many of them there were, but there were loads of them and I got the impression they were smiling at me. This sounds stupid, I know.'

She twisted back around in her seat and folded her arms. It didn't sound stupid to me and I told her so.

'So you're in this spinning silver forest and that means that whatever had happened you weren't in the twenty-seventh Aethyr any more' I said. 'Especially if you weren't alone.'

'No, I wasn't alone. I don't know how it came about, what those people had done. But the darkness had slipped away. Like something on the edge of a disk that just slides off when you spin the disk. That's the best I can do. Do you get it?'

'Yeah, I get it' I said, and I did because she'd described it beautifully. 'But how did it end?'

Toni shrugged. 'I don't know' she said. 'Because all I remember after that is sitting back leaning against that giant rock like it was holding me. And you lying flat on your back, twitching like a spas with Elke kneeling next to you and pretty much everyone else standing around you watching.'

Well that told me what I'd been interested in finding out. And it had passed a little time. In fact, we were approaching the centre of the city. More built up. Brighter lights. More people. More cars.

'Don't go back to my flat.' This was the Major, speaking for the first time from the rear seat where I thought he'd been sleeping.

'Why not?' I asked.

'Because for the best part of the last two hours, someone's

been following us.'

I have to say my blood ran cold. I'd already been abducted once in this damn city and I wasn't used to this cloak and dagger stuff. I was scared by it. I really truly was. But the Major wasn't. His voice was cold and reasoned.

'Take us to *Bahnhof Zoo*' he said. 'Lots of people. Police at hand. We'll work out what to do when we get there.'

'Do you know who it is?' I asked, working hard to keep my voice calm.

'No,' he said bluntly. 'But I'd guess they were after you. And that they don't have your best interests at heart.'

# The Story Episode # 110 (Moon phase: Day 26)

I CAN'T BE sure how the hell we got to *Bahnhof Zoo* without crashing because I think I drove all the way there through the city centre with my eyes focused entirely on the mirrors. Every car that stayed behind us for more than a block, I was sure it was our pursuers. Even though the Major assured me otherwise.

'They're professionals,' he said, noticing my alert eyes everywhere but the road. 'You'll never spot them.'

I can only tell you that I wasn't comforted by those words. This was a world I only knew from books and films and television.

'What do they want?' Toni asked.

'Him' the Major said, meaning me. 'He's standing in someone's way.'

'But I haven't done anything to anyone' I blurted out,

desperately looking for somewhere to park because the Major had told me that I should.

'You don't know what you've done or what you are' the Major explained unhelpfully. 'Whatever it is or whatever you are, you're wanted by someone. Or wanted out of the way. Now find somewhere to park, there's a good chap.'

So I found somewhere and we put the rented Mercedes in a space in the *Hardenbergstraße* car park right opposite the entrance to the underground at the corner of *Bahnhof Zoo*.

'Come with me' the Major said and Toni grabbed my hand as we followed him.

'Wait' I said and the Major stopped and turned to us.

'This has got nothing to do with her' I said, meaning Toni. 'She should go somewhere safe.'

'Where do you have in mind?' The Major said. 'And anyway, how do we know it has nothing to do with her? I'm just making an educated guess that they're after you.'

'Based on what?' I said in exasperation.

'Based on the fact that you're pursued by a dead officer of the College of Arms and based on the fact that there's something about your dead wife that's caused a whirlwind of problems. But all the same I could be wrong. We could cut her loose, send her to sit in the lobby of a smart hotel, maybe. And never see or hear from her again. Your choice.'

Actually, the way he'd put it, it wasn't my choice was it? It was Toni's. And she was adamant.

'No fucking way you're cutting me loose' she said.

The Major didn't argue. He looked beyond us, scanned the area all around us. 'Come on' he said. 'Let's move.'

We followed the Major across the busy road and into the concourse of *Bahnhoff Zoo*. The place was busy. Not as run down as it once had been, in the 1980s for example. But we weren't surrounded by jet-setters and the 'beautiful people' either.

We stood in the middle of the concourse and I'd watched enough action thriller films to understand why. Out in the open, surrounded by throngs of innocent people and able to keep a watch out for anyone who might have a focus on us. Hopefully we'd spot them before they got close to us. I hoped the major would at any rate. He was the professional. Me and Toni, we were in his hands. I was comforted by the sight of a couple of pairs of cops wandering about, going nowhere in any particular hurry. They were away from us, at the edges of the concourse, but I was glad of their presence.

'Can you see anybody?' I asked.

The Major shook his head, still scanning all the entrances. 'No,' he said.

'Do you think they've given up?' I asked.

The Major could barely disguise his contempt. 'What do you think?' he said.

I didn't answer that but I did ask what he thought we should do next.

'Get out of here' he said. 'These people are good.'

'So where to then?'

This was Toni.

'To someone I know' the Major said. 'I shouldn't do this but just in case something happens and we get separated, remember this address and make your way there if you can.'

He gave us an address in the *Wedding* district – where Heidi lived, remember – and I committed it to memory, knowing that Toni had done the same. I have to say that I was feeling more and more afraid. The thought of getting separated from the Major did that. You have to remember, Heidi and me had already been snatched off the streets just a couple of days earlier so I knew that this wasn't a game.

Right then I felt a hand placed on my shoulder and I turned sharply to see who it was, my blood running cold. But things happened too fast for me to register much. The Major's fist flashing past my head and smashing someone in the face.

'Run' I heard the Major shout, so I grabbed Toni and ran.

I looked everywhere for the cops as I dragged Toni through the crowds of startled people who all turned to look at us. But the cops had disappeared. What the fuck? I'd been counting on them. I looked back and saw the Major sinking to his knees, then slumping to the ground with a circle of people standing around watching. Oh Christ, they'd be coming for us, coming after us. We needed a place to hide even though we didn't know who we'd be hiding from. I did the stupidest thing possible as I dragged Toni into the men's toilets and into an empty cubicle before the few men in there, pissing into urinals or washing their hands, could notice or care.

We stood breathless in that cubicle for a few seconds, listening out but only hearing running water and the sound of automatic hand dryers. Until the sounds all died so that you could imagine that the toilets were empty.

My heart was racing and I could imagine that Toni's was too. I remembered something from the million films and TV shows I'd seen. I got Toni to stand on the seat of the toilet with me so that anyone looking under the door wouldn't see anything. This wasn't easy with two of us, but we managed it by leaning our weight back on to the side walls.

You've probably worked out that I hadn't thought this through. Because you probably realise that anyone looking under a locked cubicle door and seeing nothing would be immediately suspicious. I should have known that too but fear meant that I wasn't thinking straight. And Toni, for fuck knows what reason, went along with me. The stupidest thing I'd ever known her to do, to be honest. Nevertheless, there we crouched like gargoyles, barely breathing as we listened out for – well for God knows what.

It stayed silent for what seemed an impossibly long time given that this was a public toilet in a busy major railway station, but it was probably only a few seconds. The hairs on my neck stood on end as we heard two distinct sets of footsteps enter and echo around the tiles. The footsteps stopped and I listened hard for the sounds of zips being pulled down, the sound of someone pissing in a urinal. But there was just silence. Unnatural for two people to come in and stand in silence. I just knew this meant trouble. I knew it. I looked at Toni and the fear in her eyes must have been a mirror of mine. We were no comfort for each other, not then. Neither of us breathing, not wanting to give our existence away. So of course, that was the exact moment my mobile phone rang. I repressed a squeal as I instinctively reached into my pocket to pull the fucking thing out and look at the screen. It was Hesther. The fucking bitch!

# The Story Episode # 111
# (Moon phase: Day 26)

BANG BANG BANG! Hammering on the cubicle door. I was concentrating on hitting my phone's "off" button. I failed miserably and dropped it so that it clattered to the tiled floor.

There were definitely two out there because I heard one of them tell the other to break the door open. Toni's eyes were wild with fear and so were mine I'd guess. Bang! The door flew open, smashed against a wall and sprung back again but not before I'd seen the menacing bulk of the man about to come in and get us. The door did fly open again, and I saw the man step towards us and reach out like he meant to grab us. His companion standing a couple of steps behind, watching. We were fucked. No question about it. Except things didn't work out the way this pair had intended. It was all a blur, but the second guy, the one standing watching was hit by something and smashed to the ground. The first guy turned to see what the commotion was about and I could see exactly what was happening. The Major! The Major had dealt with one and I saw him stamp on the throat of this assailant even as he smashed the face of the bastard who'd been reaching out to take me and Toni. This one staggered back into the cubicle towards us, reeling from the Major's blow to the side of his face. He came towards us backwards and I somehow found the presence of mind to grab him by the ears and I head-butted the back of his head with as much force as I could possibly muster. This is much more debilitating than you'd imagine if you don't know about these things, and as this bastard started to sink to his knees, a vicious kick from the Major caught him square below the chin. That definitely put the fucker out for the count. Probably shattered his jaw. I hoped it had at any rate.

'Quick,' the Major urged us. 'Run. . . While you can.'

He sounded breathless. And I stopped in that moment and saw that he was fighting hard to remain upright and conscious. Toni squirmed past me and stooped to pick up my phone in one movement. I was frozen to the spot, looking at the Major who was sweating like a hog. He was fading fast, falling back to lean against the row of sinks.

'For Christ's sake go!' he hissed.

'Where?' I asked stupidly.

'I already told you where' he said, almost bursting with the effort of saying it.

'Come with us, I'll carry you' I said but he shook his head and from the look in his eyes I swear he'd have struck me if he'd had the strength left to do it.

'Can't,' he whispered. 'Needle. . . drugs . . . now GO!'

I turned and Toni was already at the exit, all but sucking me towards her by force of will alone. The two of us almost knocked a fat man over as we sped from the toilets and into the concourse. I grabbed her hand and slowed us down to a walk once we were deep in the crowd.

'If we run, we just bring attention to ourselves' I said, knowing that I'd only got that from some dumb film or TV show or something, but feeling that there was sense in it.

Toni handed my phone back and it had of course stopped ringing. A flashing light told me I had a message waiting. Well it could bloody-well wait. Fucking Hesther.

'The Major. . .' Toni said. 'Do you think. . ?'

Well I didn't know what to think and that's what I said. I mean, I couldn't know if he was dead. He'd told me he'd been injected. He'd mentioned drugs. Fatal or otherwise I just couldn't know, which is all I could tell her.

I found myself looking around, scanning the people and Toni did the same. Not that either of us knew what we were looking for. I mean, the way they'd come up close to us that first time without even the Major realising until the hand came down on my shoulder, well it didn't give me any confidence in my ability to spot trouble in time to do something about it. I did look carefully to try to find a police patrol but couldn't see any.

'*Achtung! Achtung!*'

Shouting, coming from the direction of the toilets. Clearly someone had entered and found three bodies on the ground. At least that's what I figured.

'Come on let's go' Toni said and we hurried without running towards the street.

Outside it was night and dark but the station was bright with white lights and coloured neon.

'You remember that address he gave us?' I asked Toni as we walked past the row of waiting taxis.

She nodded. 'Sure I do.'

'Let's go there' I said. 'That's where he wants us to go. It's the last thing he said.'

I didn't mean that to sound like I thought the Major was dead, but it did have that sense of finality about it. Toni didn't react to that though.

'You know how to get there?' she asked.

'I could probably get us to *Wedding*' I said. 'But the actual address, I wouldn't have a clue.'

'We should get a cab' Toni suggested, but I didn't want to do that.

'Let's go get a drink' I said. 'Maybe something to eat. Someplace in the city centre with normal people. Maybe some laughter. Cos you know what? I'm just absolutely fucked.'

I think Toni liked the idea because she said 'You have a place in mind?'

I told her I knew several and that I wanted to walk to the city centre.

'I just want to breathe the air' I said, and I think she understood what I meant by that because she took my hand and we started to stroll off towards the *Kurfurstendamm*, the arterial road that would take us right into the heart of the city.

Where we were going, the district of *Wedding* and the Major's contact, would be just to the north west. But they could wait. I wanted cold beer and warm hamburgers and they'd have to kill me to stop me having them. I told Toni this and she reminded me that there just might be people following us with exactly that in mind.

Well that concentrated my thoughts and no mistake so I quickened my stride and Toni did the same to match me. I could have sworn there was a smile of mischief on that lovely face of hers as she'd reminded me of my potentially fragile mortality. Definitely the old Toni. The ceremony we'd performed on the *Brockenberg Tor* in the Harz Mountains just the night before had cleared her of the remnants of the twenty-seventh Aethyr that had been haunting her and no mistake. Tom would be pleased.

Definitely the old Toni. And while I knew it was inappropriate and wrong of me, all I could think of right then was how I'd like to take her out and get us both pissed on beer and cocktails and laughter, then slope off to a hotel room with her and fuck her bloody brains out. Well, it had been a few days. Which was an age for me. Come on, be fair.

# *The Story Episode # 112 (Moon phase: Day 26)*

YOU FIND THE Hard Rock Café at *Ku'damm* 224. That's 224, *Kurfürstendamm* to those of you not familiar with the Berlin diminutive form of the name of this famous street. What's the *Ku'damm* to Berlin? It's like Oxford Street is to London. So it was busy and loud and brash and light and touristy. In fact everything I wanted right then.

The Hard Rock was busy but not absolutely crowded. All the

same there was a wait for tables that I was able to by-pass by judiciously sliding a wad of Euros in the right direction. People more often than not fuck that up by the way, but I have an instinct for it. The trick is knowing who to offer the money to, how much to offer, and above all to keep the transaction discreet. The least important of these, in a way, is knowing how much to offer. Because if you fuck up any of the other aspects of the transaction, you usually don't even get to the part where money comes into it. Anyway, I've developed this skill over time and soon enough Toni and me were sitting at a table for four, just the two of us.

I ordered large beers for us both as we listened to the chatter of the busy restaurant and something by Dire Straits playing in the background. We actually didn't say anything to each other until the beer arrived a minute or two after I'd ordered it and the way the two of us were slouched in our seats, anyone could have seen that we were knackered. As much of a mental thing with us as a physical one. You can understand that, what with everything that had happened. Still, after the beers arrived and we'd gulped a few mouthfuls down, we were a little revived.

'You going to eat?' I asked Toni as the lovely waitress stood by the table waiting to take our orders.

'Are you?' she asked right back annoyingly.

I ignored her and answered by giving my order to the waitress, finding it difficult to take my eyes off the swell of her breasts right in front of my face as she leaned in closer. I did mention that she was lovely didn't I? Yes, alright. Just wanted to make that clear. I ordered a Hickory BBQ Bacon Cheeseburger where the burger is basted with a hickory BBQ sauce and smothered with caramelized onions. The burger comes topped with crispy bacon and melted Cheddar cheese. And the reason I remember this and what it consists of is because this is what I always have at any Hard Rock Café I go to. To this day.

This did energize Toni though because she ordered the Red White and Blue burger, and for the sake of symmetry I'll tell you what that consists of. It's a burger grilled with spicy buffalo sauce and Cajun seasoning, topped off with crumbled blue cheese and a crispy fried onion ring. I ordered two more beers at the same time because we were already a good way through the first ones.

'I'm just going to go to the toilet' Toni said after the waitress had gone. 'I'm dying for a wee.'

'You sure it's safe?' I asked, teasing her as she rose from her seat.

'Fuck off' was her charming reply and she turned to go, not giving me the chance to come back with a witty rejoinder. Not that it mattered since I didn't have one.

I sank the last drops of my first beer and leaned back in my chair to listen to U2 and the incessant background chatter, realising that this was the most relaxed I'd felt in a while. This despite the fact that someone was out to kidnap and maybe even kill me, and that I'd only an hour earlier barely escaped unscathed from an attempt to snatch or murder me.

For some reason the very urbane upbeat noisy normality of the Hard Rock was a comfort. That's when I remembered the paper Elke had slipped me as I'd given her a goodbye hug before we'd set off from her place to come back to Berlin. I reached into my pocket where she'd stuffed it and took out a piece of stiff grey paper neatly folded into four. I opened it out and found that it was blank. On both sides. What the fuck was that all about? Sure, I immediately wondered if it had been written in some kind of invisible ink, but why would Elke do that without telling me how to make the writing visible? All I could think of was to hold it over a heat-source because that always worked for the invisible ink we'd played with as kids. But holding this paper over the candle on the table produced absolutely nothing. I'd folded the paper up again and was just slipping it back into my pocket when Toni returned.

'So it was safe after all' I said as she took her seat.

'Depends how you define safe' she said. 'I just got propositioned by a girl in the toilets. She wants me to go off to a party with her.'

'She asked you in German?'

Toni nodded. 'At first. Until I told her I couldn't understand her. Then she asked again. In English.'

'That figures' I said. 'So what did you tell her?'

'I told her I was with you.'

I laughed at that. 'What did she say?'

'She told me to forget you and to go with her.'

'Confident girl' I said. 'Was she pretty?'

'Pretty fucking hot actually' Toni said as the waitress came back with our second round of drinks. 'And young.'

'And you gave all that up for me? I'm flattered' I said, enjoying the banter.

'There's still time' Toni shot back. 'That's her at the bar.'

I looked over to where Toni was indicating and the girl was indeed a stunner. Short blonde hair and fabulous skin. Tall and curved, a slim waist, and wearing impossibly short and tight cut-off denim shorts. Above the shorts a white tee-shirt with horizontal red stripes that really did accentuate the positive, so to speak. She had a black PVC bolero jacket with chrome buttons and decorative fittings, draped over one shoulder. On me it would have kept slipping off making me look a total spas, but this girl kept it in place effortlessly. She seemed to be with another girl and a boy, both about the same age as her and they talked and sipped their drinks seemingly oblivious to the world around them.

I paid them no further mind as we drank and ate our way through the evening, though I did notice the girl tip Toni a nod and a wink as she left with her companions when we were looking at the dessert menus. I don't think Toni noticed though and I didn't say anything.

I have to tell you that we had a chilled-out evening there in the Hard Rock despite the raucous atmosphere, and I enjoyed myself enormously. I'm sure Toni did too. It was a couple of hours and four more large beers later when we finally left.

'You going to give Hesther a call?' Toni asked as we stepped out onto the street.

I'd forgotten all about Hesther and inside I was a tad irritated at being reminded.

'No,' I said. 'Not tonight. She can wait until tomorrow.'

Toni accepted that and we began to walk, hand in hand, north west towards *Wedding*.

'Seriously, can we get a taxi now?' Toni asked after five minutes of steady unhurried strolling. 'I'm tired.'

'Beer will do that every time' I said.

She didn't argue and truth be told I wasn't in the mood for walking either. Normally, five large beers would have me reeling but I was surprisingly in control of all my faculties. I think I must have been on an inner alert. Something keeping me switched on at any rate. So we got a cab and I told the driver to take us to the address that the Major had given us. In *Wedding*.

Fifteen minutes later and we arrived at another soul-less tenement building. Grey drab walls on the outside holding grey drab apartments on the inside. I paid the driver and followed Toni into the building. This place was a shit-hole and I have to say, a little bit intimidating. The lifts didn't work, graffiti on the walls of the entrance lobby and rubbish strewn on the floor. I was thankful there was no one about.

Apartment forty-eight the Major had told us so I guessed that meant the fourth floor. We began our traipse up the stairs in the dim light. Half the bulbs were missing or broken or simply out of commission. I can remember thinking that if the Major hadn't told us that this would be a place of refuge, I wouldn't have come near a place like this. On every landing I expected to meet a corpse or a drug-skank or some fucking gang-banging rip-off bastard. But the place was amazingly empty.

At last we reached the fourth floor and Toni took off down the landing looking for numbers on the doors. Apartment eight didn't have a number on the door but we could reasonably guess that it was the right place. Next to it, to either side, were numbers forty-seven and forty-nine. I looked at Toni then gave the door three sharp taps with my knuckles, wincing as the sound echoed through the dismal landing and potentially waking only God knew what.

The door opened impossibly, immediately, like someone had been standing behind it waiting for just this moment. And what a fucking someone it was at that. Male, and the first thing I noticed was the black beret perched on top of the head, pulled down to one side. Worn like Che Guevara in the famous posters. Even had a red star badge on it. Just like Che. John Lennon glasses, tinted blue. What I could see of the hair from beneath the beret was bleached, but it had turned out an off-white sort of yellow. Short and spiky. Amazingly no piercings in the ears or on the face. Pale skin like that of a corpse. Lips so red in contrast that you'd think it was lipstick. But it wasn't. A white shirt with an embroidered front under a grey woollen weskit that looked like it had escaped from a half-decent suit at some point. Grey silk boxer shorts. And that was it. Nothing else. This apparition stuck out a hand for me to shake.

'Harvey Beecham' he said and there was a hint of a German accent.

My right hand was in my pocket and as I pulled it out to shake Harvey Beecham's hand, Elke's note came out with it and fell to the filthy concrete floor. The handshake failed because Harvey was down there quick as a flash to retrieve the note. He unfolded it as he stood and I was shocked to see writing on it that had definitely not been there before. A strange language and the letters a jumble of colours. Harvey glanced at it and handed it back to me.

'You'd better come in' he said in English with that curiously light German accent. He stood to one side, just inside the door. 'Come on, come on. Don't stand on ceremony.'

Toni and me turned to look at each other. Toni shrugged and that was it. She stepped inside and I had little choice but to follow her, cringing as Harvey Beecham closed the door behind us.

# The Story Episode # 113
# (Moon phase: Day 26)

CLEANLINESS IS NEXT to Godliness. By the way, that's not some trite religious aphorism. It's the truth. And no matter what occult path or path of religious faith you follow, you'll get nowhere near to your God if you are a person of slovenly and careless habits. And that begins with you personally, your clothes and your surroundings.

Harvey Beecham's flat was as clean as a whistle. But you didn't get that impression from it right away. First of all it was gloomy. I discovered that curtains were drawn everywhere and that small paraffin lamps and candles provided what illumination there was. Not that the curtains were a hundred per cent light-proof. They were thin and threadbare in places. But they stopped enough light so that the place was far from cheerful with it. Something else that would have given you the impression that the place was dirty was the old, worn and tired nature of everything in the place. From the hall-runner carpet to posters and prints on the walls. The furniture. Everything. It had an air of shabbiness about it. Which, in the gloom might give you the impression that it was also dirty. But it wasn't. Not a bit of it. The whole place and everything in it was clean to the point of sterility. And that's not a word I'm using lightly because beyond the smell of the candles and paraffin lamps I could smell disinfectant. And another give away was that the place was tidy to the point of obsession.

'Through there, to the left.'

That was Harvey from behind, telling Toni in front where he wanted her to go. I followed Toni into what was the living room and Harvey followed me. A sofa and a couple of chairs were straight from the 1960s and their upholstery was worn shiny in places. A large rug covered most of the floor of the left half of the room. The other half was just bare concrete. The walls were papered but the wallpaper had been covered with white emulsion. Somebody – and I reasonably assumed it to be Harvey – had used the white walls to paint on. I mean art, not just décor. And this was the kind of art that had your brain shrieking just from being in among it. I mean, the occult stuff, the symbols, tables of correspondences - all of that stuff speaks directly to the subconscious. And even if you look at it and consciously tell yourself that it means nothing to you and leaves you cold, that's just your attachment to the illusion of material existence talking. Occult symbols do have an effect on the subconscious levels of your existence and I'm not going to sit here arguing or explaining that.

These were painted in specific colours. I mean very specific colours so that they radiated light at very specific wavelengths. Now I'm not going to try to bullshit you by saying that I could tell what these wavelengths were. The reason I know they were specific is because of the way they resonated with my consciousness. It was like an electrical firework display fizzing and popping and flashing in my mind as I gazed upon these symbols in turn. Each one having a different effect of spark or sparkle or fizz. Snap, crackle and pop. Each one stimulating complimentary colours and effects in me. It wasn't like that all the time though. Once each one had resonated and had its effect on my own personal energy, the effect on me became settled. The initial effect was just a greeting. Hey, look at me looking at you looking at me! And don't get the impression that this altered state of energy within me represented me being used or brought under a spell or anything ridiculous like that. It was rather the contrary. These symbols, painstakingly created as they had been, were announcing themselves to my consciousness as open channels to other altered states and vibrations of energy that I might want to take advantage of. They'd do that for you if your mind was open enough to understand that. But for most people it takes a great deal of occult training to reach that state. I mean, training within a group which is the training I'd received, or following the solitary path of the mystic, which is the chosen path of many these days. But enough of that for now.

'You say hello to them, eh?' Harvey said, patting me on the shoulder.

I looked over at Toni and she was enraptured. The way she

was standing looking directly at one wall of symbols I felt that she was about to stretch her arms out to either side and form a living Calvary Cross. And I felt that it would be altogether appropriate if she did.

'Come on, sit down, sit down' Harvey encouraged us, indicating the old and worn furniture.

Toni and me, we both sat on the sofa with the worn shiny fabric cover and I half expected it to be rickety. But it wasn't. Harvey sat in a chair beneath the window – shaded by thin curtains - and he regarded us for a moment.

'So you like my home then?' he said, smiling and disarmingly charming with it.

Toni said nothing and I couldn't tell you her reaction because my attention was altogether taken elsewhere. At the far end of the room, the end without carpet, I could see what was either an altar or a shrine or perhaps a bit of both. There were the usual occult Temple symbols and banners on the walls and on the bare wooden table I could see two folded altar cloths, one white and one red. I could also see a ceremonial sword, a wand a chalice and a disc. Incense burners and occult lamps too. But on the wall above this altar there was something that exercised my attention. Two lines of occult lamps on wall holders ran most of the way up to the ceiling. Between them was something remarkable. It was the pressed uniform jacket and trousers of a British Army officer. Olive drab, and not current. Maybe a couple of decades old. I could tell from the insignia that this was a Lieutenant's uniform, and that it belonged to a cavalry regiment. The Blues and Royals. Now I'd come across that regiment before, of course. The Major's old regiment. But what the fuck was that uniform doing up there? On the wall like a relic to be worshipped.

'My Temple' Harvey said and his words were accompanied

by a nervous laugh. 'You find it strange, no doubt.'

'I don't know how I find it' I said.

And that was the truth because I'd never seen anything like it. I had no idea what it could possibly signify.

'A reminder of my past' Harvey said with a shrug.

'You worship the past?' Toni said, now looking at the strange relic along with Harvey and me.

'No' Harvey said. 'I don't worship the past. That would be foolish. As you know. But I do call upon its experiences. So do you, don't you?'

I didn't think that was much of an explanation but I didn't say anything. Instead I said 'So where did you get that? It's British Army issue.'

'Yes, it is. It's mine. Issued to me.' Harvey could tell what was racing through my mind because he said 'I know, I know, the accent. I've lived here for a long time now. Don't often get to speak English. All this German – it's coloured the way I talk. But you can understand me, right?'

'Yeah.'

'Sure.'

Me and Toni could certainly understand him. The accent wasn't *that* thick after all.

'Good,' Harvey said. 'Now perhaps you can tell me just who you are.'

Toni and me looked at each other, surprised.

'You don't know?' Toni asked. 'We were given your address. Told to come here.' She looked to me for confirmation and got it. 'We thought you'd be expecting us.'

Harvey seemed to think about that for a second. 'No,' he said. 'Who gave you this address?'

'Major Richard Warne' I said without thinking that I may have compromised the Major by giving his name away to a stranger.

Harvey nodded and almost smiled. 'Ah yes, the Major' he said. 'That explains somewhat.'

'So you do know the Major then?' Toni asked.

'Yes, sure I know him.' Harvey paused for a moment, thinking. 'And you are right to come here. I believe so, yes.'

'But you don't know us. And you just let us right into your flat' Toni said. Which is exactly what had happened.

'No, I don't know you in one sense' Harvey agreed. 'But I could tell right away that you were two people who'd come to the right place.' He turned to me. 'And didn't you present your calling card?'

I knew he could only have been referring to Elke's folded paper. What the devil had he seen in those strange coloured symbols and letters? I wasn't about to find out right then because the sound of the apartment door clicking open startled us. Startled Toni and me at any rate. This could be anybody. We might be sitting in a trap.

We waited what seemed an age, watching the living room door and listening to casual footsteps coming down the hall. And then the wait was over and the newcomer was standing in the doorway, leaning on the frame with one raised and outstretched hand like a model in a fashion shoot.

'Oh, you got here early then' this girl said, but in German.

Toni and I just stared and couldn't really say a thing. Because this was the girl who'd tried to chat up Toni in the Hard Rock Café just a couple of hours earlier.

# The Story Episode # 114
# (Moon phase: Day 26)

CHARISMA IS SOMETHING you understand and use or something you either have or don't have and thus constantly wonder why things are the way they are for you. We are all of us charismatic to a great or small degree and the amount of charisma we project out into the universe is exactly the amount we tell our consciousness to project. We do this by giving signals to the subconscious which begins the process of construction and passes on the message, so to speak. It's important that you understand this because Toni and me, we were fixated by this girl as she stepped into the room. I realised after a few seconds that Harvey wasn't so fixed on her. He was fixed on us, noting the effect that she had on us. I've already described her, so you know that visually she was aggressively attractive. But charisma is something that goes way beyond appearance and you should already know that.

'Of course, you only speak English' the girl said in English, standing in front of us. She was showing off and throwaway-casual at one and the same time with her drop into our language.

I noted her height. Maybe she was a catwalk model. She had the figure and the look for it. And she carried herself naturally the way catwalk models usually do when they want all eyes upon them. Most models don't consciously do this as they're more often than not too vacuous to understand that it's a power they can exercise. But some most definitely do. And this girl certainly knew what she was doing. My God but she was strikingly gorgeous close up.

'This is Sieglinde' Harvey said not taking his eyes off me. 'You can call her Ziggy. Everybody does.'

The girl waited for a moment then turned to Harvey. 'You not going to tell me their names then?'

Harvey leaned back in his chair and shrugged. 'I can't,' he said. 'They haven't told *me*.'

The girl looked surprised for a moment then turned her attention to us in expectation.

'That's Toni' I said, 'And I'm Steven. But you can call me Stevie. Everybody does.'

I smiled, hoping I'd provided a bit of levity. But the mood didn't alter. It remained stubbornly neutral as though we were in a laboratory isolation chamber.

'Toni and Stevie,' Ziggy mused out loud in her accented English. 'I'll have to remember who is who. Two names that can be either a boy or a girl.'

Ziggy planted herself in an empty chair and draped one of her long legs over the arm. I couldn't help looking at those tight shorts and the fantastically toned thighs emerging from them and imagining the treasure squeezed tight inside them.

Harvey couldn't help noticing me looking. 'Hmmm,' he said. 'You, Stevie, are a man who desires tight young pussy above all things. I see that.'

He laughed at that. But I didn't. I was getting mighty sick of everyone I met telling me this. As if I needed telling. But Harvey hadn't been entirely accurate. Age meant nothing to me. I was attracted to sexual charisma. Young, old, ancient – it didn't matter. If a woman exuded a libertine sexuality, I'd want her. That's all there was to it. But I never got the chance to express that.

'But maybe you'll be disappointed with Ziggy,' Harvey said.

'Why,' I asked. 'Because she prefers girls?' I hadn't forgotten that Ziggy had propositioned Toni.

'Oh no,' Harvey shot back. 'I would imagine that would be added spice for you.'

I waited. Because obviously there was going to be more. But I have to say I wasn't happy with it and I was beginning to bristle with anger. If Harvey was aware of that, he didn't show it.

'Suppose - ' he said, leaning forward conspiratorially ' - I told you that she had a pussy ruined by debauchery. Forceful aggressive sex. Orgies with man after man going on for whole weekends. The repeated insertion of huge, er, you call them, I suppose, toys. . .'

I looked at Ziggy to see how she was taking all this but she merely rolled her eyes and looked away.

'. . . men and women pumping that young flexible pussy with their whole fists – '

'That's enough!' I spat out. I couldn't believe what I was hearing. I didn't know the dynamic of their relationship but I wasn't going to fucking listen to him degrading and belittling the girl like that. I just fucking wasn't.

Harvey simply laughed. And continued. 'She'd be no use to you, you know. She's got a cunt as loose as a wizard's sleeve.'

That was too much. I was up out of the chair about to show this weasel some manners and decency. But I didn't because of course without knowing how it had happened I found myself on the ground with my arse in the air, my face pressed painfully hard into the spotless and threadbare carpet and with an arm forced so painfully far up my back that I couldn't even scream. I was aware of Toni jumping up off that sofa – God bless her loyal feisty heart – but she was out of her depth.

'Back off or I break his arm' Harvey spat out at her.

I couldn't see anything, but I was sure that this had stopped Toni in her tracks. At least my arm remained unbroken. I was still held fast. Still in pain. But it had gone no further.

'Now,' Harvey hissed at me, 'Let's get one or two things straight. When it comes to violence it's stupid and dangerous to take on what you can't finish. You understand that?'

All traces of the German accent had gone and this was pure Home Counties Public School Received Pronunciation English invective. I couldn't answer though because my face remained pressed into the carpet and I couldn't move anything anywhere to signify my understanding.

'Well?' Harvey persisted, taking some of the weight of his knee from the back of my head so that I could force out the odd word or two.

'Yes' I answered feebly. It was as much as I could manage.

Harvey wasn't finished with me. 'Christ, you saw the uniform on the wall. I told you it was mine. You knew I had military training. That was really stupid.'

I should say that he wasn't using a tone of explanation. He was telling me straight, loud and clear, what a dick I'd been. And there was more.

'Harvey Beecham. Second son. Eton. Oxford. Blues and Royals. My family's been doing this for generations. You're so soft you can't see it in people. You don't know how to make that judgement. Now I'm going to let you get up but I'm not going to ask you for your word of honour that you won't try anything stupid again. I'm just going to tell you that I *will* break your fucking arm if you do.'

Harvey let go of my arm and I felt his weight lift from me. I peeled my face from the carpet and struggled to my knees. While I was on all fours, Ziggy leaned forward and placed a gentle hand on my shoulder.

'Thanks anyway,' she said. 'That was a beautiful thing you tried.'

I stood and looked over at Toni sitting back on the sofa, appearing suitably shocked. Harvey was still standing and as I turned to face him he smiled.

'No hard feelings eh?' he said. 'That was a good lesson learned. And at a very cheap price I'd say.'

'Yes, well being you, I dare say you would' I told him, dusting myself down.

'Oh, we're not going all English and class-conscious are we? Because you don't sound like you were dragged from among the great unwashed yourself.'

'That's not what I meant' I said, not really knowing what I'd meant.

I couldn't help giving him a once-over while we were standing opposite each other like that. And isn't hind-sight a wonderful thing? Because even through his clothes you could tell that he was as fit as a whippet and all whipcord muscle with not an ounce of fat on him anywhere. We're talking military-fit and that of course sent a shudder through me. Well I mean, he had been *army* after all. I steadied my emotions and let the anger and frustration and humiliation slide away.

'So what was all that about?' I asked him at last. 'Those things you were saying about Ziggy here.' I shook my head because I was genuinely puzzled.

'Come on' Harvey said. 'Sit down. Go on, sit down. I'll tell you what you need to know.'

So I sat down again, on the sofa next to Toni and Harvey sat back in his chair and started to explain.

'We all have our gifts,' he began. 'One of mine is to be a mirror. I can show you what you are. Mostly I don't. Most people wouldn't get it and wouldn't care if they did. Not the case with you though is it?'

I looked at Toni and I could tell that she hadn't a clue what he was on about either. 'Just what the hell does that mean?' I asked.

'I saw that in you the moment I opened the door' Harvey said. 'So much a part of you I had to fight to hold back from showing you right there and then. But out there in the hallway, that would've been far too ugly for you to take. And I needed to get you inside. Where you'd be safe.'

'Still not making any sense' I said.

Harvey shrugged. 'I'm not here to make sense. I'm here to play. You became part of the game the moment you knocked on the door.'

I sighed and let him continue. I knew there was more to come.

'This sexual obsession of yours. I just reflected it back to you. Exaggerated it somewhat. But essentially that was you. Your reflection distorted. I wanted you to see how ugly it can be. The more so since it's unnecessary.'

I was stunned by this. Everyone had seen that I was a sexual libertine but nobody had ever told me that it was ugly until now. That I was presenting an ugly face to the world with it. My God, why hadn't anyone told me? I turned to Toni but she just shook her head.

'You know how it goes. Mirror mirror on the wall, who's the fairest of them all? Yes, well the mirror doesn't always show us what we'd like to see. But the mirror never lies. That's the message of that part of the Snow White story. You should go to the Harz Mountains sometime, get a feel for it.'

Toni and me looked at each other at the mention of the Harz Mountains.

'Oh. So you've been there already,' Harvey continued. 'Well not everyone can see it in you, that ugliness. Not as obviously as I reflected it back to you. But most people get a feeling of it from you. And for most of them it's meaningless - if they even recognise it at all. But come on, even you know that it's holding you back.'

'Holding me back from what?' I asked.

Harvey shook his head. 'I don't know,' he said. 'Wherever it is you're headed. Look, I just wanted you to see it because you *are* in danger and this obsession may become the distraction that's used to trap you or destroy you. You have to be aware of how obvious it is. Ziggy understands. She wasn't upset by it. She knew what I was doing.' He turned to Ziggy for confirmation. 'Didn't you sunshine?'

Ziggy nodded sweetly. Then leaned towards me. 'And it was all lies anyway. I'm as tight and sweet as a Temple Virgin.' She leaned back and laughed so hard that her long legs kicked in the air and I had to look away from her to prevent my ugly side from showing through.

'Oh, that's good' Harvey said, noticing. 'That's very good. A good start. But let's get down to business. The fact you're here and the Major gave you this address means the Major's in trouble. Or worse. I don't suppose you know which?'

I glanced at Toni. 'No' we both said.

'But it didn't look good' I added. 'Not how we last saw him.'

Harvey thought about this for a few moments then said 'I think you'd better tell us what this business is and where we are with it. Start from the beginning and leave nothing out. No matter how trivial you feel it to be. Give us everything. And we'll work out where to go with it.'

'Let me ask you something first' I said.

Harvey shrugged. 'Go ahead.'

'What happened to your accent? You know, the German accent you acquired through years of living in Germany?'

Harvey suppressed a chuckle. 'Just an act' he said. 'No need for it now.'

I said nothing, wanting more, and he gave it to me.

'Look' he said, 'I open the door to perfect strangers – you - and I show you a false face until I know more about you. Just being cautious that's all. I'm sure you can understand, with all you're going through.'

'What do you know about what we're going through?' Toni asked, quick as a flash.

'Nothing really' Harvey said. 'But you *were* with the Major and he gave you this address. And I know he wouldn't give this address out lightly. The fact that you're here means someone's got to him. And that doesn't happen easily. So you're going through something. And it involves danger. I know that much.' He turned to me. 'Now if you're ready, begin at the beginning.'

I sighed and took a deep breath and was about to begin when Toni said 'Were you in the army with the Major? I mean, being in the same regiment?'

'Oh no,' Harvey said. 'Same regiment, different times.'

'But you had the same training' I said, 'I'm just going by how you dealt with me just now.' I remembered how I'd imagined he was military-fit earlier.

Harvey laughed. 'Really, you shouldn't flatter yourself. You've never been a fighter that's obvious. Any front line professional soldier would have the better of you without spilling his pint.'

He must have seen a look on my face. 'Don't take it to heart,' he said. 'Same for most people, even the bar-room brawlers you find in any town. But no, I didn't have the same training as the Major. He was field intelligence. I was seconded out. SAS. Now, shall we get on?'

# The Story Episode # 115
# (Moon phase: Day 26)

I TOLD THE whole story. The story I've been telling you. I even included the stuff about meeting my darling immortal beloved wife and our first weekend in Paris together, the way I told you. I mean, given that the Major had mentioned that he was the bearded man who'd hounded us there, I felt it to be relevant. Toni chimed in with bits and pieces where she felt I'd missed things. I even had to go into reasonable detail regarding the sex. I mean, I hadn't intended to, especially after what Harvey had done to show me this 'ugly' side of my nature as he put it. But Ziggy had insisted. She seemed to instinctively know when I'd enjoyed a sexual encounter and she'd stopped me the first couple of times where I'd skipped over these episodes to make me give the detail. If she thought she was going to further shame me into seeing ugliness in my actions she was mistaken. Because as I related the detail, without shame, I remembered the experiences as being beautiful. And my experiences with my beautiful and peerless wife aside, I remembered realising that my night of blissful delight with Heidi had been just such a one, of the most exquisite tenderness and respect and pleasure that I had ever known.

'It's not the melding of souls and bodies that's ugly you know.' This was Harvey not long after I'd finished relating the story. 'That's actually very beautiful.'

We all watched him rise and wander over to the table at the far side of the room. We continued to watch as he prepared incense-infused charcoal blocks in two large burners and set a low heat beneath them. I recognised immediately the scent of sandalwood, sweet and pretty in the gloomy air.

'No' Harvey continued, coming back to sit with us. 'It's your rapacious obsession that's ugly. Unwarranted. Unnecessary. Destructive to you. And potentially to your. . . I'm hesitating because I don't know whether to call them conquests or victims.'

I stayed calm. 'That's overly melodramatic' I said. 'Mostly they're neither.'

'Oh but sometimes they are then' Harvey shot back as quick as a flash.

I ignored that. 'You've received occult training,' I said. 'You know full well that the suppression of desire is the most disastrous thing you can do to yourself. All that New Age crap about spirituality and materialism being mutually exclusive is the greatest friction preventing spiritual progression you can possibly imagine. You know that.'

Harvey looked around the room at the threadbare shabby furnishings. 'Yes,' he said. 'I know exactly what you mean.'

I began to wonder if indeed he did. Because it's true what I said. About suppression of desire being a barrier to spiritual growth. Both eastern and western esoteric traditions teach this. They really do. It's just that most of the hippies who took off on the eastern trail from the late 1960s onwards misinterpreted just about everything they encountered. I'm not exaggerating. And the worst thing they could have brought back was the notion that a rejection of material desire is a necessary fundamental for spiritual growth. Even after the genuine eastern mystics gave them practical lesson after practical lesson to the contrary, they still never got it. Because they perceived materialism to be a product of the capitalist west they wanted to reject. They *wanted* to see materialism to be a barrier to spirituality, and that's what they slapped onto their search for their western spiritual heritage when they got back home.

Most New Age nutters now, however well meaning, still subscribe to this erroneous and retrograde thought. Which is why most of them rarely achieve anything and live frustrated and even unhappy lives. The Astral Light, the One Thing – God in self-expression – is always moving, always creating. You are a centre of expression for God. An expression *of* God actually, since existence is just one thing. You must experience. For God. Whatever can be imagined exists, and if whatever you imagine actually is your true desire, God will ensure you have it. You can only express joy and happiness through fulfilment. And this means discovering your true desire and following it, achieving it. The only caveat is one of maturity. A mature desire is one that does not involve harm to another, although it's not that simple. And that's really how it is. It's more complex than that, perhaps. But I've digressed enough. I've already introduced you to enough multi-millionaire Adepts in this story alone for you to see that pursuit and enjoyment of material things is no barrier to spiritual enlightenment. Quite the contrary, if these things are your true desire.

'You think I've rejected materialism then?' Harvey asked.

I looked around the room. 'It looks like it. But I suspect you live like this because a beautiful house was never your true desire. I'm not getting the idea that you're a spiritual failure.'

'Hmm,' Harvey said. 'I have other desires and all of them satisfied in turn. As they continue to be. Don't I simply exude joy to the glory of God?'

I could swear I saw him smirk as he glanced towards Ziggy. But I let it slide.

'That night you had with Heidi,' Ziggy said. 'Was it really as beautiful as you make it sound? Did you really do all of those things together the way you say? Two souls making love?'

I couldn't see why that was so important to her but I saw no reason not to answer.

'Sure,' I said. 'It's exactly the way I described it.' She seemed genuinely moved by it so I added 'I'm glad you enjoyed the telling of it. Why does it mean so much to you?'

She didn't have a chance to answer because Harvey jumped in. 'Oh of course, how could you know? Ziggy's bound to be moved by your anecdote. Bound to be. Heidi's Ziggy's mother. But there's no way you could have known that. No way. Not that it matters. Does it Ziggy?'

Ziggy simply shrugged. 'You did a beautiful thing for each other, I think.'

'You don't seem concerned for your mother' Toni said. 'Given that she nearly died.'

'I can't mourn death' Ziggy replied, matter of fact. 'It's just an illusion. And anyway, she didn't die. And she's with Elke. Nobody could do more for her than Elke.'

Clearly there was more to Elke than I'd even suspected. Just what was this covert cabal of occultists that Tom had thrust us into? The Major, Heidi, Elke and her group. Now Harvey and Ziggy. I was finding it hard to keep tracks on who was who and who was what.

'Let's clear the sentimentality' Harvey said, moving things along. 'We have to make plans. The College of Arms is not to be trifled with. Sable Wyvern and those agents here in Berlin after your blood – or worse – we need to keep you safe from them and move you along.'

'Move us along? What do you mean by that?' Toni asked.

'Well you can't stay in Berlin, obviously' Harvey told her. 'You're compromised here. We need to plan where you go next. And how we get you there.'

He looked at Toni for a moment then said 'You can go home.

Back to London.' Then he turned to me. 'You've been warned not to go back to London, right?'

I hadn't told him that when I'd related the events to date so I didn't know where he'd got that from. But he told me.

'It's on your face,' he said. 'I'm just reflecting it back to you.'

Toni looked at me with a face full of questions but all I could do was shrug. Bloody occult mirror.

'Come on' Harvey said, 'Let me take a look at that paper Elke gave you.'

Another face full of unvocalized questions from Toni. But I ignored her and handed over the stiff folded paper Elke had given me. And as Harvey opened it there in that room, I swear that the colours of the symbols painted on the walls sang to the coloured symbols painted on the paper. And that was just for starters.

# *The Story Episode # 116 (Moon phase: Day 26)*

COINCIDENCE IS AN illusion. No such thing. There is no such thing. I know that. I don't merely believe it. I know it. Empirically. Through experience and meticulous testing. Every one of us in that room knew it. So we all knew what was meant when Toni asked Ziggy what she'd been doing in the Hard Rock at the same time we were there. Toni didn't have to use the word coincidence. It would have been insulting to all of us.

'I arranged to meet my friends there earlier in the day. We go often. Just meet for a drink before we go off somewhere else.' She turned to Harvey. 'Tell them.'

Harvey looked up from his inspection of Elke's paper. 'What? Oh yes, yes it's true. They meet in that ghastly place. Far too vexatious for my taste. Altogether too loud.'

'So you met your friends there, and out of all the people in the place you singled me out to put the moves on?' Toni said.

Ziggy shrugged. 'I was drawn to you. I just went along with that. And you are very attractive.'

Toni wasn't one to fall for flattery. I watched Harvey and his close examination of Elke's cryptic instruction while Toni pressed on with her interrogation. 'So weren't we supposed to go to some party together? That's what you said. You wanted me to go to a party with you. So where's the party?'

Ziggy slouched back in her chair, flopped one of her delicious legs over the arm again. 'This is it,' she said. 'This is the party.'

Toni all but snorted with contempt at that. 'Really?' she said. 'You were going to bring me back here. And that was your aim all along?'

'I got the feeling that you and me had to meet. You look fun so I said there was a party' Ziggy answered.

'You and me then if you'd got me back here. And what about him?' Toni nodded towards Harvey. 'What part did you have in mind for him?'

'Oh a delicious threesome' Harvey said without looking up. 'If you could be persuaded.'

'And if I couldn't?

'Then I'd stay in here and get on with some work and leave you two to the rest of the flat to debauch each other at your leisure and pleasure.'

Harvey answered but his attention remained fixed on Elke's paper. 'You'd have had fun I can assure you,' he added.

Even Toni seemed dumbfounded by that. She looked at me but what could I say?

'You don't find me attractive?' Ziggy asked, and it struck me that it was all taken for granted that Toni would be bisexual. I mean I didn't know that myself although I'd often suspected it.

'Of course I find you attractive' Toni said. 'You're very beautiful and you know it. But that's really not the point is it? Not really what I'm asking.'

Ziggy sighed. 'Okay,' she said. 'This is how I see it. I was put in the Hard Rock at the same time as you to meet you. I didn't know that you were due to go there. How could I?'

'And yet you turned up here just a minute or two after we did.' This was me. Now I was interested too.

'I followed you,' Ziggy said.

'Why?' I asked.

Ziggy shrugged again and I got the impression that she found our interrogation tedious. 'I don't know. But perhaps I was supposed to follow you. You are in trouble right? People are after you. Maybe I was made to follow you so that I could inform Harvey if anything happened to you.'

Now I know you're going to see that as hokum, but seriously, that was probably the God's honest truth. Ziggy taking direction. Going with the flow of what something was suggesting to her. Of course the reminder that we were in such danger and way out of our depth – Toni and me I mean – did send a cold chill through my blood. But just then Harvey looked up. He held the paper out to Ziggy, who leaned forward to take it.

'I'm struggling with this' Harvey told her, 'I think we're going to need you to work your magic.'

'And now we see what part I play in this business, right?' Ziggy said and I saw her smile for the first time and my heart fluttered at the sight.

'Going to need you two to help out,' Harvey said. 'Ziggy

needs to be naked to do what she's got to do. Up to you whether or not you remain covered.'

'Naked is fine' Toni said.

Of course, I've told you before that nakedness is not an issue to any occultist, the illusion being what it is. And both Toni and me were well aware of why nakedness, the disassociation from as much of the illusion as possible, was a great catalyst in at least some occult operations. Neither of us knew what was going to be expected of us but we could take a guess that we were going to be acting as channels for certain vibrations of cosmic energy. So we all of us got naked and we sat at the table at the far end of the room, overshadowed by the uniform hanging on the wall. It wasn't a ritual in any sense that you've heard me describe them earlier in this story. Quite literally, all we did was sit at the table, which we pulled away from the wall, and we held hands. Ziggy placed the paper on the table, face up in the middle so we could see the coloured symbols painted on it.

'Just hold it in focus,' Ziggy told us and we all knew what to do. One. The Magician. Beth. E Major. House. Mercury. So we all of us unconsciously synchronised our breathing as we held hands. And while we couldn't feel it – at least I couldn't – we synchronised our heartbeats.

We fixed the image of the paper in our minds and held it there allowing no other thoughts to intrude. And we were able to manage this in short-order. We were none of us novices. Then at some point Ziggy left us. She got up and although the rest of us remained at the table holding hands and continuing to fix on the paper and the symbols, a level of my consciousness was aware of the beautifully translucently naked Ziggy gliding from wall to wall, placing the open palms of her hands on various of the brilliant symbols like she was operating the controls of some fantastic machine. If you've ever seen the classic Fritz Lang silent movie *Metropolis*, you'll get the idea. And while I'd like to describe some fantastic occult and trans-dimensional event to you, I have to say it all ended rather simply. Ziggy came back to sit at the table and said

'That's okay, I've got it.'

That broke the spell all right. We let go of each other's hands while Ziggy took a piece of paper and a ball-point pen from a draw in the table next to where she sat. As we stood I noticed that Harvey and I both had erections. That often happens to me when I channel specific occult vibrations of energy and clearly it was the same for Harvey.

'Snap,' he said, smiling and I had to laugh as Toni rolled her eyes.

Ziggy came to join us in getting dressed and once we were all clothed once more, she returned to the table and came back with both pieces of paper – Elke's, which was amazingly blank again, and the one with her translation. Harvey took it from her and scrutinized it.

'Hmm,' he said. 'A name and address. Very useful to you I'd say'

He said that to me and he was about to say more when a loud banging on the front door startled us all. Harvey passed Ziggy's note to me and told me to keep it safe so I tucked it into my wallet.

'Stay here' Harvey said. 'And keep still and quiet.'

My heart raced. The banging on the door was loud and insistent. Not the knock of a neighbour wanting to borrow a cup of sugar. I heard loud voices and Harvey answering in German. Then the sound of the door latch being opened. After that I don't really know how to describe it. The sound of banging and crashing bodies is the best I can do and it was just for a few seconds, with a couple of cries of shock and pain thrown in for good measure. I cringed with fear because we were trapped up there in that flat.

'Stevie, come quick.' This was Harvey giving the order in a whisper.

I went out and saw Harvey standing in the doorway, his feet straddling the prone and inert form of a man. I could just see beyond Harvey that another man lay similarly incapacitated in the hallway beyond the door. Whoever those two were, Harvey had dealt with them. I couldn't tell if they were living or dead and didn't want to consider that.

'Grab that one and drag him into the living room' Harvey ordered.

I did what I was told and Harvey took the one in the hallway and dragged him into the flat. I can't say I was sad to hear the door slammed shut behind us. Once we had both bodies in the living room Harvey checked to make sure they were both alive. Which they were.

'Right, so someone knows you're here,' he said. 'We're going to have to make plans on the hoof.'

'What about those two?' Toni asked, meaning the two unconscious men.

Harvey was about to answer when two beeps from my phone interrupted. I took my phone from my pocket to look at the text message just received. 'Where are you?' the message said. 'Call me. Urgent.' Fucking Hesther. Again.

# The Story Episode # 117
# (Moon phase: Day 26)

MATERIAL DESIRE IS no barrier to spiritual progress. I've mentioned that already. I'd suggested that Harvey may have been living a life of misplaced aestheticism although I did allow that Harvey's spiritual progress was such that he may have been fulfilling other true desires. Actually Harvey had suggested this himself. Fact is I needn't have concerned myself. You see, we got to see the rest of the flat. I'd been basing my opinions on what I'd seen of Harvey's flat, remember, the hallway and that living room. And the fact that the flat was in a particularly uninspiring block in an uninspiring part of *Wedding*, itself an uninspiring district of Berlin.

The rest of the flat though would have shamed Nero. Or the Sun King Louis XIV. I needn't have worried about Harvey satisfying any material desires he might have had. It's virtually impossible for me to describe this place. Fabulous *objets d'art*, incredible décor and furnishings. Everything rich and plush.

There was a second sitting room directly behind the first, that had originally been a bedroom converted by Harvey. Two further bedrooms designed for seduction and languid sexual dalliance, and a Scandinavian kitchen fitted with expensive and exquisite appliances and surfaces completed the living space.

The reason we got to see the rest of the flat was because Harvey didn't want those two agents of the College of Arms, which is what we thought the two assailants were, to remain in the living space that we'd been occupying. I realised that the first living room and indeed the hallway leading to it from the front door, were places sacred to Harvey. The aestheticism we'd encountered was indeed an expression of true desire. These were exactly the surroundings Harvey had created to compliment the energy conducive to his magical work.

So after we'd dragged the still-unconscious thugs from the Temple, we'd found ourselves in the opulent surroundings of the living room behind. Harvey had me help him tie the two of them to straight-backed wooden chairs. We're talking non-stretch rope and heavy duty tape over their mouths. The chairs were placed so that neither of them would see the other once they'd regained consciousness and the chairs themselves were lashed tight to heavy objects of furniture. I should mention that these men had been stripped bare. They'd have all kind of problems even if they did manage to free themselves. Harvey had searched them and found that neither carried identification, mobile phones, anything that could be used to tell us who they were.

'What's the matter?' Harvey asked, seeing that Toni and me were both somewhat shaken by events.

I answered for both of us. 'Them,' I said, meaning the two naked bound and gagged men. Both of them professionals, I could tell. Yes, even I could tell. They were just like Harvey. All whipcord muscle and not an ounce of fat. You'd have to be a fucking moron to imagine they were just serious fitness fanatics.

'What about them?' Harvey asked.

I explained to him exactly what the matter was. All this James Bond-Jason Bourne stuff might have been part of Harvey's professional existence and therefore a matter of no consequence to him, but for Toni and me to be tracked and targeted by professionals of this type was cause for terror. And that was the truth, really. Let me tell you, you watch a scene like I've just described in a film or on TV or something and it's ho-hum as you watch it. But when you're up close with people who mean you harm, have the skill to do whatever harm they wish, and who've been relentless in their pursuit of you, it's different altogether.

'Well these two won't be doing you any harm now' Harvey said.

'But what if there are others?' Toni asked.

Harvey laughed. 'Oh there'll be others, for sure. That's why I'd say Berlin's not safe for you. Not right now.'

One of the two men groaned. Coming back to consciousness. Harvey stepped over to him and hit him sharply beneath one ear with the edge of his hand and the man slumped back into unconsciousness. I was at one and the same time thrilled and appalled at this casual demonstration of skill. Harvey didn't seem to care at all.

'We need to get you out of here' Harvey said.

'What about these two?' Toni asked.

'Well they won't be going anywhere' Harvey answered all matter of fact. 'I'll deal with them once I'm happy you're safely on your way.'

'What does that mean, deal with them?' Toni pressed. She had her arms wrapped around herself and she looked cold.

Harvey grinned. 'You don't need to worry about that' he said.

'But what if you don't come back? I mean, what if something happens?' I don't know where that question came from or what made me blurt it out. But having asked I couldn't take it back.

Harvey thought for a moment. 'Well if *something happens* to all of us, then I suppose they'll starve to death' he said.

'Doesn't that bother you?' Toni asked. I think she was suffering a degree of shock from all that had happened to us.

'No,' Harvey said. 'Now come on, let's get you two out of here. We don't know that this address isn't compromised. We need to get to somewhere safe and neutral. We'll decide what to do with you once you're safe from prying eyes.' Harvey stopped, thought for a moment. Then said 'But first off that woman in London who keeps trying to contact you. Hesther. You should call her. Get that monkey off your back. Then turn your phone off. We don't want it going off at a delicate moment now do we?'

'What should I tell her?' I asked.

Harvey shrugged. 'Well until you know what she wants I couldn't say. But if she asks where you are, don't tell her. That's the only advice I can give you.'

'Why not?' Toni asked.

'Do you trust this woman?' This was Ziggy and it surprised me to hear her speak. She'd been relatively silent while we'd been tying the two agents to the chairs.

'Shouldn't we trust her?' Toni asked.

'I don't know' Ziggy said. 'I don't know her. I would just think that to tell what you don't have to tell is an unnecessary risk.'

'Go on, make the call' Harvey said. 'We should get away from here. Go on, get it done.'

I remembered scenarios from a multitude of action thriller movies and the thoughts didn't comfort me. I took my phone from my pocket and found Hesther's number from the missed calls log. I hit the button to dial out and waited while the phone connected. I was hoping that it would ring out and go to voicemail. Right up to the moment when Hesther picked up and answered.

# The Story Episode # 118 (Moon phase: Day 27)

AN HOUR AFTER we'd left Harvey's *Wedding* apartment, we found ourselves in the Balzac Coffee bar on the east side of *Friedrichstraße*, south west of the *Tiergarten* and just a block north of Checkpoint Charlie.

We'd driven there in Harvey's car. He kept this car in a private underground lock up garage beneath the apartment block. Another example of how Harvey acted upon his desires I have to say. The car was a Bristol Blenheim, a car so beautiful and so exclusive that the owner of Bristol Cars won't sell new models to people he doesn't consider to be of the right character to own one of his machines. He's been known to usher people who certainly had the money, out of his showroom in west London. This is absolutely true.

Anyway, Harvey had obviously passed the test because this car was near as dammit brand new and Harvey took the time to tell us that he traded up to a new model every two years. He told us this as we drove around Berlin making what seemed to me to be an arbitrary and haphazard tour of the city before ending up on *Friedrichstraße*. This is why it had taken an hour to get there. Really, it's nothing like an hour's drive from *Wedding* normally.

'Just making sure we're all alone' Harvey told me when I asked him what he was doing.

Well that made sense. I wouldn't know how to do it of course, and neither would you. But Harvey did. And once he'd deemed us to be safe, he'd parked up the car and suggested we go somewhere busy so that we could talk without being overheard.

Just before we went into the café, Harvey stopped and looked south down the road.

'That used to be Checkpoint Charlie' he said – somewhat wistfully I thought. 'They still call it Checkpoint Charlie of course, but look at it. Surrounded by tourist crap and alive with the kind of people we'd have shot dead back in the day. The Russians and us.' He sighed, fixed his attention on something we couldn't see down that road. His past. 'Worst thing that's ever happened in my lifetime' he said.

'What is?' Toni asked.

'The fall of the wall' Ziggy answered with a hint of cynicism suggesting she'd heard this all before. More than once.

'You can't mean that' Toni said.

Harvey turned on her sharpish, no longer wistful. 'Can't I? You think the world's a better place now? Safer? You feel more secure?'

Toni couldn't answer. I could see she knew exactly what he meant. I certainly did.

'They got to Gorbachev. They got to him. Made him see what he was.'

'What do you mean, see what he was?' I asked, genuinely perplexed.

'They made him see that he was one of them,' Harvey answered. 'If you put me on the spot, I'd say it happened in Reykjavik when the elitist faker went for the neutral summit with Reagan. Yes, that's when they sealed it. Americans sealed it. But the groundwork was done before that. When Thatcher went to Moscow.' He turned to me to tell me the next part directly, as though he thought that somehow I'd give a shit. 'I can tell you that Thatcher didn't know a hundredth of what was going on around her for all the time she was in office. For every petty little ideological victory they allowed her, they stripped a hundred freedoms from the very people who mindlessly cheered her on. Gullible middle England. Not that middle England could do anything about it.'

'Do anything about what?' Toni again.

'The relentless pursuit of a return to feudalism' Harvey said. 'Now come on, let's go get some coffee and get down to business.'

So that's how we happened to be in the Balzac Coffee bar on *Friedrichstraße*. Of course I wanted to ask a number of questions of my own after Harvey had come out with that last cryptic bombshell but he was already opening the door and stepping inside before I could open my mouth.

I won't tell you where we sat or what we ordered to drink or any of the details of the place because I'm well aware that there's something you're waiting to hear about and I've been neglecting it. But not on purpose I assure you. I'm talking about the phone call to Hesther back at Harvey's flat, just before we'd made our getaway. So I'll tell you now.

'Hello Steven,' Hesther said, answering my call. 'It's late. I wasn't expecting you.'

'I can hang up and call back another time' I said, knowing that she wasn't going to go for that. She didn't.

'No no, it's lovely to hear your voice' she said. 'Any time. Day or night.'

See what I was telling you about Hesther? It seems an age ago doesn't it, but she'd always looked down on me. And once I'd found out it might have been because she'd had a thing with my beautiful darling wife Helen I could understand why. Then after all that had come out into the open, she had been disarmingly gentle with me. Wonderful with me I'd say. Yet something about the way she'd been chasing me since I'd come to Berlin with Toni made the hairs on the back of my neck stand on end.

All the old suspicions returned. And her voice was formal. Friendly. But not quite approachable. I couldn't quite put my finger on it. But I was on my guard.

'I know you've been trying to speak to me but it's been difficult' I said, not mentioning that the difficulty actually amounted to nothing more than my renewed suspicion of her.

'Yes' she said, sounding like a Victorian dowager, 'Well it's good you've found the time at last.'

'So what can I do for you?' I asked. 'I'm assuming you needed me for something or other.'

'Oh,' she said, and she sounded genuinely taken aback so that a momentary wave of guilt washed through me at my uncalled for sharpness. 'Well if we must go straight to business, I just wondered where you were. I called Toni's house.' She paused for a moment here to allow me to react to that but I stayed quiet. 'Her husband – Tom - is a really nice chap and he told me that you and Toni had gone off together on some kind of business but that he didn't know where. Awfully strange, I thought.'

Good old Tom. Tom knew damn well where we were. He'd sent us there. But he hadn't seen fit to let Hesther know.

'It's been a bit of a whirlwind' was the best I could come up with. 'We've been here there and everywhere. You know how it is.'

'Quite' Hesther said. 'So where are you now?'

'Berlin,' I told her. Really there was no point lying. This was Hesther. Hesther the Adept. She'd see right through me, the state I was in.

'Oh,' Hesther said. 'I see.'

I waited, expecting her to ask what we were doing in Berlin but she didn't ask. She did ask when we'd be coming back.

'I don't know' I said. 'Not exactly. Soon though.'

Again she didn't press me on the nature of our business in Berlin and I got the feeling she was going out of her way not to ask.

'Well it's been busy here' she said. 'And we bury Professor Hanford the day after tomorrow. I thought that you and Toni would like to know. And to be there.'

'We'll try to be there' I said. 'I know how much it would mean to you. And to Toni.'

'But not to you?'

She almost had me on the ropes with that one. 'Yes, and to me. The professor was always very kind to me' I said.

'He was a kind man' Hesther said. 'I miss him. I'm sure we all do. Well please call me once you get back to London. It's been a very difficult time. Professor Hanford and Sable Wyvern passing along like that. It's been all I can do to keep things together.'

I almost dropped my phone at the mention of Sable Wyvern. What the devil was Sable Wyvern to Hesther? But she ended the call before I could betray myself.

'Well I'll look forward to hearing from you soon' she said. 'And I do hope that you can make it to the funeral. It would mean a lot.'

I didn't get the chance to ask just who it would mean a lot to as she hung up. That's when Harvey hurried us out of his flat, and now you're up to speed.

Back to the café then. One thing I did need was to go to the toilet. I made my way to the back where the toilets were located and inside I found myself alone. I couldn't see anyone at any rate. So I took a piss and washed my hands. But as I was drying them I heard something. Unmistakable. A bell-tinkle laugh that could only be my beautiful darling immortal beloved wife. I stood stark-still, seeing behind me in the mirror over the line of sinks in front of me. All I could see was the row of three toilet cubicles. Two had open doors and were empty. But the middle door was closed. The laugh again. Helen. My darling Helen. She had to be in there. Then her voice. No laughter in her words. What she said, she meant. I knew that tone. I knew it!

'You better watch yourself Stevie. It's not always like it seems.'

I turned sharply. 'What isn't' I asked the closed door.

I didn't get an answer. Just the sound of crying. Sobbing. My beautiful darling immortal beloved wife Helen sobbing her little heart out.

'Helen?' I called out. 'Helen. Don't cry.' The sobbing continued. 'Darling don't cry.'

She was in that cubicle alone and hurt and upset and I just couldn't take that. I couldn't. So I kicked that door in. Yes, I didn't even try to push it open. I kicked it in. Then wished I hadn't. Because it wasn't my Helen I found in there. It was a blond fat middle aged German man, and a slim Turkish youth. And they were standing either side of the toilet in there and masturbating each other.

# The Story Episode # 119
# (Moon phase: Day 27)

DO FEAR AND anger complement each other? I'd suggest that they do. I don't want to go into a deep discussion here but fear and anger radiated out to fill that toilet space and everything beyond it. The fat blond German man exuded fear. You could see it through the shock on his face. Fear of what? Fear of shame and dishonour that would follow if his activities were made public. Such is the result of a throw-back morality. He'd be angry though if he felt that his reputation would be safe. If he thought his grubby secret would go no further.

The young Turk was consumed with anger and no mistake. I didn't notice fear there at all. In an instant my mind was telling me that what I'd burst in on was a commercial transaction. The young Turk was going to make money from it. Perhaps he already had. Maybe he'd been promised an expectation of more to come. But my blundering action had changed things somewhat. No matter the reason he was a seething cauldron of violent fury. Even while the fat blond man was struggling to adjust his underwear, this kid had his trousers pulled up in a single move and I could see in his eyes that he was going to vent that violent anger on me.

Looking back now I can rather see his point of view. Back then I didn't have the time to consider philosophical viewpoints. The glistening object I noticed twitching in the kid's hand sent a wave of fear radiating out to the universe. Mine. The kid was holding a flick-knife.

'Look I'm terribly sorry' I started to say but I never finished because my inner Guardian Angel had other ideas and set me to turning and running. I burst out of that toilet into the back of the Balzac Coffee Bar and barged into the nearest tables as my wild eyes searched for the table nearer the door where Harvey, Toni and Ziggy were sitting. I ignored the cries of complaint from the tables I'd crashed into, spilling drinks all over the place as I raced for the door.

My companions had all turned to look at the source of the commotion but I ignored them and I was quickly past Harvey - who'd already risen from his seat - and I was pulling the glass door open in my haste to get out onto the street. But with one foot safely on the pavement outside something made me stop and turn. And what I saw was difficult to comprehend. For an ordinary man like me it was. Because Harvey had placed himself in the way of the kid with the knife who was in close pursuit and had grabbed the kid's knife-wielding arm, stopping him dead.

'Son, it isn't worth it' Harvey said in German. He let the kid go, still standing between him and me. 'Just put that away and we can sort out whatever the problem is, and if it's what you want, you can walk away with your honour intact and an advantageous bulge in your wallet.'

Now if I'd been that kid I know I'd have seen right away that what Harvey had proposed was a win-without-compromise solution and I'd have been all for it. But this kid was a slave to his base emotion. I could see in his eyes – he wasn't more than six feet away, just the other side of Harvey – that only violence would satisfy him. And well, if *I* could recognise that, Harvey certainly could.

You've probably guessed already that the kid went for Harvey with that knife. I saw what happened next and I can recall it in my memory but I was startled and astonished at the time and that sense of amazement hasn't diminished since. What Harvey did was the work of a master, and he did it at a speed I wouldn't have believed to be humanly possible. If you've ever watched those Jason Bourne films, you know, The Bourne Identity and the ones that followed it, you'll have some idea. Because it was just exactly like that. Just as fast too. And all done in-close. All I can tell you is that Harvey grabbed the kid's arm, the one holding the knife, twisted it and dragged the kid in close. From that point it was all over in maybe two, possibly three seconds at the most. The best way I can describe what I saw is to say that it looked like Harvey was attempting to tango with a life-size rag doll before slatting it to the floor where it lay unmoving.

The accompanying sounds I assumed must have been kicks and blows administered by Harvey but visually it all happened so quick and so sharp that I couldn't synchronise what I heard with what I saw. What I did hear sounded like a pro boxer landing a super-fast combination of his most vicious blows – to a cabbage. Yes, that's what it sounded like. Someone punching a crisp cabbage. Hard.

Obviously I stepped back into the coffee bar as Harvey knelt beside the kid. First thing he did was retrieve the knife, which had clattered to the tiled floor. He stuck it in his jacket pocket. He took the paper napkins that Ziggy was offering him and wiped blood from the kid's face. The kid was unconscious but breathing. The coffee bar manager was fast at the scene and he seemed more shocked than angry, constantly asking what had happened and constantly being ignored. Harvey inspected the kid quickly and efficiently, feeling for broken bones and finding – to my relief at any rate – none.

'Call an ambulance' Harvey said to the manager. 'Best you do it now' he added when the manager didn't move right away.

That had the manager scuttling off behind the counter. By this time a few of the coffee bar customers were standing over and gawping. Harvey ignored them.

'We need to get the hell out of here' Harvey said to Toni, Ziggy and me.

'Is that boy going to be alright?' Toni asked.

'Sure he is' Harvey said, already opening the door.

We followed him out and we strode after him, heading back to the car. But not before I'd turned to take a last look into that coffee bar. I saw the fat man returning to a table. Sitting at the table were a good looking woman and two children, girls in their early teens, I guessed. I don't know what I was thinking as I skipped along after the others but I remember the sense of disgust I felt. Not at what I'd caught them doing, but at the way he'd been doing that in the toilets while he was out for coffee and cake with his family.

I did get a lesson out of it. Once we were in Harvey's car and pulling out into the traffic.

'So what prompted all that?' Harvey asked, and we all know what he meant.

'I walked in on them' I said. 'I don't think they appreciated an audience.'

'Them?' Toni asked.

'Yes. There was a fat blond guy in there with him.'

'What were they doing?' Ziggy asked.

Harvey laughed. 'I'm sure you can guess that for yourself' he said.

'It was relatively innocent' I said. 'They were just wanking each other?'

Ziggy was perplexed by that and turned around from the front passenger seat to ask 'Wanking? What is that?'

Harvey laughed some more. 'He means masturbating. *Masturbieren.*'

'Oh,' Ziggy said, and giggled.

Toni didn't laugh. 'So they were just there, in the middle of the toilets, wanking each other?'

'God no,' I said. 'They were in a cubicle.'

I immediately realised what I'd said. Toni wasn't slow to pick it up either.

'So how did you come to go into an occupied cubicle?' she asked, non-judgmentally.

I was slow to answer.

'We don't mind if you like to play with men' Ziggy said, giggling. 'My God, this isn't the dark ages.'

'Oh Stevie here doesn't play with boys, do you Stevie?' This was Harvey putting Ziggy straight.

I didn't answer.

'So what did you think when you saw them?' Ziggy asked. 'Did you laugh? Is that why they chase you?'

Again I didn't answer.

Again Harvey stepped in. 'Stevie didn't laugh' he said, all serious now. 'Stevie didn't care either way. Not about what he saw in the toilet. That's right, isn't it Stevie?'

I didn't have anything to say to that either. I wasn't happy being the centre of attention in this way.

Harvey continued. 'Something you saw after wasn't to your taste though was it Steven?'

I felt compelled to answer. 'No,' I said.

'So what did you see then?' Ziggy asked after a few moments had passed in silence.

'The blond fat guy,' I said. 'As we were leaving I saw him come out of the toilet. He went to a table. And his wife and two young daughters were sitting at that table. The bastard couldn't even resist getting a bit of cock while he was out with his family.'

Harvey nodded, considering what I'd said. 'Yes, a man governed and ruled by his base sexual urges' he said. 'Truly an ugly sight to see.'

I understood right away. Harvey was telling me that the incident had been the universe holding up a different kind of mirror to me. Showing me myself. A horrible lesson. But an effective one.

'You still didn't answer' Toni said as the bright city lights passed us by, seeming to move while we stood still in the stream of traffic. 'Why did you go into that occupied cubicle in the first place?'

I leaned against the glass of the side window, looked at the glowing streaking neon outside. I was weary beyond belief right at that moment. But eventually I answered.

'Helen' I said. 'I went in because Helen was in there.'

# The Story Episode # 120
# (Moon phase: Day 28)

'WHAT DO YOU intend to do then? About your wife.'

Harvey asked this as we sat on uncomfortable seats, the public side of departure security in Berlin Tegel International airport. We'd taken a circuitous route to get there from *Friedrichstraße* thanks to Harvey's insistence on making sure we werc safe. It was beyond the middle of the night and we still had a couple of hours before the redeye flight to Heathrow that I'd booked Toni and me on to. I thought about Harvey's question for a while but I couldn't really understand it.

'I don't know what you mean by that' I said.

'Well she hasn't completely moved on has she? A great shade of her consciousness remains with you. And yes it's you she clings to.'

'Why?' I asked. 'Why does she cling to me? I'm not sure you have that right.'

'Oh yes, it's correct' Ziggy said. 'She remains to be with you. It's quite clear. I get the impression of her from time to time. At your side. And if I had to describe what I can't actually see, I'd say she's a smile when she's next to you. In a way, that's really nice, wouldn't you say?'

'You talk about her as though she doesn't know she's dead. What you're describing is spiritualism.' Toni said it before I could come up with an answer of my own.

'No, I just try to explain. Perhaps my English isn't good enough' Ziggy answered without rancour.

'I don't think Ziggy's trying to say that your wife is some sort of ghost, haunting you' Harvey said. 'Just that some of the energy that made up her personality on this plane is just – '

'I bloody-well understand how it is' I interrupted, irritated. I settled immediately, realising I'd reacted out of tiredness and fear. 'I'm sorry,' I said. 'I just want to know what you meant by your original question, you know, what do I intend to do about her.'

'No offence taken' Harvey said easily. 'I just wondered if you intended to find a way to release her essence and send her on her way or whether you intended to find a way of joining her.'

Wow. Now I understood. And I hadn't ever considered it. But what Harvey was suggesting was that I could seek out a way of joining my beautiful darling immortal beloved wife Helen. My heart lurched at the very idea and Toni – the empath once more – sensed it and placed a reassuring hand on my arm.

I had to fight for a few breaths to steady my breathing and my heart rate. But I managed it. Join Helen. It would mean death for me here. Death in the sense that you understand death, although I've already explained to you that death in that sense is just an illusion.

I should tell you that I knew that I'd never achieve it by taking my own life. Nothing could push me further from Helen than such a self-destructive act. But there were other ways. The attainment of Adeptship for one. However, don't let me lead you to believe that Adeptship is a simple attainment. Very very very few who set out on the spiritual path ever come close to achieving it. Even though in this story I may have made it seem that there's an Adept around every corner.

Still, it set me thinking; there may be other ways, more direct ways, of taking my essence on to the plane that darling wonderful Helen currently graced. I would search for the path. I'd become a seeker with a purpose and a focus.

'I have never seen such deep love' Ziggy said, and I could see she was on the verge of tears.

'Helen and me, the universe had planned and waited for a long time to bring us together' I said. 'And you know, I wish with all my heart that everyone could experience what we had with each other.'

I meant that. I really did. Ziggy had to turn away and she wiped a tear from her eye with the back of her hand.

Harvey changed the subject. 'You've been told that it's not safe for you to go back to London' he said to me. 'But you're flying into Heathrow.'

'I'm duty bound to get Toni home safe and sound. That comes before anything else' I said.

'Yeah,' Toni said, 'that's been mentioned before, you not going back to London. What's that all about?'

Harvey ignored her and continued to concentrate on me. 'Okay' he said, 'but you have that contact address that Elke gave you. Do you intend to use it?'

'Huh' I said. 'What I actually have is a piece of paper Elke gave me which sometimes displays symbols that mean absolutely nothing to me. And I have Ziggy's translation of it. I mean, no disrespect but I don't know any of you people do I? The Major, Heidi, Elke, you and Ziggy here. You suggesting I should trust you?'

Harvey shrugged. 'Your decision to make' he said. 'But I'm going to suggest that you've been told often enough recently that you need to walk away from the technical and embrace the natural. That you need – and I stress the word *need* – to learn to balance the four Ancient Elements.'

'Yes,' I said. 'I don't deny that. Earth, Air, Water and Fire. Balance them and I'll understand what's been happening. I get the picture. At least that's what I believe to be the picture.'

'That's it. Pretty much,' Harvey said. 'And I'm just trying to get you to see that the contact that Elke's given you is a wonderful gift. And absolutely where you should go.'

'That's if we can trust you' Toni said. Then she turned to me. 'Just what is this business about not returning to London?'

I sighed. 'I've been told that it may not be safe for me. That someone is out to get to Helen through me. Something like that.'

'You don't believe that' Toni said, ever the empath.

'You can see that deep down I don't want to' I said. 'But what if it's true?'

'It's true' Ziggy said. 'Truth remains the truth even if no-one believes it.'

I think I'd mentioned that one to you sometime earlier in this story. It's good to be reminded of these things from time to time though.

'Let's have a look at the paper with Ziggy's translation again' Harvey said.

I took the paper from my wallet where Harvey had told me I should put it when he'd handed it to me earlier. Harvey looked at it and handed it back.

'Keep that safe' he said. 'In case you come to realise that we're not all out to get you.'

I should have come back with a smart-arse comment but I didn't. Because something caught my attention as I leaned over to slip my wallet back into my pocket. A man standing just inside the entrance doors, maybe forty yards away from where we were sitting. Even at that distance I was sure that I recognised him. Tall. Straight back. Big bushy black beard. You know him too, right? The bearded man. From Auckland. Maybe from Paris. The man who'd been engulfed with flame as my house burned in a boiling conflagration that night back in New Zealand. *That* man, who was the absolute spitting image of the Major.

Well I was up and hurtling across that concourse and the bearded man turned and watched me for a couple of strides. Then he turned and returned to the early-morning outdoors. And when I got there he was nowhere to be seen.

'Fuck fuck fuck!' I shouted out, calming myself as I noticed two cops across the way turning to look.

I went back inside to join the others. They were standing when I got back to them, all eyes on me. I told them what I'd seen. None of them had seen it but it wasn't like they didn't believe me. I realised that Toni and me should go through the security screening and prepare for our flight. There was no way I could even begin to understand what I'd just seen and I wasn't likely to work it out sitting in the airport pre-departure concourse.

'What are you going to do now?' I asked Harvey after telling him how sorry I was to have compromised his apartment.

'I have those two creatures to deal with first of all' he said.

I'd forgotten about them and shuddered at the thought of what fate might await them. They were hired muscle and not spiritually Adept. And there were a million fates worse than death.

'And I can secure my flat' Harvey said. 'Don't you worry about that. Really, my job is to find the Major. That's what I'll do. So run along the two of you. Maybe we'll see each other again. Maybe we won't. Either way, my work here is done. That's right isn't it Ziggy?'

'Of course. Whatever you say is always right' Ziggy said

without a hint of cynicism.

So we said our goodbyes, gave each other hugs and handshakes and I had the ugly thought that I'd have loved to have spent a night with Ziggy, but I think it slipped away unnoticed.

Toni and me watched them leave before heading for our security checks. I couldn't help thinking about how Ziggy and Harvey had gone to pains to explain that they hadn't intended to picture Helen as a ghost, haunting me from an immortal love. I couldn't help thinking about it because although that's not what I'd told them, that's exactly how I saw her and that's what I wanted to believe with all my heart. My darling beautiful immortal beloved wife Helen as a ghost. Who would be by my side through all eternity.

# *The Story Episode # 121 (Moon phase: Day 28)*

DRIVING DOWN FROM Heathrow on the M4, continuing east as it became the A4. On into Chiswick, heading for Hammersmith and with Chelsea not far beyond that. Yet all of it taking an age because our plane had landed on time and the immigration and security processes had disgorged us out to collect my car at the worst possible time of day. London morning rush hour. An hour gone by the time we crawled through Chiswick, thanks to road works all over the place and a couple of accidents.

'Are you going to go to the funeral?' Toni asked me.

'Yes I suppose I should' I said. 'He was always good to me, Professor Hanford. A decent man. I respected him. So yeah, I'll go. How about you.'

'Sure, I'll be going' Toni said, but I could sense there was something on her mind.

I waited a while as we crawled a couple of car lengths closer to Hammersmith then said 'Come on, spit it out.'

Toni knew exactly what I meant – well, she was an empath after all. 'Do you think it's safe for you to stay in London? Let alone go to the professor's funeral? I mean if people have been telling you it's not safe then maybe you should take note.'

I snorted derisively, not at her but at the very notion. 'What, get out of Dodge? I'm not running.'

If that sounds like bravado to you then you're spot on the money. Because inside I *was* concerned. Maybe a little frightened. And I should have had more sense than to conceal that from Toni. Empath, remember?

'You feel there might be something in what you've been told. And you trust the ones who've told you. The Major, Heidi, Elke, Harvey. You trust them' Toni said with a finality that brooked no contradiction.

So we were definitely back to a previous square. Maybe not square one, but a square somewhere near it. Toni reading me like a book and me living on the edge of fear. Come to think of it, that pretty much *was* square one.

'You missed a name' I said, wanting to put myself on the front-foot with Toni.

'Who?' she asked, turning to me out of sheer surprise.

'Someone close enough to you' I said.

'Not Tom' she said, disbelieving it could be her husband but having no one else in mind.

I shook my head. 'No, not Tom,' I said, and left it at that.

Toni turned to look out of the passenger window. After we'd crawled another couple of car lengths along the road she turned back to me, sharpish, but with a smile. 'Come on' she said, 'who is it? Tell me.'

'Rachel' I said, not taking my eyes from the car immediately in front of us.

'Huh,' Toni said, sounding disappointed. 'And when did she tell you this? Before, during or after your fuck-session with her?'

'Oooh' I said in a tone heavy with sarcasm, 'Now that was tart.' Toni didn't respond, so I continued. 'Actually we didn't fuck for fun no matter what you might think. We engaged in a beautiful nature ceremony. In one of your basement Temples as it turned out.' Still no reaction from Toni. 'And you know how it came about?' I said, goading her.

'No' she replied, like the conversation she'd initiated had somehow become tiresome. 'Why don't you tell me.'

'It was a gift from Tom.'

That lit a fuse. 'What the hell do you mean by that?' she snapped.

'I mean that Tom, your husband, arranged to meet me down in your basement in the early hours of one morning. Only he never showed. But Rachel did. And she had something in mind for us to do. It definitely wasn't spontaneous.'

'This ceremony. . .' Toni said, confirming it to herself.

'Yes, the ceremony. Our fuck-session as you charmingly described it.' I waited, giving her the chance to say something but she didn't. I continued, asking 'Did Tom arrange that? Or was it one of those co-incidences that we both know to be delusional and illusional?'

Toni calmed herself. 'But why would Tom do that?' she asked.

I shook my head. 'I don't really know' I said, which was true. 'But maybe he sensed that there was something I needed and he knew that it would come better from Rachel than from him.'

'I don't get that' Toni said, genuinely puzzled.

'Well I'm only guessing' I said. 'But Tom had showed me that he followed a Hermetic path. When he'd shown me the Hermetic Temple you have under your house. I suppose he assumed I'd have him pigeon-holed as masculine, Hermetic, technical, and unable to see him any other way. Rachel on the other hand –'

'Would be feminine, earth, nature, elemental. Yes, I can see that. But why would Tom want to help you at all? He'd only just met you. He doesn't know you. Why would he want to arrange all that for you?'

'You're married to him' I said. 'You obviously know what he is.'

'What do *you* think he is,' she shot back.

'A man of achievement' I said, shying away from using the term "Adept." What I was really implying was that a man of Tom's spiritual and magical achievement would have a consciousness evolved to the point where it would not be able to shy away from rendering service where such service would improve the human condition as a whole, in however small a way. He must have seen that helping me would somehow be beneficial. That's how I saw it at any rate. You have to understand that what seem to be small events to you can have great significance in the elevation of humanity as a whole, in ways that can often only be seen by a consciousness much more highly evolved than our own. Or simply not devolved down to our level. If Toni got that, she didn't want to discuss it further. Maybe she was concerned that she might compromise Tom. At any rate she left it there.

'So if you're going to stay in London, at least until after the funeral, do you think you should keep a low profile?' she said and I knew that she was referring to the warnings I'd been given.

'No,' I said, 'not entirely.'

'Really?' She was not expecting that answer, evidently. 'What are you going to do?'

'For a start I'm going to see Hesther. Tonight.'

Toni was momentarily non-plussed by that. 'Whatever for?' she asked at last. 'What if she's busy? What if she won't see you?'

I smiled. 'She'll see me' I said and I just knew that she would.

'You want me to come with you?' She wanted to come, I could tell.

'No' I said with no embellishment.

Toni pouted but left it at that. I let it rest too and concentrated on the road as we'd unexpectedly started moving. It didn't last; a hundred yards or so later and we were back in the motionless snarl-up. At least our lane was. The lane next to us still had a bit of crawl left in it until eventually a black Rolls Royce Phantom VI Limousine rolled to a halt alongside us. A liveried chauffeur occupied the driver's seat but when the car came to a halt, the rear passenger window was level with me, if a couple of feet higher. I couldn't help looking to see if I could get a glimpse of the passenger. I could because that passenger was looking right at me. A man of, I'd say, late middle age. Very clean cut, slim, and sharply dressed in an immaculate charcoal-grey suit. White shirt of course, and a tie from one of one of the Guards Regiments, though I couldn't place which one exactly.

I caught this man's gaze and for a moment I swear we were peering down into each other's souls. A wave of fear washed through me because I sensed that I'd encountered this soul before. Back out on the God-forsaken twenty-seventh Aethyr when we'd gone there to save Helen. And I continued to look, held in fascination like this was the face of a cobra preparing to strike. And I could have sworn that the flesh of the face melted right away first to scales, then dissolving, leaving me to stare into the face of a living white grinning skull. The car pulled away and was soon gone before I could regain my bearings.

The sound of a car horn from behind and Toni's insistent 'Stevie!' alerted me to the fact that our lane ahead was moving too. But as I shifted through a couple of gears and caught up with the moving flow, my heart continued to pound. Because a name had planted itself in my consciousness and wouldn't leave. Sable Wyvern. Sable-bloody-Wyvern.

# The Story Episode # 122
# (Moon phase: Day 28)

NOTHING HAPPENED WHEN we got back to Toni's house in Cheyne Walk. Tom wasn't there. Neither was Rachel. Toni was a little distant with me and I think it was because I'd said I didn't want her to come with me to see Hesther. She told me that she was tired and was going to have a lie down, and that she had some business to attend to in the afternoon. It may well have been true but I smiled inwardly, knowing full-well that it was her way of telling me to leave her alone for the day. Stroppy fucking mare. I say that in all humour though – Toni didn't owe me a damn thing and we'd been through so much together and she'd made all the sacrifices. So I could see that she'd feel that I was leaving her out. But I had my reasons.

I needed to be alone with Hesther. I wanted to talk about Helen. My beautiful dead-but-dreaming wife. There were aspects of the intimacy Hesther had shared with Helen that I wanted to discuss. And privacy would afford us an openness that would benefit us both. I'm sure you understand that.

So I spent the day in London. Despite all the warnings. To tell you the truth, in the sunshine of the day I'd forgotten all about them. Traps being laid for me and so on.

What I wanted was clothes. All I had back at Toni's place was a few items of casual gear. Not good enough for me, so I headed up to the West End. To the Burlington Arcade off Piccadilly, to Jermyn Street, Bond Street and Savile Row. I took my time of course, but I went into places where I was a known regular and it pleased me to be remembered.

I ordered a couple of suits from Anderson and Sheppard in Savile Row, who kept my measurements on file, but I bought a couple of suits off the peg from Gieves and Hawkes, begging them to tailor the trouser lengths and the jacket sleeve lengths right away so that I could collect them later. Begging failed, as I'd imagined it would, but money didn't. I would able to collect the suits later that afternoon was how it turned out.

One of the suits was a very sombre charcoal grey, almost black. I'd bought this one specifically to wear to the funeral of Professor Hanford. In Jermyn Street I called in at Turnbull & Asser where I bought a dozen ready to wear shirts. Strolling down the Burlington Arcade and then Bond Street I was able to find cufflinks and ties, shoes and belts - the essential accessories for a man about town - in stores like Crockett & Jones, and Longmire. All in all a happy day. Just like old times.

One thing I will say is that once midday had come and gone, I did begin to feel a little edgy about being out on the London streets. As though the warnings I'd been given were coming to the surface of my consciousness. I tried to put them out of my mind though, and while I was ever looking over my shoulder after that, I saw nothing untoward and never felt threatened in any way. Late in the afternoon, just before I went to collect my purchases, I stopped off at the café inside Sotheby's auction house in Bond street. And it was from there that I made the call to Hesther.

Now you might think I'd left it mighty late to call if I wanted a meeting with her that very evening. And normally you'd probably be right. But I was banking on the fact that she wouldn't be going out or taking business meetings the evening before the funeral, and that she'd be glad of the distraction of talking about Helen. And I had sensed a need in her urgent attempts to get in touch with me while I was in Germany. I was right on all counts. Hesther sounded altogether pleased to hear from me and even more pleased that I'd wanted to meet up with her. That's the impression I got.

'Will you come alone or will Toni be coming with you?' she asked.

'Just me.'

She paused, ever so slightly, before saying 'That'll be nice, just the two of us. We've never really been able to relax and talk, just us. I imagine it will do us both the world of good.'

I have to admit that if anything could put me off my guard it was Hesther's voice. That perfect English Lady accent. Sent shivers through me when she wasn't using it to make cutting remarks at my expense. Still does now when I think about it. Anyway, we made an arrangement to meet at seven-thirty in her Camden Town house. I suppose she didn't want to stay in the professor's Hampstead place the night before the funeral and I could understand why. The place would be full of disparate energies that would unnecessarily stimulate her consciousness, vulnerable as she was bound to be. As an Adept she would be able to control that. But I could understand why she wouldn't want to make the effort. In her shoes, I'd have gone home to

Camden Town too.

I didn't analyse it beyond that as I made the rounds of the shops I'd visited and collected my purchases. After that I got a cab to take me back to Cheyne Walk. Once there I took my new things up to my room, hung them in the wardrobes and came back down to the kitchen for a cup of coffee. No sign of Toni but Rachel was there. I was surprised she hadn't heard me come in and I said so once we'd said our hellos.

'I heard you come in' Rachel said, 'but I was busy in here. I wouldn't have gone without coming to say hi, don't you worry.'

'What, you'd come up to my room and let yourself in without knocking to catch me with no clothes on again?' I was just having a bit of fun with her.

She looked me up and down. 'I could have your trousers off in no time if I wanted' she said. 'An' that's a big *if*, remember.'

I did catch a memory of the time we'd spent in the Nature Temple in the basement and I realised that she had a point. I did find her to be incredibly sexually charismatic. But I managed to persuade that thought to slide away. Something that Rachel noticed.

'Well you've been working hard on yerself, ain't yer?'

'I've been shown how ugly I am,' I said.

'Now who's told yer that?' she said. 'Some daft Kraut?'

'Actually he was English. Just living over there.'

'Same difference then, if he's living there. He'll have grown into their ways. People nearly always do.'

'He seemed pretty English to me once I got to know him' I said, thinking of how Harvey had fooled me with his German accent when we'd first encountered him. 'You seen Toni,' I asked, changing the subject.

'She went out about an hour ago. Didn't say where she was going or when she'd be back.' Rachel looked at me for a moment, like she was reading me. Which I suppose she was because she said 'You're off out tonight aren't yer? On yer own.'

'Yes' I said. 'I have to visit someone.'

'Well whoever it is, just you be on yer guard, yer know what I mean?'

'Why? What do you know?' I asked, a little nervous that she should have said this after the warnings I'd got in Germany.

'I don't really know anything' Rachel said with a shrug. 'Except you're vulnerable now. I can see that much. And you're a nice geezer. Wouldn't want nothing to happen to yer.'

I said nothing and the silence almost had her blushing.

'Serious' she said. 'Just you be careful. I get a feeling about you sometimes. Like there's something wants to harm you and you have no idea about it. Wish I could tell yer more.'

'Don't worry' I said. 'You've told me enough.'

I leaned towards her to kiss her on the cheek but at the last moment she turned her face so that I kissed her full on the lips and before I knew it she'd slid her tongue into my mouth. Just as quick she removed it then stood back a step and laughed.

'There' she said. 'That's a warning not to take nothing for granted. And don't pretend yer didn't like it.'

I laughed too. 'Of course I liked it' I said.

She was suddenly serious. 'You need to get out of London. You do, yer know. You need to go look for nature. Like I showed yer. Balance them elements. Like I told yer. Yer not ever gonna be safe until yer do.'

God bless her, she really did mean it and she really did care about me for some reason. But I worried about her telling me to get out of London. Seemed like everyone who professed to have my best interests at heart was telling me that. Yet still I felt there was business to finish before I could. I was definitely torn right then.

'Just you be careful tonight,' Rachel said quietly. 'Come back here safe and sound. Then decide what yer gonna do in the morning.'

I said I'd do just that. But I have to say I was suddenly afraid. I went back up to my room after sinking a cup of coffee and making small talk with Rachel and I wanted a shower. I stepped into the bathroom and stopped dead in my tracks. When I switched the light on I could see them on the tiled floor. Wet footprints. Small footprints. A girl's footprints. I knew who's footprints even before I got down on my knees, tears in my eyes, to kiss them. They were Helen's. My darling beautiful immortal beloved dead wife had been there.

I put my lips against the watery shape of the footprint right in front of me and a flood of Helen washed through me so that I sobbed and couldn't stop. Until I heard it. Sobbing, in harmony with mine. From behind me in the bedroom. Helen sobbing. I got up quickly and returned to the bedroom but it was empty. Disappointed, I wandered over to the window to look out on the Thames. On Isis. And I didn't even turn when I heard the voice behind me – Helen's voice – saying 'Stevie don't go. Don't go.'

# *The Story Episode # 123 (Moon phase: Day 28)*

I WENT. DESPITE Helen's imploring sobbing voice, I went. An hour later, after I'd spent that time standing on the embankment staring into the river, I'd calmed myself enough to know that I had to go. And actually for Helen's sake.

*Stevie don't go. Don't go.* Don't go because she was here and didn't want me to leave her? Don't go because Hesther might manipulate the memory of events? I'd see through that. *Helen I'd see through that.*

Helen you should know that. You and me, we're one and the same. No one could persuade me of a lie concerning you my darling immortal beloved beautiful wife. No one. So trust me. Wait for me. Wait for me here even though you're with me always. *Please.* Please Helen, please wait. I have to go. I *am* going.

I went. And I found myself in north London. Camden Town. Hot evening. Dark low oppressive cloud about to disgorge heavy summer rain. And maybe send some thunder with it. That's how it was when I turned up at Hesther's house some ten minutes early.

As I pressed the doorbell the first heavy drops of water started to fall and by the time Hesther answered the deluge was upon us. So I stepped inside, pressing very close to Hesther to do so and I could swear there was a glint in her eye to go with her smile as I squeezed past.

'You're early' Hesther said without criticism. 'Did you drag this weather with you?'

I smiled at that. I loved how English the comment was. A mention of the weather before we'd even said our 'hellos.' But I denied all responsibility for the rain. What I did notice was how dim and cosy Hesther had the lighting. In the hallway and from what I could see through the open door, in the living room too. Yes, amazingly I noticed this before I noticed what Hesther was wearing.

Now I normally describe what Hesther wears and I'm going to do that here, but it's not going to be as exciting as usual. Not for you I imagine. Because she was wearing a very short silk-print wrap, held together by a silk sash tied around her slender waist with a casual twist. One of those knots that if I tied it would slide open within seconds to have me looking for all the world a dismal pervert exposing my genitals. Of course the sash didn't slacken at all on Hesther and the wrap stayed wrapped and just clingy enough, without being vulgar, for me to speculate that she wore nothing beneath it.

'I was running late,' she explained as she showed me through to the living room. 'I haven't had chance to dress. I hope you don't mind. I've just stepped out of the bath.'

Now I've already told you about the effect that her voice has on me, and honestly, the way she said 'bath' with that elongated plumy vowel sound - *baaahhhth* – sent a ripple of pleasure running through me and even had my penis twitching.

I think Hesther could sense that sudden change of energy in me because she asked if I was alright. I assured her that I was as I lowered myself into the plush armchair she indicated. I watched her slide onto the sofa at an angle to me, and close so that I could luxuriate in her sexuality. Be in no doubt that she could turn that sexual charisma on and off like a tap. And she'd turned it on for me. I don't think she could help herself. She knew what I was and she loved to tease.

I was fascinated, watching her wriggle her gorgeous toes before arranging her long tanned legs on that sofa. I've mentioned Hesther's feet before and I know it makes me sound like a fetishist, but the fact is she had the most beautiful feet I've ever seen. Nothing more certain than to say she'd never crammed them into anything ill-fitting, no matter how fashionable.

'Don't you want to take your jacket off?' Hesther asked.

I should mention that I was wearing one of the suits I'd bought from Gieves & Hawkes earlier in the day. I'd sat down without taking the jacket off because I was fixated. Hesther, welcoming and friendly, had that effect on me. I stood and removed the jacket but Hesther made no move to take it from me so I draped it over the arm of a nearby chair. Then Hesther got up, swinging those fabulous legs onto the Persian rug in front of the sofa.

'Some wine?' she asked.

'I'm driving, remember?' I said.

She raised her eyebrows. 'Are you?' she asked. 'Well a glass won't hurt.'

So that was that. She headed for the kitchen leaving me to catch a waft of her perfume as she passed in front of me. And of course I recognised it. Did you seriously imagine I wouldn't? *Very Irresistible* by Givenchy, just in case you're wondering.

Moments later she was back with a bottle and two glasses. She set one glass on an occasional table and poured for me. I hadn't expected wine from a box, but I hadn't expected this either: *Chassagne-Montrachet, La Boudriotte 1er Cru, Domaine Jean-Noel Gagnard*. Now I'm no wine snob but I have spent a lot of time in the company of people who are, and some of it has rubbed off. I certainly knew what she was serving me and that it was rather special for a casual evening like this. I sipped my wine as Hesther poured a glass for herself and eased herself back onto that sofa in a single easy movement without spilling a drop.

Rain battered at the windows behind the curtains and I couldn't help but enjoy the warmth of the room, the coziness of the lighting and the rich bouquet of the wine. I became pleasantly relaxed in these surroundings, in the company of the beautiful Hesther. I hope I'm describing the atmosphere as well as the physical setting. Pure, absolute romance. And I couldn't understand it but I worked hard to control my response to it.

Even when Hesther said 'You look lonely over there in that

chair. Why don't you come sit with me?'

'I'm fine' I said without putting my guard up. Actually I was pleased with myself because sitting on that sofa with Hesther was a very attractive prospect. And I'd resisted it. Without having to work at it. I wanted to be with her as a friend. Not see her as a potential sexual partner. I realised that right then. I wanted so much for Hesther to be a friend. Because of the experience we'd shared in loving Helen. Because of her mind. Because of her achievement. Because of her charm. And yes I suppose, because she was so beautiful. Allow me a remnant of superficiality. But none of this meant anything to Hesther.

'I know you're fine,' she said. 'But please come sit with me. I'd like you to. We can forget the world while we talk. None of it between us to intrude.'

That voice. And a simple request. And me thinking that she just wanted to forget all of the burdens for a couple of hours and talk about the past. How could I resist? I couldn't. So I took my glass and went over to sit on the sofa. I lounged at one end while Hesther lounged at the other with her gorgeous legs and lovely feet stretching out to me like an invitation. And it was hard not to just move my hand a little and stroke them. But I managed not to.

'Thank you so much for coming tonight Steven' Hesther said, and I detected a hitherto unnoticed sadness. 'I didn't want to be alone. Not tonight.'

I knew what she meant. The funeral tomorrow. The secular and religious-exoteric nature of that funeral. Hiding what the professor truly was from a world that would never ever understand.

'I wanted to see you' I said, wanting her to imagine me having the need and not her. Chivalrous? Maybe. I'm not an empath. Not in the way Toni's an empath. But I can catch the mood of a beautiful woman because like it or not that's a gift I have. And I can't help but strive to give her what I feel she needs. Hesther raised a glass at any rate, and I got the feeling that she knew that I was saying what I felt she wanted to hear and was thanking me for it.

'Do you mind if I stretch out my legs?' Hesther asked. 'Believe me, I mean nothing sinister by it. Honestly.'

'Sure,' I said.

I didn't mind her putting her feet in my lap. It added to the sense of cosy romance, what with the warmth and the sound of the driving rain and the dim lighting and two friends sharing a bottle of wine. So I watched as she stretched those long slim tanned legs and placed those darling feet in my lap and wriggled her toes again. And I couldn't help but glimpse beneath that wrap and looked away quickly enough when I realised that she probably wasn't wearing underwear.

'I think we should talk about Helen' Hesther said, once she'd made herself comfortable. 'That's what you want too, isn't it?'

I did and I said so.

'You probably want to know how it was with us. How I seduced her into my life,' she said.

'I don't think it was anything other than beautiful' I said, wondering at her choice of words. 'But yes, I'd like to know everything. Everything you're comfortable with telling me.'

She took a sip of her wine. 'The two of you absolutely broke my heart, you know. Hurt me more than I imagined I could be hurt.'

Maybe it's because I held her feet in my hands and the contact allowed her to better transfer her feelings, or maybe it was because the emotional pain was still so strong within her and flooded out, but a terrible sadness washed through me. Hesther turned her face away and she was fighting hard not to cry. And all I could do to help was stroke those beautiful feet of hers.

'I can't be alone tonight Stevie. I can't. I need someone to hold me. Come to bed with me and hold me. Just hold me and we can talk. Stevie please. There is no one else.'

# *The Story Episode # 124 (Moon phase: Day 28)*

ONE IS THE All. And if the All did not contain the All, the All would be nothing. Isis labours to bring together the scattered parts of the All and fulfilment results in Horus.

Once you dedicate yourself to treading a certain occult path, you dedicate yourself to the labour of freeing the divine spark. In mystery schools throughout the ages, at all times, this has been known to result in an ecstatic manifestation, with the greatest ecstatic expression being sexual. We are made from the stuff of Titans that Zeus scattered, so of course we often react sexually to the presence of the divine. This also gives us the destructive and violent aspect of our human nature. Which I'm sure sounds like gibberish to you. Doesn't make it any less true if it does though.

At any rate, those were thoughts that crossed my mind as Hesther and I lay entwined and naked in her bed, wrapped in a soft white duvet. A room lit only by candles and fragranced by Ylang Ylang incense. Close as I was to her, I was also intoxicated by the sensual hint of Hesther's perfume, the aptly named *Very Irresistible*, by Givenchy. Aptly named because despite Hesther's claim to innocent intent – *just hold me and we can talk* – it was inevitable that there'd be more to it than that.

How could I resist? I mean we did talk. Even during. About the only time we weren't talking was when our hot mouths pressed together. But we weren't talking about my darling wife Helen. I followed as the Adept ritualized our act. Chants and songs of praise from Hesther the Adept with me the neophyte providing the responses where I could.

Now I don't want you to picture this as a formal sexual experience. Not like the ritualized sex I'd shared with Toni back in New Zealand. This wasn't ritualized sex, rather it was sex, ritualized. I do hope you understand the difference. Can see the difference. The sex that Hesther and I shared with each other you could describe as love-making. There was passion. But there was also intimacy. There was tenderness. And there was an overwhelming sense of giving. Giving to each other. Giving to the One and to the All. Flooding the room and universe with layered shades of experience; a sense of continual creation in praise of the One and All and for the One and All.

From the moment Hesther had given just the merest pull at the silk sash around her waist and the robe had fallen open we'd understood the inevitability of what would come. Understood from the way she'd shrugged and shimmied so that the robe would slide from her shoulders to expose her soft naked skin to the glow of the candles. From how she'd sat on the edge of her soft bed with her legs open, giving me a glimpse of her glistening sex between the soft black wisps of hair. From all that followed. Her reaching to loosen my clothes – trousers, shirt, tie – so that they all but fell from me. Her then taking charge to remove them. Letting me feel her warm breath on my skin where her lips passed close by. Pulling down my shorts so that only by force of will – performing complex mental arithmetic exercises – did I keep my tingling penis in check.

The world in slow motion and soft focus with me standing

naked by the bed as she slid beneath the fluffy white duvet in one movement, as exquisite as it was sensual. Responding as she reached out to take - ever-so-gently - my penis in her fingers to pull me towards her; showing me rather than telling me what she wanted. Me sliding under that duvet beside her, gasping as her fingers rolled back my foreskin, forsaking any effort I'd been making to forestall the arousal coursing through me. Both of us committing to the overwhelming need for pleasure. Pleasure given, not demanded.

Of course I held her the way she'd intimated she'd wanted to be held. And her arms wrapped around me in response, her legs entwined in mine, those soft feet rubbing against me, urging my arousal. My hot hard penis pressed against her. Her soft fingertips running the length of it so that the very energy created shifted my state of consciousness. Our mouths close but not touching. The tip of her tongue tracing my lips and retreating as I offered my tongue to greet it. Feeling her fingers reach between her legs and catching that blissful scent as it mixed with the incense and her perfume. Entering her almost without knowing, feeling only the sensation of her soft, hot, moist vagina closing around me. And rolling on that bed in this charged atmosphere, responding as best I could to the chants she whispered in vibration out into the universe.

Each of us taking the lead. Twisting and placing each other in positions attractive to us. Giving pleasure with the instruments of our sex, supplemented by our fingers, our hands, our mouths, lips, tongues, the hot breath of our lives, our feet and toes, our hair, our skin, our nails.

Touch and penetration, twin pleasures. Until I knelt upright, deep inside her with her laying back on the soft bed, almost buried in the fluffy white cloud of duvet with her legs crossed at the ankles behind my neck as she orchestrated our simultaneous orgasm; squeezing my penis with pulsing contractions of her vagina and calling out a secret name in a language I didn't recognise.

So intense was the shared orgasm that we both lost consciousness for a second or two as our sacrifice went out to the Gods. *Le petit mort*, as the French call it. The little death. Afterwards, we found ourselves in a state of bliss, wrapped around each other under the soft duvet with the thunder exploding outside and rumbling the thanks of the Gods, consecrating the blessing we'd given them.

Minutes passed before I asked in a whisper, 'Was that what it was like for you? With Helen?'

Hesther moaned, opened her eyes. 'I'd say it was closer to the intimacy *you* shared with her' she said. 'But beyond the purely physical, emotionally it was exactly the same. Exactly.'

She turned her face away and wiped a tear from her cheek. My heart lurched at the sight, welling up with compassion.

She turned to me, half-smiling. 'Don't feel sad for me' she said.

'I'll try not to' I replied. 'But you won't stop me wishing happiness for you.'

She smiled at that and said 'Happiness can be so superficial. I think that what we all strive for is fulfilment.'

I had to agree with that, wishing I'd chosen my words with more care. I could see that she was – Adept or no – in a delicate state of emotional balance. I'm not saying that she wasn't aware of or in control of her feelings and the complex balance of the structures of energy she'd woven within and around herself; just that I didn't want her to have to expend any effort in maintaining them as a result of my clumsiness.

'You know' she said, 'when I first introduced Helen to the Dionysian rituals at the family estate, I did it for selfish motives in a way.'

'I don't believe you did that out of lust' I said. 'You didn't seduce her. Not in that way.'

I genuinely didn't believe Hesther had done that. It would have been demeaning to her and to Helen. And Hesther was already an accomplished occultist back then.

She stroked my cheek, a beautiful if casual gesture. 'Lust was a factor. No point in me denying it. But the truth is I was in love with her. I didn't really know her then. We hadn't been dating, to use that childish and inadequate term; but I loved her. I knew I did. And love isn't a word I use lightly. Not then. Not now.'

I didn't speak right away. Talk of Helen and of love, well that tugged at me. Tugged at my heart. Perhaps I didn't like to hear someone else speak of love for Helen. Romantic, emotional, sexual, soul-bonding love. I think I suddenly became possessive.

'Seems Helen had that gift' I said at last, unable to think of anything else to say.

Hesther ignored it though, perhaps understanding that I'd only said it in order to give a response.

'I wanted to show her something more of the mysteries' Hesther said. 'To give her a taste. Hoping she'd be sympathetic to the energy. I wanted more for her.'

'So you thought that the frenzy of a Dionysian Maenad ritual would be appropriate?'

I smiled as I said that, stroking Hesther's hair. I was just teasing her. The Dionysian ritual is wild and utterly sexual. But executed with the proper forms and with all the guidance, experience and safeguards in place, it would have been safe. Hesther laughed.

'Was there a male sacrifice?' I asked, and I was deadly serious.

Hesther thought about it for a moment then said 'Yes. There was.'

The hairs on the back of my neck began to tingle. I could sense that something important was coming. 'Tell me' I said.

Hesther became suddenly serious. 'We milked the semen of a captive male, blindfolded and bound to a wooden frame. His head covered with a leather hood. We offered his semen as a sacrifice. Living sperm as a sacrifice.'

'So you masturbated a man as a sacrifice' I said. 'I bet you didn't have to advertise for a volunteer.'

Hesther smiled. 'No,' she said. 'The man was appropriately serious. Experienced. And we didn't masturbate him with our hands. We brought about the sacrifice with our lips.' Her eyes had brightened and her smile became lascivious.

'Go on' I said. 'I know there's more.'

'Helen was last. She had the honour of bringing about the sacrifice. And no, she didn't get him to come in her mouth.'

'Why would I have cared if she had?' I asked. It was a reasonable question. I wouldn't have cared, really I wouldn't. But I just knew that there was more to this anecdote.

'No, you wouldn't, I believe you. You're beyond that. But the way it happened was that Helen removed her lips at the appropriate moment and finished him with her fingers, directing the living sperm into a chilled silver dish. The temperature would kill the sperm instantly. An appropriate sacrifice.' A raising of her eyebrows at that. A *what do you think of that?* gesture.

'There's something else. Something you haven't told me yet' I said. I still had this tingling at the back of my neck.

Hesther turned to me, holding me with her stunning crystal-blue eyes. 'The name of the man' she said. 'It's a name you've come across.'

'Go on' I said.

'Not his mundane everyday name' Hesther whispered. 'But a

name you've heard. It was Sable Wyvern.' She paused. 'College of Arms? That Sable Wyvern.'

# The Story Episode # 125
# (Moon phase: 2/Day 1)

PERSONAL WILL IS nothing. Personal power is nothing. Belief in them is the root of failure. Reliance on them is a guarantee of failure. It's easy to understand this intellectually. But that isn't enough. You have to apply it. All the circumstances of your life come about as a result of subconscious activity. The subconscious sets in motion the creative impulse that brings about your wants and desires. Your ego, or if you prefer, your personality, is unique in the universe. The subconscious is not.

The subconscious is an aspect of the Astral Light, the One Thing. God. The subconscious is a mediator. The subconscious channels the divine will to bring about the circumstances of your *true* wants and desires. You can train your self-conscious individuality to direct the subconscious to bring about your conscious desires.

This is the secret of success. In all things. You becoming a centre of expression for the Primal Universal Will. All desires, all wants, are a gift from God. Your duty is to work to fulfil those desires. We've been through this before. And we've also mentioned that when a skilled occult practitioner uses this power of direction to control the thoughts and behaviour of another human being, this amounts to sorcery. Sorcerers inevitably pay a price for their successes brought about in this way. And even for their unsuccessful attempts. The price is spiritual. And it is terrible.

I can remember telling you when I first introduced you to Hesther that I didn't believe her to be a sorceress. Telling you that I just couldn't believe that about her. Yet lying next to her under that warm fluffy white duvet I have to say that the thought crossed my mind.

'What are you thinking?' Hesther's sleepy voice said next to me, bringing me out of my deep reverie.

'I'm wondering why I'm still here' I said, not looking at her and continuing to stare at the white ceiling.

'You're still here because you've been satisfying a desire. More or less all night. On and off.'

I could sense a smile behind those words but I wasn't going to be directed by them. 'Are you sure I haven't been satisfying yours?' I said.

She stroked my leg with the soft sole of her foot. 'Well it *was* satisfying. I won't deny that' she said.

I said nothing. Continued to stare at that ceiling. And yes, that was self-indulgent when I should have been straight and honest with her, should have told her of my suspicions. But in the end it didn't matter.

'Oh no' she said. 'You don't think that. Seriously?'

'Think what?' I asked. Disingenuously because I knew full-well what she meant.

'That I brought you to me by means of sorcery. My God, is that really how you think of me? My God.'

This was genuine surprise and disappointment. I could tell. And she was a little upset by it. I turned to her, understanding that the least she deserved was an honest exchange.

'Look, what do I know?' I said. 'About anything? It's just that I hadn't intended for us to. . .' I hesitated, not having the right words to describe what we'd done. I didn't want to say 'make love' but I didn't want to cheapen it by using some crude mechanical description either.

'No, you didn't come here for sex. I know you didn't. And I admit that the thought had crossed my mind that I might like to. . .' she seemed to be having the same descriptive difficulty I'd had. But she continued. 'But that's all there was to it. A desire. And one that wouldn't have been fulfilled if you hadn't been receptive to it yourself. You weren't bound by any sorcerer's spell.'

She was all matter-of-fact and I knew that I'd hurt her and that she wasn't lying. It was strange that, because I realised I'd thought of her as being beyond simple emotional hurt like that.

A wave of compassion for her washed through me so that I just wanted to turn to her and hold her but I held back. I knew she wouldn't be receptive to it. Not right then. And I also knew that she was right. About me. I'd been working hard to control the ugly side of my nature. But what Hesther had hoped for hadn't been ugly. It isn't ugly when two people both want that same thing; to give comfort to each other through sexual pleasure. So of course I'd been receptive to what she wanted. I hadn't made the slightest effort to fight it. And if my immature thoughts hadn't been clouded by a million other things - dark things - like Sable-bloody-Wyvern, for example, they wouldn't have taken me down this dark path of thinking ill of Hesther.

'It's safe to hold me' Hesther said gently, surprising me.

This reminded me why she was an Adept and I was just a cork being tossed about on the ocean. I turned to her and she was smiling, welcoming, beautiful, ever-so-slightly dishevelled. And I slid my arms around her as she wrapped hers around me. We held each other close, the scent of sex and sweat and her perfume seductively heavy between us. And she let me cry for a few minutes.

'You feel better?' Hesther whispered softly once my sobbing had ceased.

'Yeah' I said.

'So ask me the question you need to ask,' she said.

'I want to know the connection' I said. 'Between Sable Wyvern, whoever he really bloody is, and Helen.'

'He wanted her, I can tell you that much' Hesther said.

'Well we all bloody wanted her; or so it seems' I blurted out.

'Touché,' Hesther said. Then added 'But there is something else. Something that spoke to me but stayed hidden behind a veil.'

Now this got my interest. 'Go on' I said.

'I got the feeling that he didn't just want her for himself. Not in the way you imagine a man wanting a girl like Helen.'

'Keep talking.' I was urging her, but Hesther shook her head.

'I couldn't get to it' she said.

I knew what she was saying. She'd tried. And whatever it was she'd been seeking had been hidden from her. That would take some doing, to hide a vibration of energy from someone as accomplished as Hesther. Especially when that vibration concerned someone she shared a bond with. But why would anyone go to the trouble of creating such a veil? I sat up suddenly with a flash of realization. Yes, you know, 16, The Tower, C Major, Peh, Mars, Mouth, Iron.

'He's the reason we had to run away, isn't he?' I said. 'It's because of him.'

'I don't know' Hesther said, sounding puzzled. 'Is it? What did Helen tell you?'

I shook my head. 'She didn't tell me anything. She just said we had to go. Somewhere far away. So we went.'

Hesther looked at me in astonishment. 'Really? You ran away and left your whole life behind? Just because Helen said she needed to?'

Yes I know how that sounds. And you can see how it sounded to Hesther too. But it's the truth.

'Yes,' I said. 'I mean, I asked her. I asked her for some details. But she never told me. And there were times she seemed scared. So I did what she asked. I gave her what she needed. I loved her.'

Hesther leaned over and kissed me on the cheek. 'What you share with her transcends human love Stevie' she said.

And I damn-near cried again. But managed to control myself. 'Look,' I said. 'I can't get beyond this Sable Wyvern. What the hell could he have wanted with Helen? And why did it frighten her so much?'

'You can't be certain it's all because of him,' Hesther said.

I stayed calm. I was very calm. 'We know that coincidence is an illusion' I said. 'And this name, this creature keeps popping up. Everywhere. All the time. Even the stupid name. What's his real name by the way? His everyday name, as you put it?'

Hesther shook her head. 'I'm not going to tell you' she said, surprising me. 'I can't. You'll have to find out some other way.' She hesitated a moment. 'But you should leave it Stevie. Really, leave it. They're not to be trifled with.'

'They? Who're they?'

'I shouldn't say more. I shouldn't have said that. If the professor was still here he could. . . But for your own good Steven. Leave it.'

'What about Helen?' I said, ignoring her mention of her own loss, the professor. 'What about Helen's good?'

Hesther didn't answer that. She looked away.

'Fine,' I said. 'I understand. Somebody had Helen running scared and you feel the same about them. They frighten you. But I don't have anything to lose. I just want Helen safe. She's not moving on. She's lingering. And something's holding her. And you've near as dammit admitted that it's something to do with this Sable Wyvern character. Who keeps appearing everywhere. So I'll find out. And I'll start with the College of bloody Arms. Whatever the hell that is. That's where Tom said he was from. Somebody there's got to know about this bastard. I'll find out his real name and take it from there.'

'They'll destroy you Stevie.' Hesther looked genuinely concerned.

'What do I care?' I said. 'With Helen where she is, like I say, I've nothing to lose. And anyway, who's going to destroy me? They? Do you mean the College of Arms?' I laughed at that because I'd meant it as a joke. Some stupid barely known archaic institution full of idiotic semi-academics giving each other idiotic names.

'You'd better ask Toni's husband' Hesther said, and my blood ran cold. 'Ask Tom.'

I hadn't told Hesther anything of what had happened in Germany and she hadn't asked. And I didn't mention the Rolls Royce incident that had occurred as I'd driven back from the airport the previous day. But it didn't matter. Hesther was warning me of a danger that had already begun to manifest; on the streets of Berlin. And there'd already been collateral damage. Heidi. Maybe the Major.

If Hesther was afraid, I wouldn't endanger her by pressing her on the subject. And she was right to point me in the direction of Tom. After all, he'd first mentioned Sable Wyvern to me by announcing the bastard's death. When he'd have known the name would mean nothing to me. Why had he done that? Yes, Hesther was right. Tom would be the right person to talk to in the first instance. I sighed inwardly at the thought. Another fucking cryptic blue-blooded Adept. Things were never easy, were they?

'I'd better be going' I said, looking at my watch and noticing that it was six-thirty. I'm going to need to shower and change ready for the funeral.'

'You can shower here' Hesther said.

'But then I'd have to put on a worn shirt, underwear and socks,' I said. 'I hate that. I'd have to take another shower back at Toni's anyway.'

'Not necessarily' Hesther said, smiling and sliding out of bed to wander over to a dressing table.

She slid open a draw and pulled out a brand new white shirt, new black socks and some silk shorts. I raised a quizzical eyebrow.

'Well I did want you to stay' she said, smiling. 'So I had a reasonable expectation. It was a true desire. Honest.'

I shook my head and said nothing. Adepts eh?

# The Story Episode # 126 (Moon phase: 2/Day 1)

AT THE FUNERAL service I felt my unique individuality in a way I hadn't done for quite a while. I was aware of the people attending as separate entities. I viewed them like I was inspecting them from a remote location. Viewing myself standing among them. With Toni next to me. And Tom next to her. I don't think Tom knew the professor terribly well, and didn't hold him in great esteem from the few words I'd heard him speak about the dear departed man. All the same, he kept his own counsel about that on this occasion and in this company. As was right and respectful.

Hesther of course was the focus of attention. She wore Chanel from top to toe and it was the correct choice. Classic Chanel black dress. Straight black mid-calf overcoat despite the sunshine and the warmth. Beautiful Chanel court shoes with a discreet hint of sparkle. Quilted black Chanel handbag. And of course, Chanel sunglasses. I guessed that she'd be wearing *No. 5* perfume, but I didn't get close enough to find out.

I scanned the crowd and recognised some people. People who'd been part of the Order when darling Helen and me had undergone our initiation as Neophytes. They all avoided me of course. Averted gazes and backs being turned being the order of the day. I even got the feeling that Toni was keeping a little distance from me. But I could understand that.

Most of the people were unknown to me though. Academic colleagues past and present I guessed. Fewer people than I'd expected but still enough of a crowd to get lost in while not filling the Anglican church where the service took place. Which was Christ Church Hampstead, in Hampstead square, just so you know. Appropriately close to the professor's house too.

Now you might think it hypocritical to hold a funeral service in a Christian Church for a man who was an occult Adept following the Hermetic path of the Western Way. But you'd be mistaken. Allow me to digress. The traditions of the native mysteries were absorbed by the Christian Church – and vice versa. A symbiotic relationship with the Church establishing itself by maintaining and not opposing the native traditions, while practitioners of those traditions used the Church as a framework to carry the native traditions safely through to the future. The keepers, mediators and transmitters of the native tradition appropriated the framework of the new religion as an accessible receptacle for those traditions.

You'd be wrong to look at the church as a purely secular institution anyway; it's only chronic ignorance that would have you believe that the early Christian religion wasn't delivering a mystical mystery path to its followers. The early religion was deeply spiritual in a way that would be described as heretical just a few centuries on. The secularization of the established Christian Churches is a relatively recent phenomenon. And I wouldn't know where to begin to explain the content and meaning of the Gnostic Christian mysteries. You can look for yourself at the texts found at Nag-Hamadi and Qumran. And you should understand that some of the greatest occult philosophers were devoutly Christian. You may be amazed to hear that this wasn't due to a fear of persecution, but rather because of the access Christianity gave them to the beauty of the occult-spiritual nature that they were working with. For them there was no separation between their occult or alchemical or native traditional work and the spiritual meditations of Christian prayer and the mystery of the mass. Just what do you imagine transubstantiation to be if not an alchemical process, for Christ's sake? Look, I'm sorry. But I know how many people are dismissive of the church these days, rightly pointing out that it's an almost completely secular organization. You'll find that belief even among the dwindling numbers who regularly attend. Nevertheless, the keys to the mysteries can still be found within the established Christian Churches. And the foundation of a religion gives focus to the occult path you seek. If you indeed choose to become a seeker. I'm going to tell you right now that for my own part, *my* foundation was once Celtic Christianity and the Hidden Church of The Grail. My roots are in England of course. Having said that, you *can* create a path of your own that needs no such foundation. And more and more people are doing just that. Just don't be quick to dismiss the spiritual occult secrets held safely within Christianity and some other organized religions.

Are you still with me? Oh good. Because I know that that was a huge digression. And you want to hear about events. You want narrative. I understand that. So I'm going to skip beyond the funeral and the tasteful and restrained reception that followed in the professor's house. Because nothing of note happened. Not even knowing looks between Hesther and me.

I will just say this though. There were three men there I didn't recognise, but who made me feel a little uneasy. I couldn't say why. They hovered respectfully close to Hesther, I thought, without bothering her. And it's not like they seemed to be a little cabal. They weren't bunched together all the time. They did seem to know others among the mourners because they did their share of meeting and greeting and making small-talk. So I don't know what it was, but for me they stood out.

All of them were of late middle age, making them a generation younger than the professor. All of them dressed impeccably too. Very expensive and understated English clothing. Gentlemen's clothing. These were men familiar with the tailors and establishments I frequented. But there was something about all of them that seemed to say 'old families, old money.' Nothing showy about the way they wore these clothes.

Other than that, the funeral was uneventful. So I left after half an hour or so. I said a discreet goodbye to Hesther, told Toni and Tom that I was leaving, then drove back to Toni and Tom's house in Chelsea. I should mention here that I was starting to feel uncomfortable about staying with them. I know their house was big enough for me to hide in unseen, but all the same I was very aware of not wanting to outstay my welcome. So I decided to check into a hotel. In fact I decided to do it that same afternoon. Somewhere in the West End would suit me.

When I got back to the house in Cheyne walk it seemed cold and empty. I think this is because I'd decided to leave and I no longer saw it as home. At any rate, I went up to my room and started packing my things. I mean, I wouldn't leave until Toni and Tom got back so that I could thank them, but I wanted to be ready.

It didn't take long for me to pack of course. And it seemed so beastly quiet in the house all alone that I even opened the windows to allow some of the sounds of the city to break through. It provided a soundtrack that I actually enjoyed. Then of course I had to set about booking a room.

My favourite London boutique hotel is actually in west London rather than the West End. The Hempel in Craven Hill Gardens, W2. Designed by the gorgeous and impossibly talented Anouska Hempel, this minimalist city-centre paradise is unmatched in London as far as I'm concerned. And I *have* stayed at the Dorchester and Claridges among others. So the Hempel for me then. But could I get a room there? Could I fuck. Annoying but not soul-destroying.

I did manage to get a room at the Cavendish in Jermyn Street, W1. Absolute West End. I booked a room and a residents' car parking space and told them to expect me any time from late afternoon. Well that was that. Nothing more for me to do. So down to the kitchen for coffee. Outside my room on the landing, and my God the house did seem quiet. Almost spooky I'd say. Even though it was mid-afternoon and sunny outside. My footsteps padded on the deep pile carpet but I could still hear them. And I definitely heard the click of the door to my room shutting. I even stopped and turned to look. And there it was, shut when I'd left it ajar. But I didn't think much of it. I'd left the window open. Must have been a draft that had shut it. That's what I told myself but I did find myself looking around and keeping all my senses alert the way you would if you were wandering around a haunted house. I'd bloody well gone and spooked myself. I laughed inwardly at the thought and that calmed me.

The kitchen was empty and spotless so I assumed that Rachel had been and gone. I made some coffee and sat at the kitchen island to drink it, wondering how long Toni and Tom would be. I actually wanted to get going and move into the hotel.

I decided I'd take a nap. I'd only had sleep in fits and starts at Hesther's place the previous night so a nap would do me good. I fairly tripped up the stairs in good spirits but stopped dead when I noticed my door ajar, as I'd originally left it. Now a breeze might push the door shut. And I'd heard the click of the latch when it happened. But a breeze couldn't have opened the bloody thing. A cold chill ran through me. A sudden sense of not being alone. I turned quickly and could have sworn I glimpsed a shadow duck out of sight around a corner at the end of the landing. I could feel my heart racing with adrenaline-fuelled pounding. A click. My door. I turned again and it was closed. My skin creeping all over. A noise behind me so I turned again. And there he was. A man, beautifully suited and booted. Just by that corner at the end of the landing. He was smiling but there was no comfort for me in that.

'You're preparing to leave then Steven?' this man said. 'It is Steven, isn't it?'

The door clicked behind me and I turned again definitely expecting to see someone, expecting to be trapped. But there was no one there. I turned as the man behind me laughed. But when I turned, he'd gone. Gone! Not that it mattered. Because I knew damn well who it was. It was Sable Wyvern.

# The Story Episode # 127
# (Moon phase: 2/Day 1)

I DON'T SCARE easily. I know, I know, if you've been following this story you may be forgiven for thinking that I do. So I should mention that there's a difference between scaring easily and scaring often. For example, you may scare easily but at the same time know what things or situations scare you - so you go out of your way to avoid those things. Thus you never seem to be afraid. If people notice this at all they may imagine, since they never see you afraid, that *you don't scare easily*. On the other hand it may take quite a lot to scare you. But if you constantly find yourself in those special situations that *do* frighten you, people who notice may come to think of you as someone who *does scare easily*, since you seem to be frequently afraid. Get it?

Well the circumstances of the story I'm relating to you have constantly put me in situations that tested me. And standing on that landing in Toni and Tom's big empty house that afternoon was frightening. I mean, I *have* encountered what you might describe as ghostly visitations or apparitions. And that kind of psychic activity, that awareness of certain vibrations of the Astral Light, doesn't usually worry me. Much less frighten me. I have the ability to discern the benign from the threatening.

On that landing in Toni's house, the atmosphere was oppressive. *And* threatening. I knew that outside the sun was shining. Bright sunshine spreading love and light over the city. But it became suddenly dark on the landing. And I was afraid because my eyes were drawn to that corner. The one that Sable Wyvern had disappeared around. My heart was pounding and without realising it I had become aware of the unique projection of my consciousness. I felt alone in that dark, quiet house. Alone in the sense that there was nothing and no one there to help me.

Hairs on the back of my neck standing on end at the whispers hissing from the shadows behind me. Wondering if I'd really felt something brush the back of my neck but not daring to turn and look. And then taking a footstep towards that dark forsaken corner and almost shrieking at myself to stop.

I felt it before I saw it. Something around that corner that was the opposite of friendly. Black energy seeping around the edge of the plaster and me so afraid I could barely breathe. I could only dry-swallow while my heart raced inside my chest. Thoughts racing inside my head matching the chaotic pace of my heart. A jumble of disparate images. Helen. New Zealand. Our house there. That house in flames. The bearded man burning. Paris. Notre Dame. Hesther naked and writhing on her white duvet. A Temple made ready for some ceremony. The High Priestess. 2. Gimel. G Sharp. Moon. Camel. Silver. Then bile rising into my mouth as the familiar white face appeared around the corner. Soul-less white skin. Perfect features. Black eyes deep as the Abyss. Tight, black-lipped smile. White hand emerging from the silver sleeve of the sparkling silver cloak. Moving effortlessly, slow like a snake. Emerging. And me shaking with fear. Unable to move. And the daylight replaced with darkness so that there was only her. Her without speaking, telling me she was Lilith. Astarte. Isis. Diana. And countless other names. Istar. Ishtar. Easter. Hesther! Hesther! The white hand reaching towards me, cold breath on the back of my neck and the sense of something there. Me shutting my eyes tight. And then –

''Ello, you're back early then.' Rachel's voice calling up from the hallway downstairs, the door slamming shut behind her.

My eyes opening to perfect summer daylight, such as

managed to find its way onto the landing. Me still trembling but able to move, to look around. Seeing my bedroom door ajar. A hint of brilliant sunshine beyond it. No sense of anything threatening. No ghosts, spirits, apparitions. No Goddess. More bile forcing itself into my mouth and me swallowing it down.

'Yeah,' I managed to reply in the end. 'Paid my respects. It's all I could do.'

'Know wot yer mean' Rachel said. 'Yer can only say goodbye. After that it's morbid.' She waited a moment then said 'You coming down for a cuppa?'

A cuppa was the last thing I wanted but I said 'Yes.' Because really the last thing I wanted was to be alone up there on the landing. I'd be safe with Rachel. That's what all my senses were telling me. So I took a deep breath and raced past that corner and fairly skipped down the stairs. Yes I raced, because it was still spooking me, even knowing Rachel was in the house. She was in the house but not on that landing, you see. Anything could have been around that corner. Well it could.

Anyway, I'd calmed myself so I thought, by the time I got to the kitchen and when I entered there was Rachel putting the kettle on.

She turned and said 'Blimey, wot's the matter with you?'

I didn't know what she meant so said nothing.

'You look like you seen a ghost' she said, coming over to me and raising a hand to stroke my cheek. She held my eyes with her own then said 'You 'ave, ain't yer? You're white as sheet an' freezin' cold. What's happened?'

I told her it was nothing, that I'd spooked myself on the landing. Big empty house and all that. But she didn't buy it. Not a bit of it.

'There was somethin' up there weren't there?' she said. 'There's been something lurkin' around this house since you come. I ain't blamin' yer or nothin', just sayin'. An' it's not nothin' yer can easily put a handle on. It changes. But I can tell yer this. It ain't friendly.'

'What have you seen?' I asked, suddenly comforted by Rachel's revelation.

'I ain't really seen nothing' she said. 'I get the feelin' of it though. Somethin' behind yer in a corridor. A curtain twitchin' when there ain't no windows open. A feelin' that's somethin's in a room with yer. When yer can't see anybody else. An' it ain't a happy energy, know wot I mean?'

I knew what she meant and I told her so.

'Come on' she said, taking my hand. 'Let's go up there right now.'

I had no choice really. I let her drag me up the stairs and didn't pull back too much. But we found nothing. No darkness. No threatening atmosphere. No white-faced Goddess. No Sable Wyvern. Just an empty landing.

'Let's check in your room,' Rachel said. 'Just to be sure.'

I let her lead me into my room and we found it sunny and light and lovely and fragrant. And the sounds of the city floating in through the open window just as I'd wanted earlier.

'You goin' somewhere?' Rachel asked, noticing my packed suitcase on the bed.

I nodded, said 'Yes. Can't be a guest here forever.'

Rachel thought about that for a moment. 'Goin' somewhere nice?' she asked.

'Yeah,' I said. 'Nice enough.'

'But yer stayin' in London?'

'Yeah' I said, 'I'm staying in London.'

She took both of my hands and I'd never seen her so serious. 'You should get out of London' she said. 'It's dangerous for yer. Don't ask me how I know.'

I didn't ask her. I was shocked to hear her say that though. Because it was starting to feel like pressure on me to leave. And I wanted to leave. The pressure was having an effect on me. Yet I couldn't. Not before getting the answers to certain questions. I just couldn't.

'Remember what I told yer?' Rachel said.

I nodded. 'I should learn to balance the Ancient Elements. Follow the inner path.'

'I never told yer to follow no inner path' Rachel said. 'But that's exactly what yer should do. So go on, get out of London. At least fer now.'

'And where should I go?' I asked.

'Ain't you got no idea?' she asked, seeming surprised.

I wasn't going to say anything but something made me take my jacket from the back of the dressing table chair where I'd hung it, and search one of the inside pockets. I pulled out the piece of paper containing Ziggy's translation of the note given to me by Elke. I handed it to Rachel.

'So why don't you go there?' Rachel said.

'Do you know that person?' I asked.

Rachel shrugged. 'No. The name don't mean nothin'. But the place. I mean, yer couldn't go better than that.'

The words were hardly a ringing endorsement, yet I felt they were gold-plated somehow. I felt that Rachel giving me the okay was somehow energising the words. I stuffed the paper into my pocket.

'Maybe I will go' I said. 'But I do have some business to complete first.'

Rachel didn't like that. 'You should go now. But yer know that' she said.

She squeezed my hand and I found it comforting.

'I know,' I said.

We stood like that for a few seconds as though we couldn't work out what to do next.

'There's a woman been here yer know. In this room' Rachel said out of the blue.

I looked at her but with no sense of shock or surprise. 'Beside you, you mean?'

'I mean a beautiful girl. A sad girl. I think it's your wife.'

My turn to squeeze her hand. 'I think so too' I said.

It could have got a bit emotional right then, but Rachel to the rescue. 'Come on, let's go have that cuppa.'

I followed her out of the bedroom but just before I closed the door, I got an old familiar feeling deep in my heart. Helen was smiling.

# The Story Episode # 128 (Moon phase: 2/Day 1)

EMPTY VESSELS MAKE most noise. With that in mind I left the house when Rachel did because I couldn't trust the place to be quiet. I never did find out what brought Rachel back to the house that afternoon but I was grateful nevertheless.

Toni and Tom hadn't come back from the funeral so I didn't take my bag to go check into the Cavendish. Instead I went up to St. Paul's. And I hung around the place for a while on the steps out front with a million tourists taking in the sights and the sunshine. Helen and me used to go up to St. Paul's a lot. Sometimes we'd take food and a bottle of something and sit on those steps and talk and watch the people go by. Much as others were doing right then.

The City of London. The financial capital of the world. Was then, still is. Even the powerhouses of New York, Frankfurt and Tokyo, they couldn't match the clout and the influence of The City. Nothing could. And nothing does. St. Paul's is pretty much the western gateway to this, the most influential square mile of real estate anywhere on earth.

Helen and me, we loved walking those narrow streets of The City even though we had no business there. History in those streets. Especially the quiet narrow medieval lanes twisting their way between the main thoroughfares. I don't know why but The City cried out to Helen and me. We loved being in it even though we were never part of it. And we'd done meditations in the occasional green spaces. We'd gone there at all times of the day and night – yes, even in the early hours of the morning – in search of whatever guardian energy was speaking to us, encouraging us to come back to the place time and time again. But with no real result. Whatever guardian intelligence was responsible for that sacred space, that square mile, it told us we weren't yet ready to partake of its mysteries even while it drew us to it.

Didn't stop us from smiling while we were there though. In those narrow quiet streets. Treading softly between buildings where decisions were made that would affect – for better or worse – the lives of countless millions of people. Worse, I know now. Never better. And that by design, but I'll say no more of that here.

So, off the steps of St. Paul's and away from its precincts I walked aimlessly through The City. I took seemingly random turns – although I know there's no such thing as random – finding myself going past landmarks like the Bank of England and the Mansion House and others too numerous to mention. I stopped briefly now and then to reacquaint myself with the architecture of the churches that Helen and me had always admired and been drawn to. I don't suppose you find anything inspiring in them but for some reason they came to mean something to us. All-Hallows By The Tower, the oldest Church in The City and dating from Saxon times. St. Mary Le Bow. St. Magnus the Martyr. All the others.

I sat on the grass and spent time with my memories in open spaces such as Bunhill Fields, the graveyard where over twelve thousand dissenters are buried along with men whose lives and work obviously resonated with a would-be occultist like me; William Blake, Daniel Defoe and John Bunyon. I spent time in Postman's Park near the Memorial to Heroic Self-Sacrifice, the monument ensuring that the brave actions of ordinary people who gave their own lives to save others are never forgotten.

Mostly though I walked, not paying attention to where it was I wandered. Until at last and goodness knows how much later, I found myself in Paternoster Square looking up at The Monument, built in memory of the Great Fire of 1666. And of course I wasn't far then from St. Paul's, where I'd started.

Crossing Paternoster Square I headed south and found myself once more at the back of the great City Cathedral of St. Paul's. By now it was close-on five o'clock and I supposed I ought to get back to Toni and Tom's and hopefully – assuming they were back – say my thank yous and farewells. For some reason I decided I'd walk at least part of the way, and since they were on the river at Chelsea, I headed down to the embankment to make my way east along there. I mention this because it was an unusual choice for me to make. In the first place I wouldn't normally choose to walk, especially that late in the afternoon. And in the second place, if I was going to walk, I'd normally go directly east down Ludgate Hill and then on into Fleet Street rather than head south for the river. But head south I did.

Without knowing why I found myself wandering down Distaff Lane, which brought me out onto Queen Victoria Street. Not quite at the Embankment, I nevertheless turned right and headed east along Queen Victoria street but I hadn't gone far before I was stopped in my tracks. I found myself on the pavement next to some high railings and gates guarding entry to an old brick building set back from the road, forming an open square around a courtyard beyond the gates. the building was of a type and age you'd expect to see in The City and I suppose I must have gone past it often enough over the years without paying it any attention. I *was* paying attention now.

Looking back from the unprepossessing building and up to the railings above the gates I saw something that turned me instantly light-headed and nauseous. A large gilded crest above the gates and something majestic about it - though for some reason sinister and sickening to me nevertheless. Drawn by this crest to look back to the building's entrance at the rear of the courtyard behind the gates I saw a sight so disturbing to me right then that I had to turn away and look south towards the river. What I saw was the name of the place. The College of Arms.

All sorts of images came flooding through my mind. The grinning form of Sable Wyvern in Toni's house earlier. The white-faced Goddess tracking and haunting me since Helen had died. Hesther writhing naked on her snowy-white duvet. Tom in his Temple buried deep below the house in Chelsea. A bearded man burning to death before my eyes in New Zealand. My darling beautiful immortal beloved wife Helen dying horribly in my arms in the darkness of our living room as the rain battered our little house.

I was nearly crying and breathing hard because I couldn't bear to look at the place and I no longer wanted to walk anywhere. My eyes searched frantically for a taxi and providence, my friend right at that moment, gave me the boon I sought as a black cab came into view and I waved wild and frantic arms in an effort to flag it down.

'Bloody hell guv, you on fire or summat?' This was the driver as I threw myself into the back of the cab and made a point of continuing to look south to the river and away from the hated place.

'What?' I said, distracted as you can imagine.

'I thought you was about to chuck yerself in front of the cab, way you was wavin' with both hands an' poppin' up an' down, like.'

He was cheerful and that was a blessing. Because his cheeriness calmed me somewhat.

I managed a bit of a nervous laugh. 'Just running late' I said. 'And yeah, I probably did overdo it now you mention it.' I laughed again and hoped that that was enough to convince him I wasn't a nutter.

'Well I dare say the exercise'll have done yer good' the driver said, smiling like he'd come out with the very paradigm of humour. 'Now where to guv?'

'Cheyne Walk' I said. 'I'll show you where to let me out when we get there.'

'Right you are' the driver said and was just about to slide the dividing glass shut for a moment when he hesitated and looked at me. 'Pardon me for asking guv' he said. 'But your name ain't Steven is it?' I was instantly sick with the shock of that. 'Only I just had that name come into me 'ead like it was supposed to mean something. An I don't know any Stevens as I can think of. 'Ere, are you alright?'

# *The Story Episode # 129 (Moon phase: 2/Day 1)*

TONI'S CHEYNE WALK house wasn't an empty vessel with me in it. I'm saying that because it was eerily silent as I stood in the living room off the main hall waiting for Toni and Tom to return.

I hadn't disgraced myself by being ill in the cab but it had been a near thing. The cabbie had believed me when I'd told him I'd just felt a little light-headed and we'd made good time back to Chelsea. I'd confirmed my name to him too and it turned out that there may not have been a sinister connection between him and the College of Arms after all. It seemed he belonged to a spiritualist church in Croydon where he lived and he was active within the church as a medium.

Now I don't go much for spiritualism because I believe that spiritualists misinterpret genuine experiences and their misinterpretations then become barriers to spiritual evolution. Of course I didn't mention that to the cab driver. I did wonder if he'd genuinely channelled my name though. Wondered if my darling beautiful immortal beloved wife Helen had called out to me through him. But I didn't mention that either.

Six o'clock and still no sign of Toni and Tom. And then my phone rang. I answered and it was Hesther. She thanked me for coming to the funeral and I apologized for leaving so early. But we both knew that this call wasn't to make small talk. I asked her what time Toni had left.

'About forty minutes ago' Hesther said. 'Are you back at their house?'

I told her that I was. 'But I'm not staying' I said. 'Just waiting for them to get back so that I can say thank you. Then I'm off.'

A brief pause then Hesther asked 'Where to?'

For a moment I wondered whether I should tell her. But in the end I said 'I'm moving into the Cavendish on Jermyn Street. Do you know it?'

She told me that she did indeed know it but had never stayed there. Then she said 'Steven, I was wondering. . .' she paused as though she wasn't really sure of herself, which was unlike her. I waited until she found the words then let her continue. 'I'd really like to see you tonight' she said.

I have to tell you that there was no sorrow in that voice. Nothing needy. Nothing suggesting that she simply couldn't bear to be alone following her loss. Besides, there were people closer to her than me she'd have called if she'd felt that need, surely.

'I don't know' I said. 'I'm moving out of here this evening and I'm sort of looking forward to having some alone time. You know what I mean?'

She said she did and managed to say it without sounding slighted while seeming a touch disappointed nevertheless. Manipulative Adept bitch I thought to myself, smiling and not in the least bit angry. Honestly, I didn't think there was anything consciously magical about it anyway. We've established more than once that Hesther wasn't a sorceress.

In the end I gave an exaggerated sigh and said 'Okay, I'll come over to see you. But I won't stay long. What time shall I come over?'

'Well since you've got to settle into your new home from home, let's make it late' she said. 'Is nine late enough?'

'Sure' I said. 'Nine's fine. But where?'

'What? Oh, come to the house in Hampstead' she said, realising I'd wanted to know whether to visit her at her own place in Camden.

Just then I heard the front door open and Toni calling out 'Stevie? Are you here?'

'They're back' I said to Hesther, 'I gotta go. I'll see you at nine then.'

She said a quick goodbye but I didn't catch all of it because I cut the call, slipped my phone into my pocket and went out to meet Toni and Tom in the hallway. Toni was standing by my suitcase, which I'd brought down to the hall ready to make my getaway.

'Leaving us Stevie?' Toni said, sounding disappointed and a little peeved.

'Yes' I said. 'Before I outstay my welcome.'

'You're welcome to stay as long as you like. Truly.' This was Tom and maybe he was genuine or maybe he was saying it to sound polite, safe in the knowledge that I wouldn't be changing my mind. I mean, who ever does in such circumstances? Change their mind, I mean.

'No, really,' I said. 'You've been amazing, letting me stay here and make it my home. But it's time I stood on my own two feet again.'

Tom seemed okay with that but Toni didn't. 'Fine,' she said. 'Do whatever you feel is best.' She turned to Tom. 'I'm going up to shower and change. It's been a long day.' Then she turned back to me. 'Call from wherever you're going,' she said. 'Let me know where you are and that you got there safe.'

'I'm only going to be at the Cavendish on Jermyn Street. . .' I began. But she was already past me and sweeping up those wide stairs. Well of course I'd call her. Later. Perhaps she'd be more receptive then.

Tom remained in the hall, hands in his pockets. 'Toni's going to miss you' he said. 'But you're doing the right thing. It's probably for the best.'

'Yes,' I agreed. 'I think so.' I should have picked up my suitcase right then but the way Tom hung about I could tell that there was more to come.

'Listen old man' he said at last. 'Whatever quest you're on, I think it would be best if you'd leave Toni out of it from now on, what do you say?'

I thought about that for a moment. 'Yeah,' I said, agreeing again. 'I think you're probably right.' I didn't like being warned off but I did understand. Toni was his wife. She'd already put herself in harm's way too many times since she'd gone to fetch me back from New Zealand. And I was awfully fond of her, I had to admit. I'd miss her as much as she'd miss me. If Tom was right and she'd miss me at all.

'Glad we're in agreement then' Tom said as I stepped past him and picked up my suitcase.

I was itching to be going now that I'd seen them to say thank you and I opened the door. I was about to step outside when Tom said 'And I hope you'll be taking your dead wife with you. Toni could do without the distraction.'

I rounded on him at that and for a second I couldn't find the right words. But then I said 'What the fuck do you mean by that?'

Tom shrugged but didn't answer.

'Tell you what, I'll take Helen with me. If she's here. But I'll leave that Sable fucking Wyvern behind for you to take care of, right?'

'I don't know what you're talking about' Tom said, furrowing his brow and somewhat overdoing it. 'Sable Wyvern's dead. I told you. But I don't know – '

'The fuck you don't know!' I snapped, interrupting him. 'You know only too fucking well. I don't know what the fuck's going on or what kind of game you and fuck knows who else are playing but I'll leave you to it.' I turned to go but turned back one more time. 'Fuck you!' I said and I don't know if he ever intended a comeback to that because I left, slamming the door behind me.

I chucked my suitcase into the boot of the Aston Martin and was out onto the road on mental auto pilot. Because my mind was racing. That last exchange had me reeling. Why had Tom told me about Sable Wyvern in the first place? What was going on? And what did any of it have to do with Helen and me in the first place? Because surely it did. I wished I'd had a pop at Tom. Wished I'd had hold of him. Wished I'd throttled the information out of him. Wished I'd. . . But these were just self-destructive thoughts. And anyway, he still mightn't have talked. And he might have given me the kicking I'd have liked to have given him. I'm not James Bond or Jason Bourne when all's said and done.

I headed for Jermyn Street more determined than ever to get to the bottom of things. This business had all started with Toni coming to New Zealand to get me. I wondered now if Tom hadn't exerted a covert pressure on her to do that. I'd call Toni and fuck what I'd told Tom about leaving her out of it. I wasn't finished with Toni just yet. But I'd leave it until tomorrow. Because the way I was feeling, I needed to get my things stowed in my room at the Cavendish. And I needed to see Hesther. Yes Hesther. For some reason the thought of being with her came to me as a comfort.

Hesther, yes. I'd go see Hesther in Hampstead as arranged. And maybe I'd go early. Helen was in the car with me as I headed west past Dolphin Square. I couldn't hide anything from Helen. And Helen approved.

# *The Story Episode # 130 (Moon phase: 2/Day 1)*

CLOUDS OBSCURE THE sunlight. Dim the daylight. But they still belong to the Astral Light and as such we should see in them and their effects, illumination and not obscurity. We live in the illusion and we only see obscurity in clouds. That's how it was with me as I drove to Hampstead through central London and up onto the Finchley Road past St. John's Wood. Dark clouds forming low, to dim the otherwise azure sky and cast a pall over the city.

Looked like rain again. Was bound to be rain. Reminded me of the previous evening and the night with Hesther at her house in Camden. It had rained all night. Heavy rain.

I smiled. Perhaps I should read something into the combination of Hesther and me and rain. I mean, I know there's no such thing as coincidence, but surely it would be vanity to ascribe the formation of clouds and the deluge of rainfall to Hesther and me coming together.

Meeting up with Hesther then. Looking forward to it. Finding comfort in it. But in the back of my mind there was always that parting exchange with Tom, who'd previously been so decent with me. I kept it there. On the back burner. Wondered instead what Hesther would be wearing when I got to the house. She'd have changed out of the Chanel of course. She'd looked stunning in it but that look wasn't Hesther. Just a sheet of silk print wound around that astonishingly proportioned body, shaped and curved to perfection, was what I was guessing. Bare feet, no jewellery. And no underwear. *That* was Hesther.

I even wondered if I'd spend another night with her but

quickly pushed that thought away. Let it slide into the ether. The poor woman was in mourning after all. And she had so many burdens to bear. It was unworthy of me to think such thoughts.

Rain was falling as I pulled up outside the professor's house. Hesther's house I supposed it would be, once the professor's will came out of probate. I couldn't imagine things any other way. So I trotted up the steps, up the path to the front door and pressed the bell. I was undercover so I didn't mind that it took Hesther the best part of a minute to come to the door. When she opened it I couldn't help smiling. She was dressed as I'd imagined with just a colourful sheet of floral-printed silk wrapped around her and tied in an exquisite knot just above her breasts. Bare feet. No jewellery. And definitely no underwear.

How did I know that last part? Oh come on. She wore that silk-wind like a sheath. I remember thinking exactly that. And like a dirty schoolboy, following that thought with another; 'sheath' is the English translation of the Latin noun, *vagina*. Did you know that? Well if you didn't before, now you do. And the next thought that occurred to me was that this word, one you'd expect to be unambiguously feminine and female, is actually a male label for that exclusively feminine attribute. Think about it. A sheath is a case or covering; a receptacle. Any way you define it, a sheath has no intrinsic value. It only has purpose and value when it serves something else. Something you put inside it. I wonder if early radical feminists would have been quite so insistently shrill in using this word – *vagina* -as their weapon of choice when they were out to shock a prim and proper establishment in the early 1970s - and later - if they'd known this etymology. It's probably time feminists invented a new word for it. I don't know whether it was a man or a woman who first coined the term 'pussy' to describe it. But personally I hate that. I'd say any new word needs to be beautiful and unambiguous. And feminine. I won't hold my breath waiting. Now that was a digression I hadn't expected or intended to make. You just can't beat a classical education, can you?

Back to Hesther though. 'I'm so glad you could come' she said, leaning forward to kiss me on the cheek.

For a moment I sensed a sadness within her and instinctively put my arms around her and pulled her gently to me. I gave her a hug as we stood there in the doorway with the rain at my back. Sensations flooded through me. Feeling her soft yielding body pressed close against me, feeling the soft smooth texture of her silk wrap beneath my fingers, hearing the rustle of the shifting fabric, catching the scent of her perfume – most definitely Chanel No. 5 – was nothing short of transcendental. I had to fight to stop my mind from shifting three levels into an otherworldly reverie just basking in the aura of this most incredible woman.

I held her close to me for a second or two longer than I should have, I suppose, lingering over the blissful proximity to her loveliness. And she made no effort to pull away from me. I felt an overwhelming compassion for her right then and I so wanted to be able to comfort her. Sex didn't come into that equation at all, even if genuine human contact and warmth did.

'Come in' she said, looking past me to the rain getting heavier behind me. 'It's been such a beautiful day' she continued, gently shutting the door. 'Perhaps it's us. Perhaps the rain is meant to be our chaperone.'

She smiled and so did I. I didn't bother to mention that I'd been having almost identical thoughts on the way over to see her. What would be the point? It was mere whimsy after all.

She took my hand as naturally as if Helen were doing it and my chest tightened painfully with the memory of my beautiful dead wife. That, however, passed quickly. I wasn't slow to see what had brought it on. I was strolling hand in hand with the woman who'd been my darling beautiful Helen's one true adult love - before me. And nothing wrong with that, I might add. Me hand in hand with Hesther, I mean. I felt no guilt, nor should I have. Nor did Hesther. We were becoming close, I felt. Developing a friendship based on mutual interests and a mutual love and respect for both my darling Helen and the recently departed professor. We were both emotionally evolved enough not to see anything salacious or immoral about sharing sexual pleasure with each other as we had done the previous night. We were at a place where we could divorce physical closeness from any sense of loyalty we might feel for those we'd lost.

'So why did you need to see me?' I asked as the pad of her thumb rubbed innocently against the back of my hand.

She stopped and turned to me. Held both my hands in hers. 'I didn't,' she said. 'I mean I did. I'm glad you're here. But that's not why I called you.'

I was intrigued. That was the second time I'd heard her seem to struggle for the right words.

'Where shall we go to sit and talk?' I asked gently. 'In this place we're spoiled for choice.'

Hesther looked away. 'Come with me' she said, and we walked together, hand in hand, through to the back of the house. Beyond the study, down the broad corridor leading through to the kitchen.

But we weren't heading for the kitchen. Hesther stopped in front of a white-painted door. She opened it and stepped aside for me to enter. I knew what was behind that door. A wide and well-lit staircase. Leading down to a massive basement. Well it had to be massive, housing as it did the Temple of the mystical and magical order the professor had founded and Hesther now headed, and that Helen and I had been introduced to.

'Where are we going?' I asked, but as I've just mentioned I knew full well where we were going.

'It's an appropriate place to talk' was all that Hesther said, following me down the stairs.

I said nothing more. She wanted the comfort of the Temple. Well I could understand that. No different than a member of an orthodox exoteric religion finding comfort in a church or whatever other place was sacred. I hadn't expected it of Hesther. But as I've said, the woman was under a great deal of pressure. And I was familiar with the Temple. It wasn't the first time I'd been there. I wasn't the least concerned.

'Go on, go in' Hesther said as we reached the huge double oak doors.

I pushed them open. The scent of frankincense drifted out, heavy and sweet and pleasant. Dim light beyond. All of which would make a comfortable atmosphere for us. Inside, Hesther closed the door softly behind us. Then I realised it. We weren't alone! At various points around the Temple, strategic points I might add, were the three discreet but well-dressed men I'd seen at the funeral earlier in the day.

The hairs on the back of my neck stood on end. This wasn't right.

'I'm so sorry Steven' Hesther said from behind me. 'I didn't mean to trick you. But they really need to speak to you. They insisted.'

I turned to face Hesther and immediately I could see that she meant every word. What shocked me first though was the idea that anyone, let alone these three, could bend Hesther - the Adept - to do their bidding. But second, and far worse, was the feeling I got that these impeccably dressed English gentlemen hadn't summoned me here to enquire about the state of my health.

# The Story Episode # 131
# (Moon phase: 2/Day 1)

'YOU SEEM WORRIED Nolan.' This was the deep authoritative aristocratic voice of the man seated in the Temple Master's chair on the raised area down at the far side of the Temple. 'There's no need. Really.'

Easy for him to say. I reserved the right to remain worried without saying so. I turned from Hesther's apologetic face back to face the voice. Then I turned my attention to his companions in turn. One seated against the wall to my left, and the other seated against the wall to my right. Draw lines between them and you've got an equilateral triangle. These were strategic positions and they hadn't arranged themselves spontaneously. Another effect was to have me twisting my head this way and that when responding to one or another of them, denying me a true focus if I had something I wanted to say to all of them. I'd deal with that last part though. I was smart enough to be wise to that. I'd keep my focus on the one directly ahead of me if I ever had anything to say.

'Very good of you to come at short notice.' This from a second voice, the man seated to my right. I turned my head to face him.

'Yes, we can understand that you may have been reluctant.' This from the third voice, the man seated to my left.

So you can see how I'd be twisting my head this way and that throughout this exchange, interrogation, laying down of the law, or whatever it was going to be.

'You know my name' I said, addressing my words to the first man directly in front of me. 'Are you going to tell me who you are?'

'Oh I don't think that's necessary' said number two, to my right.

'Then you have me at a disadvantage' I said.

'Yes – ' this from number three ' – we do, rather.'

I turned and aimed a questioning look at beautiful Hesther who seemed embarrassed. Embarrassed at this exchange or embarrassed for having tricked me into being there I couldn't say. I just found it strange to see her embarrassed at all. And it shocked me when I realised that this was the first time I'd ever seen Hesther in anything but complete control of herself and her surroundings. Just who were these men?

'You should leave now' number one said and I could see from Hesther's reaction that his words were addressed to her.

I rounded quickly on the man. 'She needs to stay' I said. 'I want her to hear anything you have to say to me.'

I turned back to Hesther but she seemed subdued in the presence of these men whoever they were. She was slowly shaking her head.

'No Stevie, I should go. I'll only be upstairs. In the professor's study. I'll be waiting there for you when your business here is done.

'That's a very good idea.' This from number three.

Hesther wanted to stay with me I could see that. But she just couldn't defy these men. She took a step back from me and I reached out a hand to grab her, to stop her, but she stepped back again, too sharp and too quick for me.

'I'll be upstairs Stevie' she said; then she was gone, closing the door behind her.

I turned my attention back to these three men. 'Why shouldn't I just leave now?' I asked.

They seemed to consider this for a moment, then number one said 'Because you're curious. You want to know what we have to say.'

Horrifically he was right. I was curious. My feet remained rooted to the spot.

'You are of course free to leave any time you like,' number three said.

Easy for him to say. And I was certain he knew that to be disingenuous. But I was going nowhere because to tell you the truth, they made me uneasy. I looked from one to another of them, took in all three. Homogenous, I thought. They all looked the same. Solid men. Sober suits. A very casual gravitas about them. They looked like very senior civil servants. Permanent Secretaries. The true power within government. The sort of men who provided stable continuity in the running of the country's affairs. The sort of people who'd been doing this for centuries while governments came and went. Even as systems of government came and went.

Can I tell you what it felt like in that dim Temple right then? It felt like I was in the presence of *Spectre*. Yes, that's right. The organization invented by Ian Fleming for the James Bond stories. Yes, *that Spectre*, the one with designs on taking over the world. If that bastard right in front of me had suddenly pulled a cat out of a bag and sat stroking it, I wouldn't have been surprised. But I shouldn't make light of this. I don't want you to lose sight of how nervous I was. Nervous verging on scared.

'What do you want with me?' I asked, trying to sound confident and not really succeeding.

'You've come to our attention' number two said. 'You have abilities.'

'What abilities?' I said. 'Is this something to do with this?' I waved a hand ostentatiously around to indicate the Temple. 'Because I can tell you I have no abilities regarding these matters.'

'I'm sure I don't know what you mean' number one said.

'Well I'm sure you do' I fired back. 'You know full well what this place is. You know the purpose it serves.'

'Do we?' Number one again. 'Well if you say so. If it makes you comfortable to believe that.'

'Are you with the government?' I asked, not knowing why.

Number two laughed and it sounded deep and sinister in that dimly lit and fragrant Temple. 'We are custodians of a certain status quo,' he said. 'Can we leave it at that for now?'

He asked, but I knew damn well that it wasn't a request; it was a statement of how things would be. But what could he have meant by that. Custodians of a certain status quo?

'We're very sorry for your loss' number one said.

'You mean the professor?' I said. 'He was an acquaintance. A friend you might say. But we weren't close.'

'I didn't mean the professor' number two said.

'We're talking about your dear wife.' This from number three.

A chill ran through me. Fear, anger, I felt them both at the same time.

'What do you want with me?' I said in a low voice devoid of passion.

Number one looked from number two to number three and I followed his gaze, saw both of them nod imperceptibly.

'We want to interview you' number one said.

'And why did you mention my wife?' I asked. 'She's been gone three years now. What's she to you?'

Number two joined his hands and flexed his fingers. 'Gone three years,' he said. 'And she still lives with you. And you with her. That's a gift. A skill. A very special ability.'

'But this isn't the place to explore it fully' number three said. 'We'd like you to come to us. Tomorrow morning. Or at any rate at your earliest convenience.'

'Will you come?' This from number two. 'We've been searching for you for quite a while, and now we've found you. . .' He let his idea trail away.

My heart was racing. My Helen. This was about my Helen. Of course it was. Just who the hell were these people? I was suddenly frightened. What with everything that had happened to me. And now the mention of my darling beautiful wife who seemed to be at the heart of all things. My poor immortal beloved Helen. Helen. How can I save you? How can I save you?

They were waiting for my answer and they got it. 'Yes,' I said. 'I'll come. Yes, we'll talk. And tomorrow morning's fine. I can be there at ten. Just tell me where, and who to ask for.'

'Oh you won't have to ask for anyone' number three said. 'You'll be expected. You'll be shown through.'

'Through to where?' I asked. 'Where should I show up?'

'Come now, don't play games. I thought you'd have realised by now' number one said. 'The College of Arms on Queen Victoria Street. I think you'll find it easily enough.'

I was rather expecting that in the end as I'm sure you were. The College of Arms. They'd got me. I'd been running from them and here they had me. I felt sick and giddy. Emotional. On the verge of sobbing and tears. But I maintained a degree of composure.

'We'll see you tomorrow then. At ten.' I couldn't tell you which of them said that. Just that it was a plummy voice. And not Received Pronunciation. Not typically Public School. But I knew what it was. You would too if you heard it. If you've ever heard members of the British Royal Family speak, or ranking members of their households, you'd know it alright. Not a voice of the merely Upper Class. The voice of the *ruling* class. And I knew damn well that there was a difference. A voice from the rulers of Empire. Of country. A voice that had just dismissed me.

I left that Temple. I couldn't wait. I fairly flew up those stairs and along that wide corridor leading to the tiled hallway. I didn't even stop to look in the study where Hesther waited for me in my haste to get out of there.

'Stevie?' I heard her call out after me but I didn't hesitate. I was out of the door before Hesther could catch me and I slammed it behind me. I ran down the path and jumped into my car with Hesther still calling after me from the door.

I started the car and I shot off into the road, not caring which direction I was taking. But just outside Hampstead village, I stopped at the side of the road. I took my wallet from my pocket and removed a piece of paper. The one that had Ziggy's translation of Elke's note. I looked at it. Inspected it. Noted the name. Noted the address. The College of Arms at ten the next morning? You've got to be fucking joking man. Let the fuckers wait. They'd be waiting an eternity. I had other ideas.

*END OF PART TWO...*

# Coming Soon...

# The Story part three
## – Earth Air Fire Water -

...I was standing in Glastonbury High Street right outside a door between two old and jolly shops; exactly where I was meant to be. I knew that behind the door there'd be a narrow dim passageway leading to the front door of the flat or townhouse or whatever arrangement of property mapped to the number I'd been given. Question was, what time would be a fit and proper one to go ringing the bell? In the end I decided not to wait despite the earliness of the hour.

The passageway behind the door was indeed dim but I was able to negotiate my way to the end, which was only a few yards in. There I found a black oak door and the push-button for an electronic doorbell.

I didn't hesitate. I pressed the button. And heard nothing. Something that always irritates the hell out of me, because you never know whether the damn thing isn't working or whether the ringing part of it is so far into the house that you can't hear it at the door. I've got to the point where I don't stand waiting;

I knock on the door right away if I can't hear the bell ring. So this is what I did. Bang bang bang. Fairly loud really. Louder than I should have knocked if I'm honest.

I stood around waiting for a while. I don't know for how long. And I was just about to knock again when I heard a woman's voice call out from inside the house somewhere saying 'I don't know. That's why I'm going to find out.' This was followed by the sounds of padded footsteps approaching.

Soon enough I heard the sound of a chain and a bolt being slid back. I took a step back as the door opened to reveal a dishevelled woman wrapped in a midnight-blue woollen dressing gown worked with exquisite embroidered symbols. Bare feet of course – I'll come back to that presently – and pale hands, and a just-woke-up-and-got-out-of-bed look on her face. She rubbed her eyes and looked at me.

'So you're not the rozzers then?' she said.

I shook my head. 'No. Were you expecting them?'

'Who else comes banging and hammering at the door in the middle of the night?'

She had a point but I said 'It's not the middle of the night. It's –'

'Yeah,' she said, 'I know the time. Middle of the night. Middle of the night somewhere in the world at any rate.' She suppressed a yawn then turned to go back into the house saying 'I suppose you'd better come in. Shut the door behind you.'

That was unexpected and I did as I was told, following this woman up half a dozen wooden stairs and onto a small landing then through into a living room.

'Who is it?' A girl's sleepy voice calling out from somewhere.

'I don't know' the woman called back. 'Perhaps you'd like to come and see for yourself. If you can drag yourself out of bed.'

'But it's the middle of the night' the girl's voice whined, and

I got the feeling I'd gone round in a circle.

The woman turned to me. 'Right,' she said. 'Sit down. Anywhere you like. I'll put the kettle on and we can have a cuppa and take things from there.'

She smiled at me as I chose an extravagantly deep and richly upholstered arm chair then turned to leave, presumably to go to the kitchen and put the kettle on. That smile brought her face to life and I was able to properly take her in at that moment. Dishevelled and barely awake as she was, she had auburn hair cascading in thick curls and waves over her shoulders. Green eyes, as far as I could make out in the dim light and through her early-morning squint. She was tall and curvy beneath the dressing gown. Mumsy but very sexy. It was in her posture, the way she carried herself. I'd say she was in her forties and she had a charismatic aura that fairly drew your eyes to her.

Watching her from behind as she went to the kitchen I found myself wondering what she'd look like beneath the dressing gown. Wondering if she was naked beneath it. And I realised right away what I was doing, the road I was going down. I stopped myself, giving thanks to my inner guardian for pointing it out and for giving me the chance to do something about it.

Instead I took in this living room. Because I have to say the décor was overwhelming and I'm sure too much for most people's taste. Deep rich polished hardwood floors with scattered rugs here and there. The walls and ceiling were green. Again, I'm not talking pastel shades or white with a hint of apple. They were green, for real. Pale blue pleated drape curtains. A chandelier hanging from a plaster rose in the centre of the ceiling. Pale green throw-cloths over the deep and sumptuous armchairs and sofa. Large rosewood-framed mirrors on two walls. What looked like a Chippendale table in the middle of the floor. Period wooden chairs, though I'm not expert enough to say which period - old will suffice. Detail detail detail. Eveywhere I looked, decorative detail. And the smells of spice and incense. Which incense? Who knows? The scented residue of a multitude of varieties. Middle class suburban tastes would hate this room with a passion. But I loved it. Revelled in its richness.

The woman came back with two cups of what I presumed was tea. She hadn't asked me how I took mine but since it was chamomile tea it was just boiling water infused with the aromatic dried leaves. I mean, how else would you serve it?

She noticed me taking in the room and must have caught the smile on my face or a glint in my eye or something because she said 'You like it I see. Not to everyone's taste.' Which it wasn't, as I was just explaining to you.

'It's very comfortable' I said. I was still a little wary. Because it was strange as hell the way she'd just invited me in. Sat me down. Brought me tea.

'So who are you then?' the woman asked.

'I was given your address –' I began, but the woman cut me short.

'No' she said, interrupting. 'What's your name?'

I had to smile at that. 'Steven' I said. 'But you can call me Stevie. Everyone does.'

'Not everyone, I'm sure' she said.

I waited, expecting her to give me her name. And after a couple of second's thought she said 'You can call me Darnelle.'

The thought occurred that she'd hesitated because she had a hidden name. A secret name. Though she was never going to have revealed that. She was just being careful, not yet fully awake. Thinking before she spoke. Evidence of an evolved mind in my book.

'Darnelle' I said. 'Unusual name' 'At least, I don't know any other Darnelles.'

'It's old English' the woman explained. 'I suppose it's uncommon. I don't know any other Darnelles either.'

'What does it mean?' I asked, knowing that all old names had meanings. But before she could reply, something made me turn to look at the doorway I'd come in through. And I saw the most captivating girl leaning in through that gap, holding onto the door frame. Late teens I guessed. Tall, slim, wrapped in the shortest silk kimono you could imagine and with strawberry hair cut pixie-short, and blue eyes and the longest sexiest legs. And she gave me a little wave that perfectly matched her grin and it was all I could do not to mirror the silly little wave right back.

'It means "secret place" or "hidden place." Take your pick.' This was the young girl and she had a sweet happy voice to match her looks. 'I bet you're wondering what her hidden place is' the girl continued, sashaying into the room and draping herself in another armchair. She threw her legs over one arm of the chair, all the time watching my reaction as the soft silk kimono rode up her thighs, stopping just short of revealing everything. I can't tell you what my reaction was but this girl giggled again and it must have been because of me. So I suppose my eyes were popping out or something like that.

'Yes well I didn't keep it hidden enough or we wouldn't have to put up with you now would we?' This was the woman and she'd spoken with a smile so that I understood that this was mere banter. I also understood that these two were mother and daughter.

The girl pouted, pretended to be hurt, then turned to me. 'Don't you want to know what you call me?' she asked.

Before I could answer, her mother chipped in. 'You can call that one Ellie,' she said. 'It's short for Eletta. Another old

English name. And before you ask, it means "mischievious." In case you couldn't guess.'

Another pout from the girl as her mother made an elegant job of lowering herself into the sumptuous sofa.

'Now' Darnelle said, 'since you've got us up at an ungodly hour, I think you have some explaining to do. Whenever you're ready. Stevie...'

# The Story part three
*because true love is immortal*
# – Earth Air Fire Water -

available from Fire Gate Media
in 2017

visit
www.facebook.com/FireGateMedia
for the latest updates

"like" **The Story Facebook page** at
www.facebook.com/TheStoryPeterLancett

Fire Gate Media - the world beyond imagination

34010426R00170

Printed in Poland
by Amazon Fulfillment
Poland Sp. z o.o., Wrocław